WAKING
IN
TOMBSTONE

Marilyn Brown

WAKING IN TOMBSTONE

WALNUT SPRINGS PRESS

Walnut Springs Press
4110 S. Highland Drive
Salt Lake City, Utah 84124

Cover design by Tracy Anderson

Text copyright © 2014 by Marilyn Brown
Cover design copyright © 2014 by Walnut Springs Press
Interior design copyright © 2014 by Walnut Springs Press

ISBN: 978-1-59992-925-5

This is a work of fiction. Except as stated in the author's note, the characters, names, incidents, and dialogue are products of the author's imagination and are not to be construed as real, and any resemblance to real people is not intentional.

Acknowledgments

Thank you to the kind people at Walnut Springs Press, especially editor Linda Prince for her support. This book would not have been written without her encouragement. Thank you also to Simeen Brown, Elaine Flake, Elaine McKay, Clare Johnson, Lynne Larson, Veda Hale, and all of those who kindly urge me to keep writing.

Author's Note

The Art of Historical Fiction

Stories are exciting because we can enter into the minds and hearts of other people, living "lives" in other times and places, experiencing conversations, feelings, glances, etc., that connect us more intimately with the past than dry historical facts can do.

The difficulty with this "art of historical fiction" is that the reader wants to know what's really true and what isn't. I took the risk of shaping Cotter after a real person whose name was Endicott Peabody. Friends called him "Cotter," but I changed his name, because everything can't be true in a novel. Most of what I write about him follows the facts of his life as clearly as I could discover them. And of course, the Earps, their friends, the lawless cowboys, and the shoot-out, are all of record.

What in this story is fiction? I invented Libby and the Barons, and I've taken certain liberties with time. Early in the story I introduce true characters at a fictional card game in Denver. Most of them played cards in Denver, but not at this time. I also took the liberty to make a composite of the many robberies in one fictional robbery, placed at a time when Libby and Cotter could experience it. However, most of the story events happen in chronological correctness. For example, the timing of the fires is accurate, and there truly was a corpse discovered in the Cosmopolitan Hotel ruins after the fire of May 26, 1882.

When I found out about the man "Cotter," I felt he needed acclaim for his contribution to Tombstone. He was one of the great leaders in Massachusetts, the founder of the exemplary Groton Boys' School, and the father of six leaders whose progeny became senators, educators, and other professional men and women of great service to our country. The church he built in Tombstone still stands.

1

Before she left, she caught an image of herself in the mirror on the hall tree. The light from the swollen moon gave her a pasty, middle-of-the-night glow—flickering in the pools of her eyes, bathing her sallow cheeks with the gloom. She looked at her mouth. Jacob Stuyvesant had always focused on her mouth. "Your mouth is a red bow shootin' the arrows of Cupid, little wench. Don't shoot them arrows without expectin' me to follow through."

It was over now. She didn't dare take much with her. She dressed in a pair of the gardener's overalls he left on a hook in the shed when he and his wife left for Denver. In the deep pocket of her overcoat she had stuffed a chemise, two pairs of panties, silk hose, and a handful of walnuts in a bandana. And the money. She had taken all the coins—both gold and silver—from the sauerkraut jar in the kitchen, wrapped them tightly in a handkerchief, and deposited them in her mother's tiny leather sack.

Libby grimaced in the glass. She knew nothing of what would happen now, only that it would be better than what had happened since her mother dropped dead over a bucket of water cleaning the Stuyvesant cellar. In the pantry, perched on the scullion's stool, Libby was lifting a potato skin with the paring knife when she heard the spine-withering cry. Swinging down the cellar steps, she found her mother lying buckled into a knot beside the overturned bucket, the soapy water creeping along the edge of the gray bandana, loose on the strings of lanky hair. Barefoot, Libby ran to the neighbors, who brought the coroner and the police.

When the master, along with a couple of his crony bookkeepers, showed up from the law offices, they found a house full of neighbors, and city officials hauling the body away on a gurney. The gardener and his wife were frantic with tears at the housekeeper's death, agreeing to stay with Jacob Stuyvesant because there was no other choice. But when they left for Denver and the master hired the new woman, Libby's world broke apart. Hetty Moffitt crossed the threshold, squinting in the brown light, her hair so tight in the bun on the back of her head, it pulled her eyes into slits. When Libby opened the shades, Hetty drew them shut with a snap and said, "I'm in charge."

But it was over now. Libby wanted to spit at the mirror. So she did. The spittle blurred her image. As soon as she crossed the doorstep, this girl in the glass would be gone forever.

Rummaging in her huge pockets, she felt past the underwear for the money sack. She clutched it. She wanted something to conceal everything, pack it down, safely deep. Pages of newspaper lining the bottom of the small middle drawer in the hall tree would do. She divided the papers into two wads and tamped them down into her pockets to protect everything precious she was taking.

Because the door creaked, she opened it slowly, gritting her teeth, praying Jacob Stuyvesant or the cruel Hetty would not wake.

The moon was so huge it gave the world a golden glow—enough light that Libby could see the curve in the front driveway, the clump of mulberry trees, the road to the gate, and beyond the gate—freedom! She glanced back, hoping no lights would suddenly burst on in the master's bedroom.

The imposing Victorian mansion, its turrets, the shingles along the upper windows, the huge weathervane on the black roof—the bulk of it seemed to loom over her like the massive claws of a giant monster hungry to grip her back into its grasp.

But she would not let it keep her. She ran. She ran across the cobblestones, around the clump of mulberry leaves to the gate. She stopped and carefully lifted the latch. It must not make a sound. Once Jacob Stuyvesant had been startled awake in the night by a stray cat slipping off the roof and falling into the rain barrel. The slightest noise in the yard might wake him.

Outside on the road, Libby closed the gate. The world was silent. The towering houses along the Kansas City streets stood like sleeping tombs, without life or light. She would make as much progress as she could before dawn.

She knew the general direction she wanted to go. West. And she knew the railroad station was west. But she didn't know what phantoms stood in the shadows, or what would happen if Jacob Stuyvesant sent some of his men, or even the police, out to stop her.

She walked in a blur, the memory of her master's foul breath in her face spurring her on. She prayed she could get far away quickly enough. As the light began to rise in the east, she could see the road, and, next to the road, the railroad tracks. There would be a train she could catch in the big city—she wasn't sure how many miles away. Ahead she saw a sign: "Mulvaney Stables." She wondered how much it would cost to get a ride.

The huge red barn looked purple in the dawn, and the stables loomed like a whaling ship. Libby pushed her fingers past the clump of newspaper, past her underwear, to the small sack of coins at the bottom of her pocket. She prayed she had enough to get out of town.

Crossing the field to the barn, she felt her nerves fail her. She had robbed Stuyvesant of some of his precious gold. When they found her, they would put her in jail.

She clenched her teeth and ducked behind the field rake at the back of the barn. No sound came from the barn, except perhaps the clop of a horse's hoof or its snort as it slept. Huddling outside, on the other side of the red slats of the barn wall, Libby trembled with the late-spring cold.

It seemed like hours before Mr. Mulvaney came out of the house, wrapping his scarf around his neck. He blew his nose, spit, and wiped his lips with his sleeve.

"Mister," Libby cried out, glad her frozen limbs unwound so quickly.

"What?" He drew back, his eyes wide.

"I'm sorry, mister. I have money. I'll pay for a ride to the train station."

His eyes narrowed. "Whoa there, boy!" Had she disguised herself that well?

"Please, sir. I need to get out of town."

"Where you come from?" He looked at her with a narrow gaze, taking in the knotted-up caramel-colored hair, the coat, the bulging pockets at her sides.

His stare reminded her of Stuyvesant's penetrating scrutiny, or the sharp eyes of some of his attorneys who followed him home almost every night to work the books in the office. Libby feared them all—one in particular, Mr. Grenville, who always seemed to be there, peering with his black eyes under his dense eyebrows, black like the burly hair of his head, watching, watching, as though he read through every harsh command Stuyvesant barked at her. But, she reminded herself, she was free of them all now.

"Does it matter?" she said to Mulvaney.

His gaze was suspicious, his eyes still bursting with surprise above the red wool muffler that covered his mouth and neck. "We don't leave for the train station until nine this morning."

"I can wait, sir."

His hands and fingers were thick, like the stubs of cigars. He stopped and leaned away from Libby to look at her overalls, the shoes. "You tryin' to fool me? You ain't no boy. You runnin' away from home, girl?"

"Please, sir. I have money." She reached below the folded newspaper inside the pocket of her coat. She had lumped the coins together in a handkerchief and stuffed them inside the little leather sack.

The man's eyes jerked at the sight of the gold coins. "Well, yeah. Was it stole?" he drawled.

"Sir, I earned this money."

After a pause he sniffed, screwing up his nose. "Well, all right, Miss Runaway. Wait at the house. Mrs. Mulvaney will feed you breakfast." He cocked his head and looked at Libby sideways, as though he might have second or third thoughts about dealing with this vagabond.

He hit on the right note, because her focus shifted when she heard the word *breakfast.* She had not touched the nuts in her bandana.

"Ermagard is turnin' up pancakes this minute," Mr. Mulvaney continued in his oily tone.

Pancakes. Libby hadn't known how pleasantly the sound of the word would drop into the hollow of her stomach.

Mrs. Mulvaney was a stocky housewife in a huge, dirty apron, flipping cakes on the black griddle. When the woman turned around, Libby took a quick breath. The square face was a gray color under the white cap. "We got us a runaway girl, Ermagard," Mr. Mulvaney said.

Mrs. Mulvaney narrowed her eyes, looking through Libby with a scowl. "She tryin' to be a boy on purpose?"

Libby wished she hadn't stepped into the kitchen. She thought about doing an about-face and running, but the waves of fragrant maple syrup and hotcakes paralyzed her. She ate as much as she could under the penetrating gaze of Mrs. Mulvaney. She ate what the husband might have eaten if he hadn't left, stomping off down the steps and spitting on the grass. "I'll get some after a while," he called back.

It was only after three or four pancakes that Libby looked out the window and saw Mr. Mulvaney walking across the back yard. A sudden fear shot through her. With him was a man in a long black coat. He looked formidable, like an officer of the law, or some important government official. He wore a black top hat, and a large black wool scarf wrapped around his throat. He was carrying a brief case. *That was quick,* she thought. *Where did Mulvaney find him so soon?* He looked vaguely familiar to her, but there wasn't time to ask questions.

She stuffed her mouth with the remaining cake and drained the cup of milk. "Thank you so much, Mrs. Mulvaney." It crossed Libby's mind that this meal may be her last on earth.

The woman didn't say much, just stood at the stove breaking eggs. Tiptoeing softly, Libby found her way through the narrow hall to the front room. She raced to the door that opened out to the front road. She heard the two men open the back door. Mr. Mulvaney said, "Well, where is she, Ermagard?"

Frantic, Libby stooped down to look at the lock on the door to see how it worked. There was a brass knob on the deadbolt, which she moved. Luckily, the door opened. In a flood of relief, she put her coat on and slipped out just as she heard Ermagard say, "She was here two minutes ago." Libby closed the door quietly and ran. For a while she ran without looking behind her. But when she did glance back, she saw Mr. Mulvaney and his shifty-looking companion following her. They began to move swiftly over the field. The man with the case outdistanced Mr. Mulvaney. His legs in the black trousers seemed to swallow up the length of the meadow as though he had the stride of a giant. Out of breath, Libby ran into a copse of sumac and burrowed under a pile of dead leaves. For a few moments all she could hear was the thump of her heart.

Buried in the leaves, she could see in the distance the tall man in his black coat pausing to allow Mulvaney to catch up with him. *Who is he?* In a brief moment she thought she recognized him. The two men stood on one leg and then the other before they began to move toward her out across the field. She stayed quiet, but the newspapers in her pockets made a crackling sound. She should pull the noisy wads out, she thought. Once out of her pockets, both balls of news opened up. They seemed to bloom like roses.

"TOMBSTONE SHOOT-OUT: THREE KILLED," the headline said. There was still enough light coming through the leaves to make out the words, and Libby was a captive audience. She dare not move, hearing the voices of the men not far away.

On October 26, 1881, old rivals, the Earp brothers and the Clantons and McLaurys faced each other in a shoot-out at the OK Corral. Three are dead, several wounded.

Libby moved slightly in the leaves. She pulled some of them away so the light shone directly on the words.

Frank McLaury yelled, "If you come after me, you will never take me."

*Morgan calmly replied, "If circumstances require it,
I would arrest you."*

"You will never arrest me! You'll die first!"

Libby was hooked on the story now and wanted to know what happened next. But she heard the men drawing closer. Through the leaves, she saw them approaching, so she ducked farther down. As still as she was, she wondered if they had seen her. For a few moments she did not even breathe. But sideways, she glanced at the story in her hands.

*Wyatt reported that at least nine or ten men told him
they heard threats from the ranchers against the lives of
the Earps.*

There was more, but Libby could see two broad backs through the leaves. The men had evidently decided not to come all the way into the woods. They had turned around as though circling the meadow. She wondered if she dare try to get away.

Clutching the pieces of newspaper, she slowly pulled out of her hiding place, trying to muffle the noise. She crawled along the ground and then looked back. The men were on the other side of the meadow. She got on her feet and ran through the woods.

When she was out of breath, she sat down in a copse of sumac vines and pulled out the broken newspaper. One piece was about to tear away, but she managed to hold it together.

*With the law on their side, the Earps have been after
the cowboys for good reason. So far the renegades in
southeastern Arizona are having a pretty good time
robbing and murdering and putting the blame on the
Indians.*

Close to the tracks now, Libby heard a *clack clack* sound shaking on the rail. A train was slowly crawling nearby. She slipped out of her hiding place and wove her way cautiously through the trees to the tracks. *Clack clack.* Slow. Slower. Libby folded the newspaper story carefully, this time over and over until it was a neat little packet she could stuff into her pockets with the money and the underwear.

The last few cars were high coal bins decked out with shiny metal fittings. The train was making such tentative progress, it was easy for her to run beside it and catch hold of a ladder. Once fastened to a car, she breathed a sigh of relief. The Mulvaney people would be far away.

But the railroad station wasn't so far away. She barely felt she had gone far enough when the cars came to a faltering crawl, and finally stopped in a vast fenced yard filled with bins and pillars of steel. In the yard, a man in a navy blue uniform, wearing a hat that looked like an upside-down kettle, began running toward her waving his arms.

"Sonny! Sonny!" he cried out. "Police!" he shouted. "Stowaway! Stowaway!" He made a dash for the tracks.

Libby got off the ladder and scooted around in back of the caboose. She raced toward the station. But she wasn't quick enough to disappear from view. Ahead of her, groups of would-be passengers stood in clumps: ladies in high-topped shoes and big petticoats, wearing little fox tails on their shoulders, gentlemen in frock coats and stovepipe hats—even a preacher with a starched white collar so bright it flashed like the sun into her eyes.

She slowed. Speed would definitely draw attention. She was hoping to reach the protection of the crowd, but when behind her she heard, "Stop that boy!" she knew she wouldn't make it unless she dashed. So she made a run for it. It was a moment of quick decision. And she chose the preacher.

2

Gasping, Libby ran to the man with the white collar. She lost her footing, so she clutched his sleeve to keep from falling.

When her weight hit him, he looked down at her with surprise. "Hey, hey, boy!"

This preacher was tall. He might be as tall as Stuyvesant's attorney, who, Libby remembered, was the tallest man she had ever seen. It was a blessing to be so tall, she thought. However, the preacher was so tall that when she stood close to him, she couldn't see his face. When she turned to pull away enough to see what he looked like, she caught a glimpse of the man in the black kettle hat. He was gaining on her. She buried her face in the woolly shelter of the preacher's armpit. There was a murky odor of wet sheep, and a surprising scent of faint lavender.

"Hey, what?" the preacher's voice boomed in his rib cage and floated somewhere from above.

"Please, sir, help me," Libby squeaked.

Under his hat, the station man's face was steaming, his nose red below knit brows. "All right, sonny," he growled. He stopped when he saw the man with the white collar. "Sir preacher, sorry about this. But this here ruffian was caught hitching illegal." He glared into Libby's face. "Don't you know it's a crime . . ."

She'd better be quick. Cocking her head, she leaned against the preacher's arm. "He's my brother, sir," she got out clumsily, the words rolling around in her head. "Our parents is dead. I was left by mistake. He's been expecting me." Libby dared not look up into the sky-high face to see the preacher's surprise.

For a moment the railman pulled back. "Oh, good heavens!" He caught his breath. He leaned close and examined her with a fierce glare. "So you ain't a boy? What are you?"

"There's just one other option." It was the preacher's voice high above her. The preacher! When he spoke, some heaviness as thick as fog seemed to lift from her.

"This your sister?" growled the man with the black kettle hat.

"Yes, sir," the preacher said.

"Well, I don't believe you. If you wasn't a man of God I'd say you was lying."

The preacher's retort was as smooth as butter. "I'm her brother. That's not a lie."

"My hell, man. This here boy . . . this here gal . . . is a stowaway. If the crazy tale she's tellin' is anywhere close to truth, I'll eat my hat."

Libby tried to hold back imagining the sweaty-faced agent chomping on the kettle hat with his tiny, rotten teeth. She swallowed a giggle that erupted in "Yuck."

"What did you say, you little . . . why, I'll . . ." The railman thrust his face so close she practically choked on the stench of his tobacco breath.

"Look, I'll pay her ticket," the voice from on high said. "Will that do? How much was it?" He turned and leaned down to look at her face for the first time. "When did you get on that car?"

As the preacher looked at her, she felt some ripple of nervous tension clamor down every limb of her body. He was like a bright pillar, she mused. All light. The light brown locks of hair that had escaped from under the brim of his felt hat framed the light brows and the light blue eyes. All light. A strong nose, high cheekbones, and lips so light they blended into the general impression of a wisp of cloud in a morning sky. Libby was too surprised to speak.

When Mr. Kettle Hat saw Mr. Preacher taking out his leather purse, he backed away. "Oh, no. That's not necessary, if she's in your custody, sir."

The preacher's eyebrows and eyelashes were so light she felt for a moment she was looking at the sky through a window dressed with white curtains, blowing, shimmering. What was beyond the curtains? She was not sure. "She's a paying customer now, sir," the preacher said.

"Well, all right, all right." Kettle Hat backed away.

When he left, there was almost no sound. Except perhaps for Libby's ragged breathing.

"Well . . ." the preacher began.

Libby was still trying to process everything.

"So . . . what does my little sister want to do?"

"I'm grateful, sir," she stammered, standing apart from him. "You don't really need to pay for me. I have my own money." She motioned toward the ticket office. "I'm going west."

"West?"

The preacher, with his clear blue eyes, glanced around at the knots of travelers in the station. "We're all going west." He paused. "Just west?"

"You going on this train west?" Libby wanted to know.

"How far are you going?" the preacher grilled her. But his look was kind. He leaned down as though intent on seeing into her soul—to see if she would be honest with him.

"Oh . . . far," Libby mumbled. She plunged her fists into the pockets of her coat. The panties, the money bag, the packets of newspapers were still there. "Maybe to . . . Tombstone."

"Tombstone, Arizona?"

Libby glanced up. The preacher had turned away, but from the tension in his cheek she was certain he was smiling.

"Tombstone?" he finally repeated.

"Well . . ." She hesitated. She had thought about somewhere as close as Burlington. And she had thought about Denver, where she might look up the gardener and his wife. But she had her hand on the papers in her pocket. Tombstone was on the tips of her fingers, and had somehow just suddenly burst to the tip of her tongue.

"I'm . . . not sure. But if that's far, that's where I'm going."

The preacher seemed amused at Libby's pronouncement, but he did not say anything.

"Do you know about Tombstone?" Libby finally asked him. There was something faraway in his eyes, as though he were not really present. There was no answer.

"Did you read about what happened there a couple months ago?" Libby hoped she wasn't being a pest.

"I read about it," he answered, still somewhat vacant from the conversation.

"What do you know about it?"

While they dallied in the rail yard, dozens of people passed them: boys hauling carts with luggage, women in silk skirts, herding little children dressed in sailor suits and ruffled dresses. One woman wore a feathered hat so large, the crowd pulled away from her. From the rail station, bells rang out, echoing in the cavernous hall.

A short little man came up to Libby and the preacher. "You ready with your tickets?" he said through his nose. "The train stops is at Topeka, Salina, Burlington, all the way to Denver, Colorado."

"Are you going all the way to Denver?" Libby pressed the preacher, fully aware she was bordering on brazen. When he didn't answer, she said, "If we're going all the way to Denver, I ought to know your name."

It seemed he was forcing himself to look at her—transparently struggling to maintain the kindness he had been taught to show to everyone. "All right. My name for yours." He smiled. "I'll buy your ticket as far as Denver." He reached into his pocket.

"Keep your money," she said like she meant it. She drew her heavy brown brows together over the hazel-gold eyes and rose-tinted cheeks.

"And so who are you, then?"

"Libby. Libby Campbell. And so who are you?"

"Call me Cotter," he said.

"Cotter? That's the strangest name I ever heard."

"My last name's Cotter. I have a first name, but I'd prefer . . ."

"Well, what is it? I don't think it's smart for me to go all the way to Colorado with a stranger. And you certainly don't have to buy my ticket. I have money. I took it out of Mr. Stuyvesant's bottle in the pantry. I earned it. He never gave it to me. There's gold coins in the stash. I knew I was going to need it. So I paid myself. I earned it. And I got what I deserved." She stopped, knowing she had said too much, and finally muttered softly, "I am afraid they are after me for taking the gold."

Mr. Cotter did not seem to notice she had admitted she was a thief. Libby breathed in and kept her head down as they began to move toward the door of the railway station. The cavernous hall echoed with the conversation and footsteps of hundreds of passengers. They had drawn close to the ticket office when, glancing behind her at the sunny entrance, she gasped. She quickly averted her eyes. Could she have been mistaken? She peeked again and caught sight of the same towering man she had left in the meadow with Mr. Mulvaney. No! Libby's body seemed to jump a foot high. She slipped around to the other side of Cotter and hid her face in his sleeve.

"Stand still," she whispered. "Someone is . . . someone knows I am here."

The preacher balanced himself.

She took the coin bag out of her pocket and thrust it into his hand. "Shh. Here's the money. Keep it with you. Just buy my tickets and get on the train."

For a few tense moments the ticket master in the booth examined the gold coins. He wrinkled his nose and peered over half spectacles. "This yours?" He looked up at them.

"It's valid," Cotter said.

"Well, I ain't seen coins like these this century."

This century? The old codger looked like he had also lived in the last century. Libby watched anxiously while he slipped the coin between his stained teeth and bit on it. *Hurry, hurry,* she thought to herself.

"All right. Just one ticket. Yours, boy?" He glared at Libby. "You say you want to go to Tombstone? No train to Tombstone. Train stops at Benson. Any farther, you have to take a stagecoach." While the clerk rattled on, he continued to eye Libby: her knotted hair, the rosebud mouth, the overalls, the heavy wool coat.

"That's right—Benson," Cotter replied. "That new route that opened up last year thirty miles north of Tombstone." He put the change into the bag of coins.

"Mining country?" the old man said. "You gonna try your hand at silver? It's a rush there, that's a fact."

Cotter didn't say more. But when he turned to give Libby the coin bag, she pushed his hand away. "You keep it," she whispered. "Please. Keep it safe for me."

The money was contraband, but no one would think to search the preacher for it. Libby gave up the money easily, but tucked the ticket into her pocket. Then, glancing around at the crowded station, she sidestepped so quickly and bumped into Cotter so hard, it seemed to throw him off balance. When he moved away from her, she cast a glance back at her pursuer again. For the moment, he had turned his back to them.

"Do you see that man in the long black coat?" she whispered, clinging to Cotter's sleeve.

"Who?" The preacher turned around.

But she dare not point. The man was looking her way again. There was something about his stance, the briefcase, the gleam of the black curls under his hat that jarred her memory. She knew this person—even before he began chasing her at the Mulvaney farm.

"I believe," she began, but so quietly that Cotter may not have heard her, "I believe that man is one of Mr. Stuyvesant's men." She forced the words between her teeth, then pulled at the preacher's sleeve until they passed through the station door and reached the boardwalk.

At the line of passengers waiting for the conductor, she slipped behind the woman with the huge hat festooned with red ostrich feathers. Under the hat, a silver netting covered dark hair that framed a white face. The woman's lips were painted bright red.

The line moved swiftly forward, with Libby still hiding, still watching for the man she believed was eyeballing her from the station yard. The conductor, standing on the boardwalk beside the yellow step to the door of the train, took the tickets without looking into anyone's eyes. It was not long before the line of passengers was in a closed, narrow passageway flanked on both sides by baggage cupboards. When they reached the passenger car, Libby ducked and looked through the window. The man she called "Stuyvesant's man" was walking swiftly toward the end of the line of passengers.

"Pray the train moves out fast," Libby breathed. As those ahead of them began to fill up the car, she fell hard onto a bench on the left side, one seat back and across the aisle from the woman with the red mouth. In that moment, Libby was sure Cotter—who now carried her fortune—would sit beside her. And he did.

"Burlington?" The conductor finally made his way down the aisle and checked the ticket stubs.

Libby didn't say anything. After the conductor passed, she lowered her face into her hands. With the bench beneath her, she felt a spiraling sense of relief. But as she tried to breathe, her body shook, and she could not hold back her tears.

Mr. Cotter leaned forward and laid his hand on her shoulder. "Are you all right? Do you want your purse back?"

"No, no. I want you to keep it for me." She tried to collect herself. When she looked up at him, it was through wet eyelashes over tear-stained cheeks. Strands of her hair were wet across her brow. "It's just when you can't take it anymore and you have a chance to sit and think about everything, you break down."

"Do you want to tell me about it?"

No one has ever asked me that. I would say too much, Libby thought. So she stayed quiet. She sniffled and wiped her cheeks with the edge of her coat sleeve. There was a long period of silence until the engines began to rumble.

"You're safe, now, aren't you?" Mr. Cotter tried again.

Through the window of the train, she saw the towering, black-coated man standing by the ticket taker, gesturing intensely. But he had no ticket. After a few more moments, as the train began to grind forward in clouds of coal smoke, steam, and the stench of tobacco, Libby settled herself back in her seat and closed her eyes.

"That's the man who is looking for the gold, isn't it?"

I've already said too much. Libby nodded. "I need to get as far away from here as I possibly can."

Over the steam, Mr. Cotter began to speak, so softly she almost didn't hear him. "Tombstone is far. I didn't tell you." He paused. "But that is also my destination."

3

The preacher said the words quietly, but not quietly enough. Over the clamor of the wheels on the track, and the shuffle of the conductor taking tickets, his was still the only voice in the car, and the overdressed woman in the big feathered hat—seated one bench ahead of them across the aisle—turned and stared at him.

Libby caught her breath. *Mr. Cotter is going to Tombstone? Did I hear him correctly?* She could not help but notice the astonishment of the woman across the aisle. When Libby's eyes traveled from the woman to Cotter, she saw they were exchanging glances. Libby was not naive. The woman's red mouth said everything that needed to be said. She was glad when the woman turned away from peering at them.

"You said Tombstone," the preacher continued. "I have an appointment there."

Tombstone? That's what Libby thought she heard the first time. In the formidable silence, she was too shocked to speak for a moment. "You're going to Tombstone?" she finally asked.

"I am," he replied. "And you said . . ."

"You were not telling me, just because . . ."

Cotter did not answer her. They gazed out the window, and Libby saw Stuyvesant's man still standing by the ticket taker.

"No. No. I have been called to the church there." He stopped. "It is nothing you said, except that I am supposed to be a man dedicated to the truth of God, and here I am a new pastor and already I've lied for you a couple of times. I've taken into my possession your entire fortune. And if I'm not mistaken, it's . . . questionable funds." Cotter gave a small smile. "I'd like to help, but I'm a bit nervous—expecting at any minute to be struck by lightning." He laughed as if trying to cover up his fears.

It seems we both have some explaining to do, Libby thought.

"I haven't yet graduated from the institute," he offered. "A miner from Tombstone who wants to marry my cousin told me there is a pulpit vacant there. It's only for six months."

"Six months?"

Though his head was down, Cotter looked at her sideways, seeming to test her feelings. "I'd like to know your story."

There was no way Libby could begin to tell him anything: her mother's violent death, Hetty's whip, the thrust of Mr. Stuyvesant's rough hands into her bodice, the sick smell of incense, the occasional knock of the visiting attorneys on the door, and their glaring eyes when she let them out at the end of the day. She would rather cut out her tongue. This man was training to be a pastor. He taught purity, chastity, honor. He would balk at her story.

As the train slowly began to move on the track, she dug into the pocket of her coat and pulled out the packet of neatly folded newspaper. "I just read this. I just pulled Tombstone out of the air." Libby had stopped sniffling.

She handed him the packet. He took it and found the edge that would yield the secrets. While he pulled the corner away, the woman across the aisle leaned out of her seat and craned her neck toward them.

"I got to here," Libby indicated. "You can read it yourself."

As Cotter unwrapped the articles, the headlines glared at them. "I already know about this," he said. "'SHOOT-OUT AT THE OK CORRAL: THREE PEOPLE KILLED.'" He glanced at her. "This is serious trouble. Are you sure you want to entertain the idea of . . . I mean . . ." He fumbled for words. "Going to a place of such danger?"

She cocked her head and studied his eyes. They were like blue glass, intense and bright, resembling the light that shimmers on water. "So why are you going?"

Her question stopped him for a moment. "My cousin . . . my cousin Frances . . ." He said each word slowly as if he needed to think about it separately, and he dare not come out with the entire thought. He began again. "The man who told me about the church job in Tombstone is a very wealthy miner named Grafton Abbott." Libby thought she could hear anger in Cotter's voice as he mouthed the name. "He wants to marry my cousin Frances. Because he just invested in a mine in Tombstone, he was aware the church there needed a . . ."

"A new pastor," Libby finished for him. "You didn't really want to come."

It was quiet. "No," he said finally.

She thought she saw a tremor in his cheek. "So is your cousin going to marry him?"

He smiled at her as though amused. "Who knows?"

"Why not? He's rich. But you don't want her to marry him?"

Libby looked at Cotter's profile, the strong nose, the light eyebrows, and the blond hair falling across his forehead. She felt an urge to reach to his face and put her fingers in the light hair to smooth it back from his brow. But she stayed still.

"Why didn't you want her to marry him?" she probed.

He turned to the story in the newspaper and began reading aloud keeping his voice low.

Because several lawmen were after some escaped prisoners, Sheriff Behan was short on deputies when the shoot-out happened on October 26, 1881.

Had Libby asked too many questions? She changed the subject. "He was short on deputies? But there were deputies there to fight. If the deputies were gone, who was there?"

Cotter didn't speak for a moment. "It was the ex-lawmen still in town who participated in the shoot-out."

Libby tried to digest it. She pulled at the tops of her fingers one by one until the tips were white. "They just murdered each other?"

"In a matter of seconds."

"Oh." Libby thought about biting a nail, but kept her hands to herself.

A while later, with Cotter so intent on reading, she was about to fall asleep. Her eyelids were becoming very heavy when all of a sudden there was a distraction across the aisle. The red-lipped woman suddenly stood up, raised her arms to unpin the bouncy hat with its profusion of red ostrich feathers, and tried to balance herself on the rocking floor. As she reached up to put the hat on the high shelf, the car pitched to one side. She grasped for the pole, but missed. When she stepped back, the hat flew from her head like a red bird, and her feet danced while she tried to gain her balance. But it didn't work. She fell back, her arms waving to grasp the air.

Suddenly, a tall figure in a long overcoat came up from behind them. He appeared miraculously as the woman rocked back on her heels. She fell against him, and he caught her just in time. There was laughter and a few inaudible words between them. The man turned slightly, and Libby gasped. It was Stuyvesant's attorney! For an instant, she couldn't breathe.

Though Cotter had taken notice of the woman stumbling, and the man who caught her, he returned to reading aloud.

> *"You're a fool, Doc, a pistol-totin' fool. I oughta shoot your head off."*
> *"Well, get your gun out and go to work."*
> *Deputy Morgan climbed over the lunchroom bar, took Doc by the arm, and—with Ike following—led the pair out to the street to fight. Virgil Earp promised to arrest both Doc and Ike.*

All during Cotter's steady reading about the conflict between the cowboys and the lawmen, Libby sat close against the window, clenching her hands in her lap. *Stuyvesant's attorney is on this train!* Up close, she knew his face. He had been a shadow in the Stuyvesant house. She even knew his name. Charles Grenville. He wore the same top hat perched on the same waves of black hair that shone slick as coal. After helping the woman in red feathers to stand, he guided her into her seat and sat down beside her. Stuyvesant's attorney was now sitting in front of Libby—only one bench ahead.

She had stopped listening to what Cotter was reading. He must have known, because he was half murmuring. She clenched her hands in her lap and asked, "How tall are you?"

Her seat mate lowered the newspaper and searched her face.

"How tall are you? I'm five foot six. How tall are you?"

He smiled. "Does it make any difference?"

"Difference? I just wondered. Sometimes people are so tall they think they're above everybody else. They look down on people. You're not like that, are you?"

Cotter's smile softened. "No, no. I'm supposed to . . . I am called . . . My job is to teach people that they should love everyone. We are all God's children. Tall and short, lean and fat, bond and free, black and white." The preacher spoke as though reciting a litany. But when he brought the newspaper to his face again to find his place in the story, he slyly continued the conversation. "Hate is easy to come by. That's how murder happens." He put his finger on the newspaper in front of him and continued to read, this time with more timbre in his voice.

Ike Clanton was full of hate. He wanted to fight Doc Holliday. He couldn't let it go. When he left the street scene, he had been so angry he headed to the edge of town for his horse and picked up his pistol. It was illegal in town to carry arms, but he was ready to fight now.

This time he followed Wyatt into the Eagle Brewery. "This fighting talk between the lot of ya has been going on for who knows how long? So I guess it's about time it came to a close."

Wyatt did not let Ike's testy speech ruffle his feathers. "If I was you I wouldn't fight if I could help it," he drawled. "There's no money in it." He walked away.

Shouting after him, Ike said, "I will be ready for you in the morning."

Ike kept following Wyatt until he was tired of it. So he finally joined a poker game with the sheriff and Virgil Earp. The cowboy Tom McLaury was also present. The boys played poker until the sun came like a red chip into the eastern sky.

"That was one of the problems," Cotter said to Libby. "The men who took part in the shoot-out were deprived of sleep. They hadn't been to bed all night."

Libby was not concentrating on the story. Her eyes could not leave the dark head in front of her. Stuyvesant's man had removed his hat. His hair was so thick it sprang into a globe, like the map of the world. She watched to make sure he did not turn her way. She sat close to Mr. Cotter, trying to hide behind his shoulder.

"Why did you become a pastor?"

The noise of the train seemed to intensify. Cotter lowered the news to his lap. "What?"

"Why did you become a pastor?" It was the main reason she trusted him.

"My cousin Frances and I . . ." He stopped. "We were close." Something hidden in his voice told Libby he was holding on to his true feelings. "My parents were worried that my cousin and I . . . To keep us from . . . becoming involved." He hesitated. "My father moved the family to England. I played ball in a churchyard and hit a homer through the cardinal's window. The cardinal was the reason."

"You hit a home run through the church window?"

Cotter smiled at her. "Yes. He called me to his office. There was broken glass all over the floor. He sat me down and said, 'You must be quite a hitter.'"

"So did he punish you?"

"Yes." Cotter looked away. "He confronted me with it. He said, 'Are you ready to pay for that window with a few jobs around here?'"

"So did you work for him?"

Cotter was silent. Libby could hear some groaning sounds from the engine.

"Yes. And I stayed for two years. He was the kindest, most loving man I have ever known."

"And you wanted to be like him, so you are following in his footsteps?"

"Yes." Cotter smiled. It was a faraway look. He raised his eyes to the window as if he could see something no one else on the car could see. But whatever it was, he could not have foretold the danger Libby faced.

While they talked, there was another disturbance across the aisle. The painted lady suddenly stood and tried to reach her hat or purse on the shelf overhead. When she stood, the attorney beside her turned to place his feet in the aisle. He scanned the passengers in the car, his eyes wandering. Then he looked directly at Libby. She jerked.

It wasn't a coincidence. He had followed her.

4

Libby's heart slammed against her ribs. She tried to turn into Cotter's shoulder again while he continued mumbling the words of the newspaper. As the noise of the tracks and his voice overwhelmed her ears, she could still hear the pounding of her heart. She wished she could go to sleep and escape the torture. But her eyes were wide open, and she could not stop the little gasping sound in her throat.

After his penetrating glance of recognition, the attorney did not turn back again. But when the train slowed at Tecumseh, the woman with the disarray of profuse shiny black hair stood up in front of the attorney's knees and began to climb over him to get to the aisle. This time, when she stood up, Mr. Grenville stood to give her more room to get by.

Libby thought back about how she had remembered him, this great figure much like a monstrous black bat shadowing the afternoon with its dark wings. Nervous with frustration, she turned her head against the window, pulling the coat collar against her cheek. When she managed to peer out, she saw the attorney's face. He was saying something to the hussy now, smiling, and nodding as she lurched unsteadily to get down the aisle—probably to the powder room. He turned again. This time he did not look at Libby.

But the damage had been done. Their eyes had met, and both of them knew it. As he began to sit back down, she felt the urge to get out of there. Abruptly, she stood up to follow the woman, wherever she was going.

"Excuse me," Libby said to Cotter. By now he had stopped reading out loud. He moved his knees to the aisle so she could get through. She climbed out and tried to stand steadily on the floor, adjusting to the movement of the train. She did not look behind her, but hurried to follow the big skirts that swished ahead. At the water closet she stood, shivering with the cold, waiting for the locked door to open. When the woman finally emerged, she looked flushed. Libby had already decided this was a woman of ill repute. But then the woman caught her eye and smiled at her. "It's cold in there," she said good-naturedly.

Libby didn't know how to reply. It was hard to believe this gaudy creature was just another woman taking a long journey. Libby looked up shyly and gave a faint grin.

"I noted you have no baggage. If you need a dress, I have some extra. I would be happy to lend something to you."

Libby was speechless. *A dress?* The woman was observant, and unexpectedly friendly.

The woman gave a little laugh and said slyly, "Don't let me keep you from your present pursuit."

The woman graciously smiled and turned to walk back to her seat in the car, leaving Libby standing frozen with her hand on the toilet's wooden door.

Once she was in the small closet, she hurried everything—completely taking down the overalls, feeling the shock of the cold under her thighs, thinking a dress would have been infinitely easier.

As she made her way back through the passageway without windows, the car seemed to darken. With her head down she watched where she was going as the train rocked. But suddenly she stopped. There appeared before her in the dusky hall of the passage, a pair of huge shoes. They were more like boots— massive black leather boots with heavy toes. She believed one kick could have broken her legs. She lifted her eyes and felt every nerve in her body crawl. It was the attorney, standing over her like a heavy cloud.

Paralyzed, she dare not look up. Yet she could not walk through him. Trembling, she stepped forward with her eyes down. "Excuse me, sir."

The man did not move. Without daring to look up into his face, Libby calculated the distance between his body and the bank of compartments on both sides. They were in a narrow hall. It was not possible to pass him.

"Where do you think you are going?"

The voice was familiar. But she had never heard Charles Grenville speak to her alone. It was a sound so deep it almost disappeared from the normal range of hearing.

She could not help it. She raised her head. His dark eyes beneath his knit brows were challenging her. His thick black curls grazed the collar of his greatcoat. He was so close she thought she caught the fragrance of the same white foam Mr. Stuyvesant had always insisted she use for his shave. Once this attorney had come to the door while she was shaving the master, and Hetty had let him in. He had stood in the doorway of the kitchen with his top hat in his hand. "This is important, Stuyvesant." His voice had been insistent, piercing.

Libby was shaving the master. His cheeks twitched. She felt it under the razor she carefully dragged across his jowl—feeling as she always did, the urge to cut his throat.

Grenville leaned against the doorjamb in the kitchen. He was tall, the size of one of the gray statues on the monument in the park: chiseled nose, high cheekbones, and eyes of steel. These eyes seemed to cut her flesh to the bone. It was hard, if not impossible, to complete Stuyvesant's shave under this scrutiny. Libby's hands began to shake.

She wondered what Grenville knew about her bondage to Stuyvesant. Did he know that as soon as the house echoed with emptiness, as soon as there were no attorneys, as soon as Hetty left the premises, it would be time to climb the stairs to the upper room, dim the light, and lie on his bed? In the beginning, when Libby screamed or pleaded for her life, he had held her down. But when she had learned to accept it, to gain his trust, she suffered through it for the sake of her room and board—until she found the gold and silver coins in the sauerkraut jar deep behind the pickled onions on the bottom shelf of the pantry.

Libby knelt at the cupboard, and the light from the pantry window seemed to bloom above her as though some ethereal figure metamorphosed from another world. She remained silent and thrust the jar back into its dark recess, all while hearing the beat of her blood sound like drums in her head.

Out of a fog of anxiety, now captive in the rumbling car of the train, she heard the man before her speak again in his direct, low voice. "You know why I'm here, don't you?"

The fog lifted from her mind. *No, I really do not know why you are here—on a train you hadn't planned to take, hoping to find Stuyvesant's gold.*

She took an instant to congratulate herself on the fortunate transfer of her treasure into Cotter's hands. Grenville would never find it.

She prayed for someone to come by. It would have been nice if it were Cotter. Even the woman with the red lips would have been welcome. But no one came. Libby would have to navigate her way through his interrogation on her own—to survive the glare of his gaze. She gathered her courage and looked him squarely in the face.

"No, Mr. Grenville, I really don't know why you're here. Why are you here?"

For a brief time, he did not answer. She tried to hold his gaze. He was standing close, and then he moved another step closer. She was appalled. He loomed above her like a huge mountain she had no hope of climbing or passing.

"You really don't know, do you?"

He spread his arms above her and flattened his palms against the compartments on both sides, then leaned toward her. He was so near she could feel the heat in his face. There was more in his eyes than the question he asked.

For a moment she defied him, not moving. She could stand up to him. But the frustration in her body took a leap that totally surprised her. The close proximity of such a large, forceful presence alarmed her. When there was only an inch from his challenging eyes, her hand, almost without warning, flew up from the pocket of her overalls and slapped his cheek. The tension in the air snapped with electricity.

"Excuse me, please." She forced the words through her teeth.

"Ah, I see," he drawled in an oily voice. "You really do want to go back to Jacob Stuyvesant."

"Excuse me, Mr. Grenville," she repeated, stepping forward. But when she walked close into the curve of his body, the blood in her head pounded.

He backed away just enough to prevent contact.

"All right," he said. "We'll see. We have all the way to the pit of Arizona's murders to find out, don't we?"

At these words he stepped aside, and as she passed under his chin, she felt an almost visible bulwark of power crackle around her. It was the most extraordinary sensation she had ever felt. So he was planning to follow her all the way to Arizona, was he?

Wordless, she took a second to compose herself and then walked purposefully through the opening Grenville had created. What was happening in her heart? She did not look back.

On the way to her seat, she felt dizzy from the encounter. Images whirled in her head of her first introduction to this man. Stuyvesant hired Grenville a week and a half before Christmas. Libby's mother was still alive then. It was less than four months before her death on the cellar floor.

On Christmas Eve, Stuyvesant had transported Grenville and several other of his cronies to the mansion through the snow in the purple dark. Some carolers had stopped in the street, and Libby's mother brought a basket of apples to give them. When the master and his men emerged from the carriage, they hurried past the carolers as though the wet snow would melt them all into puddles. Inadvertently, one of them bumped Libby's mother, and the basket of apples tumbled from her arms into the snow.

"Oh," Stuyvesant said, swinging the front door open. "Libby, can you get those? We have a matter of business." He disappeared inside the house.

Libby and her mother bent over to pick up the apples. But someone had already been picking them up and returning them to the basket. Libby noted it was the new attorney, Charles Grenville. She caught his glance toward her in that moment—a piercing stare.

Later in the evening, when the men left the house, while she was helping to scrub the pans, she asked her mother about the attorney.

Her mother was quiet for a long time, watching the door warily to be sure no one came back into the scullery. "He graduated from Valparaiso. He's from somewhere in Kentucky. He's been here with Mr. Stuyvesant for a short time. There's a rumor he is running from something, wants to go west to practice law, or find gold. There's a rumor that he killed someone, a woman in white gloves in a rose garden. But I do not know any of the details."

He killed a woman in a rose garden. The words rang in Libby's head.

On her way back to her seat in the train, her memories seemed scrambled. In the passenger section she did not see Charles Grenville. But she saw the painted woman in the aisle, now hatless, her copious dark hair in profuse disorder on her white brow. She was leaning over someone at the left. It was Cotter.

Libby saw a gleam in the woman's eyes. As she drew close, the woman transferred her effusive smile from Cotter to her. "Hello," the woman drawled. "Miss Campbell? Libby Campbell?"

Libby nodded. What else had Cotter revealed besides her name?

"Hello. I've been talking with Mr. Cotter here." The woman referred to him with a bright look. "When I learned you were all headed for Arizona, I thought we ought to get acquainted."

Libby narrowed her eyes. The face before her came on with such brilliance, she mentally backed away.

"My name is Marcella Baron. I'm glad to make your acquaintance." She extended her hand. The fur piece, dangling with little fox feet, still lay on her arm.

Libby was not sure she wanted to respond, but the woman's friendliness was so compelling, she put out her hand. The fingers she grasped were stronger than they looked.

"Mr. Cotter has told me about you," Marcella said.

What would he tell? That I am a thief? That I named Tombstone my destination on the whim of a paragraph or two in a crumpled old newspaper?

"Tombstone is a long way from Kansas City, and twice as far from New Brunswick, New Jersey, where I'm from." Marcella smiled. "If you need a place to stay, I can help."

If I need a place to stay? "I thank you," Libby stammered.

"It's a long journey. We might as well be friends."

5

From then on, as they clattered across Kansas, Libby looked out of the corner of her eye for Charles Grenville. But she did not see him. He did not enter their car and sit down by Marcella Baron. Everything changed after the confrontation at the powder room. For a long time Marcella sat on the arm of Cotter's bench and began to propel her way into their lives.

The lady talked about China. She said her parents had been Christian missionaries in China, just like Mr. Cotter was a missionary to Tombstone. "My mother and father were secretly holding gospel meetings," she said. "The Chinese government sent their bulldog warriors wielding scimitars that flashed in the sun. Three short men with long black braids hanging down their backs came to a meeting my father was holding in their paper house. The intruders were short and stocky, bulging with muscles that stretched their skin so tight their bodies glistened like glazed pottery in the sun. They cut up my father and mother while my sister and brother and I cowered behind a curtain."

Libby felt a stab of horror and saw Cotter shudder. She tried to find a trace of the wound it must have left in a little child living in a foreign country, watching the destruction of her family through the film of a curtain in a paper house. But

Marcella had probably lived with the tragedy for so long that she had become immune to the trauma.

In Tecumseh, Libby followed Marcella and Cotter to the market where, in a little Chinese shop, Marcella showed them how to eat the dumplings with two sticks. Libby separated the sticks with her fingers and tried to make them chop like the jaws of a dragon, but it was so much easier to grab the dumpling with her fingers and stuff it into her mouth. She ate four dumplings. They were delicious.

Cotter tried the chopsticks too, but gave up after his third attempt. Marcella laughed at how awkward he and Libby proved to be, as she used those sticks skillfully with a small bowl full of curling noodles.

At Burlington, during a longer stop in the station, Marcella looked around for the baggage master. When she found him, she ran in her voluminous skirts to flag him down. "Oh sir!" she cried out. Libby and Cotter stayed behind a few feet. Marcella pulled out a little stub of a ticket from her purse and waved it under the man's nose. The conversation was animated, but finally he nodded and agreed with her over something. So she beckoned to Cotter and Libby to come and follow them into the baggage compartment a few cars down.

Inside the close, musky space, the baggage master raised his lantern over a row of upright trunks. He stopped at one and said to Marcella, "This should be it. Does it have the right number?"

She checked the stub of her ticket and nodded, suddenly animated with excitement. "This is it," she beamed. "So, Cotter, help him pull it out for a few minutes. We'll have to hurry before the train decides to start up again."

Cotter took one side of the upright trunk and the baggage master the other, and they pulled it out of a long row of big trunks and boxes the passengers were taking west. Libby watched, uncertain.

"There are several dresses you could wear," Marcella declared. "But for now we'll find the lavender gingham." She fiddled with a key tied around her wrist until Cotter came to her rescue and untied it for her. "You will look very pretty in the lavender." She bent over the lock and hassled with the key until the clasp opened. Then she plunged her hands into the dresses hanging smashed together on their velvet-covered hangers along a polished brass rack.

"Here it is!" It took skill to maneuver the crushed gingham out from among its companion dresses, but Marcella was skillful and steady until it burst through, a little wrinkled, but responding to its freedom like the petals of a rose.

"You see . . . your nut-colored hair has red in it. And this is the perfect color for you." She placed the fabric against Libby's cheek. "You are a beauty, young lady. Hasn't anyone ever told you that before? Such a shame to hide it in overalls!"

Libby glanced at Cotter and the baggage man, who stood like two rubbernecks, seeming completely confused and slightly embarrassed. When Marcella produced a pair of white chambray bloomers trimmed with lace, a blush appeared on the men's cheeks. She grinned. "I have so many of these, and I hardly use them."

When the bloomers came out, the men made affable excuses that it was time to leave. "Oh, the whistle is blowing," the baggage man declared.

With the dress and other pieces on her arm, Marcella closed and locked the trunk, stepped down from the baggage car, and walked swiftly behind Cotter to the door of their coach. From there she hurried Libby back through the hall to the room with walls of lockers, and put the clothes on the arm of a box near the door of the water closet.

Libby observed all of this with some trepidation. Was she really ready to give up her overalls?

"This is going to be such a good time," Marcella gushed. She picked the dress up by the shoulders and shook it out. Libby gave a little gasp. The gown was beautiful. "This is lawn. It will shake out," Marcella explained. The puffed sleeves expanded as though some hovering spirit blew air into them.

Libby wasn't sure. The neck seemed deep. But it was sewn with thick purple velvet ribbon. A filler of white lace all along the neckline, repeating the ruffles on the sleeves, might be enough to cover her. "But your dress . . . are you sure you want to . . ." Libby mumbled.

"There are plenty more where this came from. Here, let me help . . ." Marcella unclasped the metal on the gardener's overalls and peeled everything off Libby until she stood naked in the cold. She prayed no one would come by. When the train lurched, she fell forward, catching herself on the lockers, wondering how she had ever let herself fall into this woman's wiles.

As Marcella chattered and gave directions, she pumped water from the water closet basin into a piece of towel, helped Libby sponge off some of the dirt, and then began piece by piece to gild her with fine items of clothing: underwear, chamois, the hose, and the petticoats. In the scrubbed metal of the mirror above the pump, Libby watched herself change from a bleary-eyed hoodlum into someone who resembled a lady.

"We'll tie your hair in back," Marcella said. "There are enough short pieces in front to make wet curls against your cheek."

Libby stiffened when the woman spit copiously on her forefinger and plastered the hair from over both ears into crescent curls on her cheeks. She would have stopped her, but she didn't want to cause a problem.

"There!" Marcella stood back to admire her work. "Miss Libby Campbell, you are a work of art." Her hands flew to her cheeks. "You will put all of us to shame!"

Libby wanted to ask Marcella whom she referred to when she said "all of us." Was she talking about herself and the people she hoped to meet in Tombstone? She was still a mysterious figure. Cotter had asked her a few questions earlier: "What happened to the children? To you and your brother and sister when your parents were killed and you came out from behind the curtain in the paper house?"

But Marcella had simply smiled and said, "It's a long story. I'll tell you sometime." At that moment the conductor happened to walk down the aisle, and they got into a discussion with him about their arrival in Denver.

"There will be time to stay overnight at a hotel in Larimer Street," the conductor told them, "or you may stay in the coach."

Libby believed she would stay in the car to save money, but a few miles before they reached Denver, Marcella insisted the three of them must go to a lounge she knew of in the Windsor Hotel.

Since Libby's transformation, Cotter did not seem to be the same. He moved to the far end of his seat. When he first saw her, he smiled. She caught his eyes skimming nervously to the décolleté of her neckline. With a glimmer of surprise in his cheeks, he said in a timorous voice, "You look very pretty, Miss Campbell." But he grew wary over the miles as the engine belched and struggled over the rocky hills. He buried his nose in his Bible, or a slim book he had brought, *The Sonnets of Edmund Spenser.*

Most of the distance passed in silence, with Libby feeling crunched and uncomfortable in the dress that seemed to encroach upon Cotter's trousers and the sleeve of his coat.

"You will have a chance to see the amazing city streets of Denver," Marcella told them, often leaning from across the aisle toward their seat, or sitting on the arm of Cotter's bench. "Believe me when I tell you the opulence of Denver will prepare you for the grandeur of Tombstone. When the mines build the towns, you will see more than you ever saw in Kansas City."

Cotter raised his eyes and murmured polite phrases, but Libby could tell he felt a little uncomfortable under Marcella's effusive gaze.

"It has been so long since I was with all of my family in Hong Kong," she finally revealed. "Nora's in Tombstone. But it will be eighteen years since I have seen my brother."

"Your brother?" Libby ventured. She was not sure if Marcella would want to talk about it.

"He's been in the territorial penitentiary in Laramie, Wyoming." Marcella gazed past Libby and Cotter through the window as though she could see her brother in the patchy snow of the yellow fields. "Horace," she murmured. "Horace Baron is his name. A dancer and actor. He was indicted for stealing the neighbor's horse. He's been incarcerated since the 4th of April."

There was a pause, and Libby wondered if she ought to say something, but she didn't know what.

"It was nothing short of a miracle when a friend of mine saw his name on a list of prisoners in the Kansas City post office and called my attention to it. I did not know he was alive. When we found each other and corresponded, he told me he would be out of prison in January, and to meet him at Nora's in Tombstone."

Oh, so that is why she is headed for Tombstone, Libby mused. Her sister was there. And her brother was on his way. Libby looked at Cotter. He seemed oblivious to the conversation.

6

When the train drew into the Denver station, Marcella pulled
down her hat from the overhead rack and pinned it over her
shiny curls in perfect position without looking in a mirror. "Are
you ready for some fun?" She grinned.

Cotter seemed uneasy. "Come on, let's go," Libby said,
pulling on his sleeve.

"The Windsor Hotel is just a few blocks from the Union
Station," Marcella explained. It looked like a few other passengers
were headed there. "Only the people who've been to Denver
before know about the Windsor." Marcella quickened her step.

Cotter was still sluggish, but Libby did not leave him. It
was tricky watching for the red-feathered hat ahead while,
with her hand on his arm, she virtually pulled Cotter through
the crowd.

The large, imposing hotel sat regally on the busy Denver
street flooded with people entering and exiting restaurants,
theatres, and saloons. As the three travelers entered the Windsor
near dusk, the gaslights in the foyer began to flicker and
illuminate the lower lounge, which was draped with gold lamé
curtains studded with silver-edged porcelain rings. Large live
trees lined the lobby, their leaves polished by someone hired to
rub each one of them with what looked like butter or milk.

Beyond the giant stained-walnut doors, Libby heard music. Someone was playing a grand piano, and another a harp. The strains of a Stephen Foster song drifted across the crowd. Groups of opulently dressed men and women sat at or milled about among the tables, or lined up at the bar. Staring at them, Cotter backed away shyly.

Marcella batted her eyes at him and giggled. "You're afraid of this, and you're going to Tombstone?" she teased.

Once they were inside the room, she scanned the crowd as though confident she would find someone she knew. And she did. "Follow me," she beckoned, leading Cotter and Libby back to the southwest corner.

A large gaming table gleamed under an amber light, with seven or eight players laughing and chatting while they concentrated on playing their hands. Smoke from half a dozen cigars and pipes curled up under the lamp over the center of the table, wafting like a cloud into the stained glass of the decorative shade. Libby had never seen anything like it. As her party approached the table, she glanced warily at the faces of the players. She did not recognize anyone.

"Yoo-hoo," Marcella called. "Johnny Holliday! I didn't expect to see you here!" She ran forward to one of the gamblers, who sat back against his chair as though he could see through everyone's cards and had the capacity to wait forever. John Holliday was a straw-haired, lanky man with a scrubby short beard from ear to ear. Perhaps his most remarkable feature was his mutton-chop mustache, so dark and large it swept downward on his narrow, jutting chin and gave him the look of a maharaja in a version of the *Arabian Nights.* Next to him, hanging on his arm, so near she could have seen his poker hand and betrayed his secrets with a twitch of her brow, was an oval-faced woman with a prominent beak of a nose that might have rendered any other face unattractive. But this was a magnificent nose that served as her icon, and she wore it with dignity and an amazing sense of self-assurance.

When he heard Marcella's cry, this Johnny Holliday raised his eyes, and a spark of recognition flickered in them. It was obvious he was trying to keep his gaming face together, but when he saw the woman in the red hat, his mouth opened just enough that the cigar lost its support and began to dangle from his lip. He took hold of himself quickly, pushed his cards face down on the table and stood, his cigar still dangerously leaning from the side of his mouth. "The baroness," he exclaimed. "What are you doing here?"

The woman at his side pulled back and eyed Marcella with an uneasy gaze. "Marcella! What brings you to Denver?" Libby thought she noticed a sneer in the woman's words, although they were somewhat lost in the faint music still hovering over the noise of the crowd. "And your party?" the woman said, looking over her nose through sharp brown eyes at Cotter and Libby.

"We're on our way to Tombstone to see Nora," Marcella replied. "Mr. Cotter is the new preacher at the Episcopal church." She presented him with an open palm. "And Miss Campbell, his ward."

A break in the sound of the piano brought a few seconds of quiet to the corner of the room. Libby felt uncomfortably like an animal in the zoo. Some of the other players at the table, and their accompanying women, turned to look at them. Some nodded their heads and smiled. But noticeably, one of them turned away from them and kept his head down. It was a disturbance that caught Libby's eye immediately. When she turned her head to discern the contrary movement, the man looked up and caught her gaze. His piercing stare struck her with a jolt. It was Grenville!

The man Marcella called Johnny Holliday muttered, "Well, Miss Baron, you came to tell the world Johnny Holliday is a killer. The fastest gun in the West?"

Marcella's eyes focused directly on him. "Are you always going to run from Kansas?"

"They've all been self-defense, Baroness." His voice was steady and low.

"Sure." She grinned.

While they stood across the table from one another, the players fell silent. Libby may have been the first to see the clandestine motion when it began, but she had issues of her own to deal with and would never have blown a whistle on a card player. The woman whose nose suggested she might have the inclination to enter into other people's business had slyly slipped her hands over Holliday's cards and moved them. She picked a couple of the corners up while her man was engrossed with Marcella. Libby saw the motion, but did not move a muscle.

But the man next to Holliday's girl must've also seen the movement, for he leaned above the cards.

Suddenly a crack broke the silence. The blast was so powerful it rocked the stained glass chandelier. Holliday, as smooth as though he had done this a thousand times, had removed his pistol and shot clean through the table. Smoke rose into the light and blurred the shocked faces. He was still watching Marcella when he swung his pistol on his fingers and replaced it at his side.

The girl Kate stood up at the crack of the shot and backed away from the smoking scene. "Johnny!" she cried out. Then she leaned forward and thrust both hands on the edge of the table as though she would fall. "Oh, I thought . . ."

"You didn't think," John Holliday said contemptuously. Without moving a muscle, he directed a comment to the cheater. "Kate's my business. But Curly Bill Brocius, you're in trouble." Never looking at his opponent, Holliday stayed as stiff as a gun barrel, his red-rimmed eyes smoldering. When he replaced the pistol, he pulled a kerchief from his pocket and coughed into it several times. When he withdrew it, it was stained with blood.

The cheater, Curly Bill Brocius, backed away from Kate. His eyes had opened so wide Libby could see the white around their black centers.

"You can hold your tongue, can't you, Marcella?" the pale-faced Holliday smirked.

"Sure, Doc," she said.

Libby watched Marcella's face. She smiled a crooked grin, as though she knew she had information that could put Doc Holliday behind prison walls for the rest of his life.

Libby was surprised to feel Cotter's hand on the small of her back. "We'd better go," he said.

Marcella looked watchful.

"See you in Tombstone," Doc Holliday said in a voice so low and piercing that it crawled like electricity up Libby's spine. She again caught the dark eyes of Charles Grenville and turned at the pressure of Cotter's hand as he steered her away from the table.

Coming toward them was the atelier at the hotel. "What . . . ?" he said to Cotter.

By now Marcella had also turned and smiled. "An old friend," she said to the host. "Anybody who allows Doc Holliday in their place has to expect a little fun."

Libby thought Marcella would want to stay at the table, but surprisingly, she turned and began to walk out with them.

"Don't go just because . . ." Cotter hesitated. "Don't you want to stay?"

"And get shot?" Marcella looked straight ahead to the exit. "No." She turned, smiling at Cotter. "John Holliday started his shenanigans some dozen years ago as a dental student at Valdosta, Georgia. He joined a bunch of friends who set a keg of powder off under the steps of the courthouse at a campaign rally for a Republican congressional candidate, J. W. Clift."

Cotter and Libby remained silent, and Marcella continued. "His father presented him with an 1851 Navy Colt revolver at his graduation from dental school on his twenty-first birthday, and the rest is the beginning of mayhem."

Ahead Libby saw the elaborate light of the train station winking in the dusk. She felt Cotter close behind her. She listened to Marcella's story, and she and Cotter interrupted only to ask an occasional question.

"He had a promising career in dentistry set ready for him with his cousin Robert, but suddenly John left Atlanta for Dallas, Texas. Nobody really knew why . . ." Marcella paused. "But I do."

The streets were busy with partygoers in tall hats and hoop skirts. Couples decked in ermine and feathers were making their way to the Windsor Hotel, or stepping out of taxis at the saloons.

"So why did he leave Atlanta?" Libby asked.

At that point a buckboard swung through a puddle at the curbside, and Marcella leaped back into Cotter, clutching her red hat. "Excuse me, preacher," she chimed a little too flirtatiously, Libby thought. She waited for a moment before she decided to ask her question again.

"Why did Mr. Holliday leave his promising dental practice with his cousin Robert?"

As they were nearing the train station, Marcella picked up her skirts at the street and concentrated on getting across. At the other side she stopped and turned to Cotter and Libby. They stood in a little circle as though to find some protection from the crowd moving around them.

"It was only ten years after the Civil War," Marcella said in a whisper so low Libby could barely hear her. "Georgia was not yet used to free blacks running about. Johnny found a group of them at his old swimming hole that he and his buddies had carefully dug out of a spot of land on his uncle's farm between the Little and Withlacoochee Rivers."

Libby moved forward to hear what Marcella was saying.

"Johnny and his friends told the black boys to leave—this was their swimming hole. The black boys mouthed him and threw clods of mud into the water to foul it purposely. So Johnny got out his new gun. His uncle claimed he just wanted to shoot into the air to warn them, but . . ."

"He hurt them?" Libby said.

"He killed two of them."

In the silence that followed, Marcella's words were suffused by the huge train station looming over them. And in the doorway the echo of her voice bounced off the granite walls and high ceilings.

Libby was not looking forward to sleeping cramped in the bench of their car, so she hung back inside the station, eyeing one of the long benches as a possibility. But Marcella and Cotter seemed to be moving forward to the tracks.

"He wanted to marry his cousin Mattie, but the family wouldn't hear of it . . . and he contracted tuberculosis." Marcella looked back at Cotter and continued, "The cousin became a nun."

Libby slept restlessly on the hard bench in their car, thinking about the thin doctor who spit blood into his handkerchief, and about the cousin he loved who became a nun. Libby would be glad when this journey was over. The dress and petticoat mounded and crackled when she stirred, waking her at odd times during the night. Often she opened her eyes briefly just to see the same electric lights out of the windows. She realized the train was not moving.

She had asked Cotter earlier, "Did you want to marry your cousin Frances?"

He had only murmured, "She's my cousin. My family is very strict."

"Does she really love that miner?"

Cotter did not answer.

7

The mountains frightened Libby. Sometimes the track was so narrow and the cliff at the side so precipitous, she believed she could feel the car leaning over, threatening to drop into the ribbon of river below.

"Once you said you would finish your story," she said to Marcella. "What happened to you and your brother and sister after the Chinese police killed your parents?"

"When we get to Tombstone, you'll find out soon enough," the woman replied evasively. "Did you think about what you're going to do to keep yourself alive when you get there?"

Libby still had the money in Cotter's pocket. Marcella didn't know about the gold. Still, the journey seemed endless, and the meals were expensive. Libby wasn't sure her resources would last. But she held out one great hope—Cotter. He would not let her down.

Finally, after several long days, they reached the desert. Libby had never imagined so many miles of nothing. There was an occasional cloud in the sky—even a skiff of January snow. But the land passed below her window in a blur of scrubby weeds and patches of sand and lava rock. The hills in the distance were thin strips of blue and gray. An occasional black dot on the horizon—cattle, deer, or even wild buffalo—represented the only sign of life. She dozed, or listened to Cotter mumble verses from the Bible.

They responded when Marcella left her bench to lean over them and ask how they were doing.

"You like reading that dull stuff?" she asked Cotter once.

"Tool of my trade." He smiled back at her.

"Cotter thinks all you have to do in this life to do well is to obey those commandments." Libby pointed at the pages.

Cotter tipped his head to her. "That's right. You're learning, Libby Campbell."

"I always thought that book to be dry gibberish." Marcella threw back her stock of raven hair and laughed. "There are many ways of doing well."

"Oh, there are no guarantees," Cotter said. "But there's a straight path—and a safer chance if you stay in it."

"Spoken like a preacher," Marcella quipped. "But there's nothing straight about Tombstone. If you don't finally let it corrupt you, I'll eat my hat."

Cotter didn't hesitate. "I'll take you up on that." He grinned back at her. "Get a hat you can chew on."

Sometimes passengers from one end of the train walked through their car to the other end of the train, or to the powder rooms. Libby found herself watching for Charles Grenville, but she did not see him again. Perhaps he stayed in Denver to finish the card game. She tried to replace the image of his piercing eyes. But sometimes, when she dozed, she saw him standing above her, his dark hair coarse on his brow, and his eyes boring through her.

"Benson, Arizona! End of the line!"

The shout was so thunderous, Libby lurched forward out of a dream. In her subconscious, she was flying over a dark cliff on the edge of the sea.

A short little man in a navy-blue uniform two sizes too big stomped down the aisle, shouting into the smoky air. "End of the line at Benson! Anything farther is on your own! Tucson, Phoenix—you'll have to hire a coach!"

Marcella stood and reached for her hat.

"Don't move until we stop," Cotter said to Libby. "Sometimes after they warn you, the train rattles on for another five or ten minutes."

Farmhouses sped by outside the window. The cattle in the fields looked wasted in the sun. The town of Benson was not much of a town. Straining to look out of the window, Libby saw a collection of dusty brick buildings on a wide street clogged with coaches and wagons. Horses were stomping and swatting flies with their tails.

"Benson! End of the line!" the man bellowed again. "Coaches leave every two hours!"

Libby sat back with Cotter and watched Marcella across the aisle tie a thin silk scarf around her hat brim and under her chin.

"So, the only way to get to Tombstone is by coach?" Libby asked Cotter.

"It's not much more than twenty miles, if that. At least that's what they told me."

When the cars moved more sluggishly into the station, the brakes squealed and metal clanked against metal, accompanied by the sound of heavy chains. Red lights flashed, and railroad personnel ran about moving bars and shouting orders as they changed the location of the engine along the cluster of tracks.

"They're serious," Cotter observed.

Marcella stood above them now, bundling her belongings in her arms. "You ready for the ride of your life?" She grinned.

"Ride of my life?" Cotter quipped. "Or ride *for* my life?"

"Both." Marcella laughed. "I've heard about these western stagecoaches. Cowboys and Indians, broken wheels, robbers!"

It took a few minutes for everyone to disembark from the train—and longer for the baggage to exit the storage car. The same squatty man who yelled "Benson" helped Marcella with her huge trunk.

About half a block ahead Libby saw two coaches parked in the dust. Some men stood around the vehicles, looking in the direction of the passengers. One of the coachmen hurried forward. "Tombstone?" he called, and Marcella waved and nodded. He enlisted one of the little wooden carts that stood by the tracks, and Cotter helped him lift Marcella's heavy trunk, take it to the cart, and tie it to the back of the coach.

"We have an hour and a half delay," the coachman said. "The Owl and the Pussy Cat Café serves good beefsteak, if you're at all hungry."

Marcella looked at Cotter. "They get your business in Benson. One way or another."

Libby wondered what kind of food they served at a restaurant with a name like that, but she was so hungry it didn't matter.

Several yards ahead, a couple of other coachmen and customers at the saloon stood talking, or just waiting. As soon as the trunk and other luggage were tied safely on the coach, and their tickets purchased, Libby followed Cotter and Marcella to The Owl and the Pussy Cat. One of the shorter men standing in front of the doorway to the saloon suddenly stepped away from his conversation and looked their way. He shaded his eyes with a hand that looked too large for his lean body.

Marcella stopped. Cotter and Libby didn't move ahead either.

"What's wrong?" Cotter asked.

"No!" Marcella's voice was husky with emotion. "No, it couldn't be!"

The small man, dressed in dapper pinstriped gray tails, wore a tall matching gray fur hat similar to the top hats Libby saw at the Windsor Hotel. A white cravat at his throat set off what looked like sun-leathered cheeks. "Marcella Baron?" He walked forward, his smart patent leather shoes hitting the boardwalk like the clack of a drum. "Marcella, is that you?"

"Horace? Horace Baron?" she said warily, holding herself back by reaching out for Cotter and Libby.

He started forward but must have seen her hesitancy. The crisp January air hung between them, wavering, until he threw back his properly hatted head and laughed. "Yes, I'm Horace. Unless somebody slips and calls me Horse. I'm used to it."

Libby noticed the ropy neck standing loose in the glaring white collar. The leathery color of the man's cheeks made quite a contrast to the fine clothes.

"I been called Horse Baron, and that's fine with me." He gave another sharp cackle. He had a little voice to match his dried-up body, which seemed almost invisible swimming in the dapper clothes. "If you want to know my longest name, it's Honest 'Horse's Mouth' Baron." When Marcella looked too dumbfounded to reply, Horace chortled and said, "Whatever comes from the horse's mouth? It's always true!"

Libby was stunned by the reunion scene. It was so sudden, it seemed to surprise them all.

Finally, Marcella graciously presented her hand to the man, and he leaned over to kiss it with a flourish. "You're a beauty, Sis, and I'm better'n horse glue. Stick with me and we'll go places!" He laughed again.

"Horace! It's hard for me to believe . . ."

"You sent me which train you was taking, and I been waiting here for you a day and a half. It's me, Sis. We been apart for thirty years!"

"But . . ." Marcella seemed to be recovering from her shock. "I thought you were going to meet me at Nora's in Tombstone."

"Well, ain't you lucky to meet me before you end up with some Tombstone? Ha ha!" There was only a brief pause. "Or are we already ghosts? Goin' to the graveyard?"

Marcella wasn't keeping up with his metaphors.

"If we are ghosts, you'll find out I'm transparently honest! You can see right through me! Ha Ha."

Marcella looked at Libby and Cotter now. "These are my friends, Cotter and Libby."

"Well, folks! Pleased, I'm sure. At least I dressed up for you."

"You certainly did," Marcella began. "Don't tell me . . . are these your duds, or did they give them to you when you got out of prison?"

"Hey, Sis, I earned these duds, cookin' at Hundred Mile Hotel. I worked for two businesses in Laramie before my wife got sick and I stole the neighbor's horse to go fetch the doctor."

Marcella was silent, and Libby could tell she was trying to size up her brother. But Marcella scowled when he mentioned he had stolen the horse.

Horace didn't seem to be bothered by her disapproval. He had more to say. "Yep. But I stole it from the wrong neighbor! An old biddy who made charges."

Libby couldn't take her eyes off the little brother. He looked like a parsnip floating around in a sea of fresh cucumbers.

"I had a wife." He got suddenly nervous. "At least at one time I thought I had one, anyway."

"Horace, I had no idea!"

"Spent eight months at the penitentiary, got released three weeks ago, came back, and she was gone! I sold the house and bought these clothes. Like 'em?"

Clearly, he wasn't searching for his wife. He had sold the house and spent most of the money on clothes. Marcella seemed wary. All she could say was "Horace. You look very nice."

Yes, Libby thought. *Nice like a scarecrow.*

"But I didn't expect . . ." Marcella continued.

"You was expecting a bum?"

"No, no."

"Ha! Maybe like the famous Englishman, James Lucas, who never washed?" Horace whiffed his armpit with a flourish. "People for miles around came to see him caked with grime."

Marcella frowned a little "No. No, I didn't know. I didn't know anything. And it will take a while to catch up."

"So . . . ask me anything. Anything out of the horse's mouth. I'm an honest horse." Horace chuckled. "A horse of a different color. Whatever you want to know. Yes, I was shot in the leg at Bunker Hill, played drums for the corps. Stole teeth out of the mouths of Confederates and sold them to dentists. I made a pretty good purse out of a sow's ear, so to speak."

"You fought with the Yankees?"

"Then left for Wyoming. We heard trains give you nosebleeds if they go fifteen miles an hour. But Elvira and me, we took our chances . . ."

"Was she your wife? Is she still your wife?" Marcella asked.

Horace turned away, probably not wanting to put on an emotional display in front of strangers. "I would tell ya' if I knew," he finally told his sister. "I would. Honest I would. But I think she's left me for good."

"Oh, Horace. I'm so sorry."

"When you seen my name in the paper in Kansas City and wrote me, I was sure that you was my family."

"Horace." Marcella looked him over carefully, still seeming undecided about many things.

He tossed it off with a laugh. "I've checked out The Owl and the Pussy Cat. I'll buy you some dinner. Bring your friends." He turned to Libby. "Do you want boiled cats or barbecued owl?"

Libby was speechless, but she noticed he put his hands deep into his pants pockets.

He laughed. "You look like the cat that ate the canary. Well, they stripped the fur and the feathers, young lady. Come on in, it ain't so bad. The dogs I used to cook at the Hundred Mile Hotel weren't nearly as good."

As they walked toward the restaurant, they passed the two other men still standing on the boardwalk. Horace called out, "We're going to the dogs!" The men grinned and waved. Horace murmured to Marcella and her friends, "Before you come along, I was talking to the fellow that runs shotgun on our stage. His name's Bob Paul. Ran for sheriff of Tombstone and lost."

"Shotgun on our stage?" Marcella said.

"That means he holds the shotgun all the way there. Usually sits up with the driver," Horace replied.

Marcella's brows rose. "Accompanied by a gunman? Does that mean we're in danger?"

Horace laughed again. "In this country? Always, Sis! Always in danger. Ain't you heard of Geronimo? In '58, a Mexican killed his family, and he's been on the rampage in this area ever since. Kill, kill, kill. We're livin' on the edge, Sis."

Marcella clearly didn't think it was funny. She kept her head down in the dim restaurant where a big Mexican with a tuft of beard on his chin asked them what they wanted. Libby ordered a baked potato. Cotter ordered a steak.

"No dog?" Horace teased. "You know, leg of dog? And I'm not pulling your leg." He laughed again. "In early spring the Chinese rubbed the doglegs with rock salt, squeezed out the blood, and packed 'em in a wooden tub, and on the fifth, tenth, and sometimes fifteenth day, they turned 'em over and rubbed 'em again."

Libby watched Marcella. She was deciding on a piece of fish and a tomato pie.

"They rubbed 'em down with salt every five days, for maybe twenty days. Then hung 'em in the breezy shade for six months. Sometimes they coated the thighs with sesame seeds."

Cotter turned away slightly, and Libby thought she detected a grin on his lips.

"But maybe that isn't the yummiest dish in history. Not many people know that Louis Fourteen's mummified heart was stolen by the French rebels and eaten by a biologist by the name of William Buckland. Now that ought to have been a dish!"

Libby wasn't listening anymore. Her meal had come and she was mashing the hot baked potato and adding a huge dollop of butter. She would insist on paying for it herself, so she asked Cotter for her money bag. She notified him with a jerk of her elbow and a whisper while she still watched Horace politely, nodding when it was appropriate.

Marcella was staring at her brother, and from her expression, Libby guessed she was wondering, *Is this my brother, the one my sister and I knew long ago?*

Cotter also listened politely. He reached into his shirt for the money bag and passed it to Libby under the table. After setting down her knife and fork, she put her hands under the tablecloth to take out a small coin to pay for her dinner. Then she drew the string tight and put the bag back on Cotter's knee.

Now the subject had changed, and all of them were involved in hearing Horace talk about his life in China. "I was only six years old about the time the British forced the Treaty of Nanking at the end of the first opium war and leased Honk Kong for ninety-nine years. Ha! When they come through and killed our mother and father—since they was not Chinese, and was Christians to boot— the rogues sold me to a fisherman. What'd they do with you, Marcella? I never knew."

She smiled and glanced briefly in Libby's direction. But Marcella did not answer her brother's questions or respond to his outlandish expostulations. "Oh, it's a long story. I'll tell it sometime."

While they were talking, Cotter suddenly pulled away from the table and leaned over to the floor to pick up his napkin. Libby noticed that it took him a while. Maybe he had to tie his shoe.

"Shall we go?" Marcella asked.

But just then, one of the men from the sidewalk entered the saloon and hailed Horace. He was the tall one—huge, as a matter of fact. He wore a graying beard, and a white mustache with black marks in it, thick under his nose like an old broom. His wrinkled brown wool suit looked like it had been dragged through the dust. But a smart gold chain hanging from his vest indicated he had a watch with him. And when he pulled it out and squinted at it, he looked like a comfortable old gentleman used to flipping that watch cover every few minutes as though it was his responsibility to share his superior knowledge with those around him.

"Mr. Paul," Horace exclaimed, then introduced him. "This is Mr. Paul from Tucson, who was the sheriff of Pima County. They been having trouble on the Well Fargo stage, so he comes here to help from time to time. The Wells Fargo stage was attacked last month. They think bad people was trying to kill the newspaper man, a Mr. Clum. So that fella got off the stage when nobody was looking and walked all the way to Tombstone." Horace chattered on cheerily in his usual manner, as though he had known Bob Paul for years. "He was the one I told you about who ran for sheriff in this new Cochise County. And he should have won. There was some hanky panky countin' the votes in that election. They was a group of cowboys in San Simon who stuffed the ballot box. They gave names to all the dogs, poultry, and burros, and then all those creatures got a vote! The election commission found them out, though, and discounted San Simon. I believe it was the same group tried to kill that newspaper fella, Clum. Ain't that right, Mr. Paul? Curly Bill Brocius and Johnny Ringo. Somethin' like that."

Libby vaguely recalled hearing the name Curly Bill Brocius at the poker table in Denver. She remembered it because of the man's curly hair. When he had peered at John Holliday's cards, the quick-drawing gambler put some lead straight into the table.

Mr. Paul didn't respond to Horace's historical information. He'd probably already heard it many times before. "Are you folks ready?" Mr. Paul asked.

"Sure. Any time," Horace said, then turned to speak to everyone. "He should a' been sheriff. This man's a pot shot. He can take care of us if anybody can."

"I . . . wanted to let you know," Mr. Paul began. "There's a young man I know from Tombstone who wants a ride. We might be a bit crowded. Hope you folks won't mind?"

"No, we're as friendly as sardines, ain't we?" Horace laughed.

Cotter said, "All right, fine. We're not hard to get along with."

When Mr. Paul led them out of the restaurant, one of the other men who had been waiting came toward them.

"It's okay, Bill," Mr. Paul said. "Let's go."

Bill? It wasn't Curly Bill Brocius, was it? Libby would wait. She couldn't see any curly heads in the group.

8

At the coach, Mr. Paul climbed up beside Rex Phillips, the driver, and set his shotgun on his knee. Phillips was a clean-shaven young man wearing chaps and a red shirt. With his long fingers he handled the reins with the touch of a piano player.

Mr. Paul was right—the stagecoach was crowded. There were two facing seats, room enough for four, but Libby found herself stuffed between Cotter on her right and this new man, Bill, on the left. She pinched up her dress and tried to settle it around her legs, all the time wishing she hadn't traded her overalls for it.

Horace smiled at the man. "Well, good afternoon, cowboy."

"Name's Bill Byers." He was leaning against the window in as tight a space as he could inoffensively put himself. He had a toothpick in his teeth.

"Happy to have you with us," Horace said.

Maybe he is happy, Libby thought, but she was miserable, feeling cramped and overcome by what smelled like hot cows.

"You livin' in Tombstone?" Horace probed.

"If you call it livin'," Bill Byers said. He leaned his head back and seemed to peer at them from tiny slits of eyes, all the while keeping a straight face with the toothpick jumping around between his lips.

"Gonna be the tombstone of all us? Ha ha."

Horace's laugh didn't affect a single muscle in Bill's face. "You know what's goin' on there, I trust?" the cowboy asked.

Marcella and Libby were quiet. But Libby turned to look at the man crushed beside her. His face looked like hog leather beaten with the blunt point of a knife.

"No law there," Bill Byers continued. "The lawmen are killers."

"Is that so?" When the coach rocked Horace forward, he looked at this Bill with a question in his eyes.

"Last October the sheriff's deputies killed three men at the OK Corral."

"Nora wrote about that to me," Marcella said.

"Did they just shoot them down?" Horace wanted to know.

"Yep," Bill drawled, looking out of the coach window. "Big war."

"A war?" Horace leaned forward.

"A big war," Bill Byers repeated. "Them law people, them Earps down there . . ."

Marcella piped in. "What about the Earps? How did it start?"

Bill Byers looked down at her through the slits in his eyes. "Dumb government mules. They wandered onto Tom McLowry's land. Some of Tom's hired hands killed a couple of them mules and started to skin 'em. The Earps come and say they are government mules and will arrest Tom and his men if they don't return 'em."

"Did they return them?" Horace asked.

"No. Two of 'em was swolled up, putrid flesh without skin on 'em. Infested with flies. Government didn't want 'em." Bill laughed.

"Did they return the rest?"

"No. Tom said the mules come by their own on his land, and he don't hold with no trespassers on his property."

For a moment there was quiet. Libby digested all of this information without looking at the source. The man was so close to her she thought she could feel his heartbeat.

"So then what happened?" Marcella wanted to know.

"War. The Earps harassed the boys when they brought a gun into town."

"No guns allowed in town?" Marcella asked.

"No guns allowed in town." Bill Byers bit on the toothpick and looked out the window. No one said anything for a moment, until he blurted, "It don't hurt none to bring a gun into town once't in a while effen' you don't use it."

"You ever used it?" Horace goaded him.

"I tried once," Bill drawled. "I'm a quick shot with the Mexicans. But when they jumped us at Guadaloupe, thinkin' Old Man Clanton had some of their cows, they was quicker. They was killin' my buddies and strippin' off clothes. So's I stripped naked and got flat on the ground and pretended I was dead. And I came out okay." He turned to look straight across the coach at Horace and Marcella. His eyes opened and Libby glanced over to see a sly light in them. "The old Clanton father and four of my buddies was killed that day. We didn't see them ambushers, but we think it was the Earps and Doc Holliday. They was there in that area at the time."

Horace and Marcella were quiet. But Cotter peered over at Mr. Byers and said, "So I was reading about a Bill who killed that marshal, Frank White."

Bill Byers's eyes snapped, and he turned to Cotter in a quick jerk. "No, that ain't me, if that's what you're thinkin'. No, I ain't that Bill. That was Bill Brocius, Curly Bill Brocius, whose other names are Bill Allen, or Bill Breakenridge, or whatever.

You think Mr. Paul would let that Bill ride on this stage, you got another think comin'."

Libby heard an entirely different tone in Bill Byers's voice, as though he had been accused of being Brocius once or twice in his life, and he could fight back if anybody called him on it. "Have you ever met him?" she asked Byers.

"Oh, I know Brocius, one of the . . . rancheros."

They waited for more.

"That Curly Bill killed Marshal Frank White," Byers went on. "Stupid Wyatt Earp's fault for trying to disarm him."

"Stupid Wyatt Earp?" Marcella repeated. "My sister Nora thinks the Earps are the only ones making the law stick down there."

Byers lowered his head until his glance looked sinister below his tight brows. "You don't know nothin', lady. The Earps are killers."

"What happened to Curly Bill?"

"Well, it weren't his fault!" Byers declared. "They tried him and let him go. It was too bad. Frank White was a reasonable lawman, not like them killers, the Earps. Them Earps have got to be taken off the face of the earth." He paused briefly. "At least we keep tryin'. My friends Johnny Ringo, Ike Clanton, and Johnny Barnes shot up Virgil a couple weeks ago at the Oriental Saloon. But it didn't take. He's still gallivantin' with his brothers—wounded, but alive as ever."

No one said anything for a while. Horace looked out the window. Libby saw him bounce with the rough motion of the coach. He seemed to be thinking something through.

Byers suddenly leaned forward and began to whisper as though he would share something with these strangers that he didn't want anyone else to know. "You know that big fellow up top of this coach, Bob Paul?"

"Talked to him this afternoon. Learned a little about what's been goin' on around here," Horace said.

"You learned his spin on things. He's an Earp fan. The Earps wanted him to be the sheriff. But us cowboys got together and elected John Behan."

Horace raised his head. "Was you cheatin' to do it?"

Bill laughed. "Ha! You heard the truth. We named all the chickens and livestock, and you never seen such smart animals in all your life! Voted out the murderers—Earps and that John Holliday."

"John Holliday?" Marcella said. "We saw him in Denver?"

Bill looked wary now. "Yeah . . . that Doc Holliday is a killer, right with the Earps. Killed Bud Philpot robbin' this stage."

"Holliday robbed this Benson stage?" Horace sat up, an alert look in his eyes.

"Yep, this Benson stage," Bill said. "And because he's a mining partner with Wyatt Earp, nobody does nothing about it."

Libby turned her head toward the other window. She watched Marcella's eyes. They were wide open, fastened on Bill Byers.

"They robbed this stage coach?" Marcella repeated.

"Yes, ma'am. It was Doc Holliday who killed the driver, Bud Philpot. It was Doc's girl, Big Nose Kate, who ratted on him."

"Holliday?" Horace squinted his eyes at Marcella. "Didn't you say he was the one who killed the black boys at the pond?"

Bill grimaced. "See what I mean? He's a killer. He was at the OK Corral shootin' and killin' Bill Clanton and two McLowry boys. All of 'em shootin' so fast nobody knew who killed who."

9

Libby did not look at Bill Byers's face. Feeling very uneasy, she kept her gaze out the window. Cotter's arm was close to her, and she wondered if he shared her reservations. She dared to raise her eyes to his face. He returned her gaze, and as he looked away, he brought his hand up in a gesture of dismissal, as though to say "Don't believe a word," or "It's all right, Libby." She took the gesture to mean she ought to relax. So she calmed herself and peered out of the window to see where they were.

Suddenly the stagecoach slowed down. Outside on the road, a sign read, "Drew's Station." It was a cluster of hastily built structures, an outpost furnishing fresh horses along the road. The travelers were surrounded.

Libby's heart leaped as she saw two men with black bandanas tied around their faces. When they pointed their guns at the coach, the air went out of her lungs.

"No way!" Horace muttered. "Oh my!"

"Now, we don't want no one to get hurt," Bill said, the toothpick no longer in his mouth. He had drawn a small pistol from his pocket. "Just get out slow. All we want is money."

Libby couldn't believe it. The man Bill had known what was going to happen all along. Their worst nightmare was taking place!

"It's just money. We ain't murderers," Bill declared. "Just follow directions."

Marcella looked at the ceiling of the coach. "Where is that Mr. Paul?"

A shot rang out.

Marcella's eyes grew huge with fear. "What's that?"

"They're shootin' the rifle out of Paul's hands. He ain't got a chance, lady. Just do as we say and you won't get hurt."

Libby shivered.

"Keep your hands high. No talkin'," Bill ordered. "Get out of the coach and stand in a line. Come on, come on. Don't be shy. If there's no trouble, there's no killin'."

Libby's heart knocked around in her ribs. She noticed the sky—how blue it was, and the hills in the distance. Other than the outpost, there was not much here, just unlimited fields of sand-colored dust dotted with green sage and an occasional cactus. At least now she could breathe without smelling the barnyard odor on Bill's clothes. And he would not be crowding her in the seat again.

Bill stood guard with the pistol in his right hand, while one of the masked men hustled Bob Paul and the driver off their perch. Mr. Paul was holding his right hand with his left, and blood was coursing through his fingers.

"I ain't done this before," Bill said, "which is why Bob Paul was fooled big time. But he should know Wells Fargo gets robbed at least once a year. Ain't that right, Ike?" Bill spoke to one of the men training his rifle on Bob Paul. The young driver Mr. Paul called Phillips looked terrified, and dropped the reins.

"The rich guys are movin' in on us cattlemen, so we're entitled to some of this," Bill continued. He rummaged around in the luggage and pulled up a pouch that looked like it was chock full of coins pushing through the canvas. "We'll take this, thank you very much. But we know you folks has got some, too."

While Bill blabbed, the man who forced Paul and Phillips off the high coach seat handed his gun to Bill. He began at one end of the line, patting his big hands down Phillips' red shirt and then his trousers. When he did not find anything, he did the same to Bob Paul. This time he hit pay dirt, finding Bob's watch. He took it out and grinned. "Well, lookee what I found. You may not have beat Johnny Behan in the election, but you still got a fine watch!"

Libby tried not to show her shock. "If you are ever afraid, don't let it on," her mother had told her. "Fight back by thinking positive. Nothing can hurt you if you don't let it." Her mother ought to have known, since she had survived the murder of her husband and the cruelty of John Stuyvesant, who had practically purchased her as a slave. She had learned to be quiet in his house and do what she was told until he trusted her completely and made her head housekeeper.

Libby's heart raced like a quick drumbeat. She had been so afraid she had not thought about her own treasure inside Cotter's pocket until the villain reached the preacher and began to press his hands down his coat. *My gold! The thief will find it!*

But there was something about Cotter that intercepted the rage in the young man who approached him. Libby had felt it. Cotter was one who could radiate confidence in the midst of chaos, like coming upon a still pool of water in a dry forest raging with fire. As he began to pat the preacher's suit, the masked man almost visibly shook. "You a man of God, mister?" He sneered. "It don't mean much when you ain't got any money, does it?"

Libby kept still.

"I don't bring a lot with me," Cotter said.

The man found Cotter's wallet in his lapel and brought it out. He rifled through it and took out the paper bills.

Horrified, Libby couldn't breathe. But she held steady.

"Five lousy bucks?" the masked man mocked. "Well, you ain't well heeled. But you're thinkin' God will take care of you, right?" He laughed.

"He always has," Cotter replied.

It seems like a joke, Libby thought, *but it is probably true.* She wished Cotter hadn't honored him with any statement at all. Why was he so calm in the midst of pins and needles?

As she watched the man continue to pat Cotter down at his belt, and now into his jacket pockets, she said a prayer in her heart. If they found her gold, she would be penniless in Tombstone. Her mouth and throat went dry.

But in a move she had not expected, the masked man suddenly stood back and counted the five dollars he had already retrieved from Cotter's wallet and then moved on. He was passing up Cotter without the gold! He moved to Marcella with a hungry look in his eye and began feeling her ribs. Libby was not sure what had happened. Where was her little bag—the only resources she had? The robber would have found it.

Marcella didn't flinch under the thief's touch. She actually joked, as though she enjoyed being felt up and down. She must have known she had hidden her fortune well, for they could find nothing on her—at least nothing they were willing to go for. Marcella had probably hidden her purse inside her "bustier," and Libby figured the thief was too shy to open that up. But when they reached Horace, they found a thin wallet and robbed him of several hundred dollars.

Mr. Paul glanced at them with a painful look, clutching his wounded hand. Blood still dropped to the ground. He stood silently, as did Rex Phillips and the passengers, while the robbers talked among themselves. Finally they nodded to the trembling Phillips, as though giving him permission to take the coach away. The gang mounted their horses. Bill Byers, grinning, looked back at Bob Paul and said, "Don't you wish you would a' won the election to be sheriff instead of working as a stupid shotgun on Wells Fargo?" He waved largely. "Thanks, Bob, but not even John Behan will find me, for I'll be off to Colorado!" He mounted a horse the others had ready for him, and the three robbers rode away, hooting their success at the top of their lungs.

Mr. Paul had a swollen face that already looked as though it had been pockmarked by grief. "I'm so sorry," he said to them as one by one they climbed the steps back up into the stage. He held his handkerchief around the thumb that had taken the hit, untied one of the horses from the team, climbed it bareback, and waved to the driver to get the coach into town. It was only a dozen miles now, he had told them as he mounted. He would get Sheriff Behan to go after the gang as soon as possible. But Mr. Paul had added, "Not that it will do much good."

Stunned, Libby did not say anything until they were again seated inside the coach. "I can't believe it!" she said finally. When Horace and Marcella commiserated over his losses, Libby whispered to Cotter, "What happened to my gold?"

Cotter, with a quiet, steady gaze, let a smile play on his lips. "Do you remember when you gave me back your little bag in the restaurant?"

She did. She had put it on his knee.

"And I leaned over to pick up my napkin?"

Now she remembered. It had taken a long time for him to come up for air.

"Well, I slipped your money into my shoe. Didn't you see me stagger to the lineup?"

Libby grinned.

10

With the young driver at the helm, and one horse missing, the stagecoach crawled the last twelve miles to the city of Tombstone. All around them, the land rippled into distant blue ribbons of hills through barren sand, spotted only occasionally with sage or cactus. The sky hovered like gauze in the wavering slats of the low-lying winter sun.

From the window Libby saw occasional groups of cattle standing against the raw brown landscape, grasping for some morsel from the dead ground.

"This land ain't much," Horace muttered. "Wonder if it was worth the four cents an acre the gov'ment paid for it."

In the distance the town came into focus like a collection of small dice thrown together in the folds of a burlap feed bag. As they drew nearer, Libby saw a collection of tombstones planted haphazardly on a small rise.

"Looks like some of them Tombstone people is sleeping with tombstones now," Horace exclaimed.

No one else commented.

Among the gravestones, a silhouette bent over a placard in the dry ground. Soon Libby could see it was a small Chinese woman placing flowers one by one on a grave.

"Hey, what d'ya know," Horace mused. "Ain't she from . . ."

"There's lots of Chinese here," Marcella said. "Nora tells me that there is one woman in charge of every one of them. China Mary. Nobody does nothing unless they ask her. Especially her . . ." She hesitated. "Especially her girls."

Before they reached the graveyard, a group of men on horseback appeared through the haze and dust like the teeth of a comb rising into view.

"Oh, oh," Horace said. "A welcoming committee?" He seemed to be the only one still lively after the ordeal they had just suffered. The others seemed to be in shock, or waiting to see what would happen next.

Libby recognized Bob Paul on the leading horse, one different from the animal he took from the team. His right hand was wrapped in a large white bandage, and his left clutched the reins. Beside him rode a slender man with dark eyes, thick brows, and a small chin and ears. Libby guessed he was the sheriff of Tombstone. Four others rode behind him.

"That fella dead or alive?" Horace began. "Or are they doin' that Spanish trick—an El Cid, strappin' the leadin' corpse to his horse?"

Whatever that was, Libby thought. "That's another fellow riding beside Mr. Paul." Curious, she focused her eyes on the blur of dust, faces, bodies, and legs that hurtled toward them. Were these the lawmakers Bill Byers had called "killers"—the Earp brothers? Remembering Bill Byers and his lies, she thought she could smell a whiff of cow dung.

When the posse surrounded the coach, Mr. Paul shouted through the window, "We're going after them. Doc Holliday will see you back into town."

The man who now separated himself from the posse turned his horse so quickly on its hooves, the dust rose into a column of gray. His face loomed white under the wide-brimmed hat. He was dressed in a natty black suit of clothes over a white shirt and a solid red silk tie. Libby knew he was the same man they had seen in Denver playing cards. John Holliday. How had he come here so quickly, ahead of them? A brief thought that he might have been behind one of the black masks at Drew's Station flitted into her mind. "He is the worst killer," Bill Byers had said.

John Holliday stayed just ahead of the coach and exchanged a few words with the driver, Phillips. When the stagecoach reached the graveyard, Holliday raised his arm, and Phillips brought the three horses to a stop. Libby strained to see this Doc Holliday's face. His skin was a pasty color against the dark roots of his hair. He moved into the cemetery on his horse, not paying much attention to whose grave he trampled. When he reached the Chinese woman, he leaned over and appeared to speak to her. She rose quickly. Libby could see that under her loose clothes, the woman was buxom, and round like a billiard ball, her face as white as a mask and as flat as a frying pan. Mr. Holliday pointed to the coach, whereupon the woman gave a wide smile and began walking toward them, her feet shuffling away on the ground in embroidered slippers. She had left all of her flowers and carried only the basket.

"China Mary, folks," Mr. Holliday said, drawing his horse close to the door of the vehicle.

"Ah sung! Velly happy meet you!" The woman smiled. "I speak little English." She looked into the coach, then glanced back at Mr. Holliday. "No room, no room."

But Libby moved her mounds of crinoline closer to Cotter—again. And China Mary smiled and climbed in, saying something in what had to be Chinese.

Libby was stunned when Marcella responded in the same language. She could speak Chinese! *Of course.* The words struck something in Libby's heart. Marcella's parents had been killed in China when Marcella and her little sister Nora had been nine and seven years old, and their brother Horace had been four or five.

Libby shouldn't have been surprised when Horace also spoke to Mary in Chinese. When he finished, he quickly said to Libby, "I asked her if she has a loved one in the grave."

Libby glanced at Cotter, who seemed to be enjoying every word of the musical tongue.

China Mary's eyes lit up with excitement. "Oh, speakee Chinee. Oh, wunnerful. Yes, Foo Kee."

Horace asked her another question in her language, then translated for Libby and Cotter, "Did someone die?"

"Foo Kee." Mary's happy expression disappeared. "How you say mis-take. Mistake?"

"Mistake."

"Wing Lung's best friend was stab." Mary gestured toward her heart as if holding a dagger. She made several quick pounding motions against her ample bosom.

Marcella looked at Libby and Cotter. "Wing Lung was Foo Kee's best friend. Some robbers came to Foo Kee's store and tore up the place. He went after them, and in the confusion he accidentally killed his best friend."

Horace shook his head. "His best friend made a mistake and stabbed him dead."

Extremely cramped now, with the little round China Mary lodged in the coach, Libby turned to the window. Staring at the sky, the dust of the bare hills, she felt a tremor in her bones. What was this place, where so much shooting, so much fighting, so much anger happened that one could make a mistake and kill his best friend?

Thinking of mistakes, how was it that Libby had decided to come to Tombstone?

11

When the coach pulled into the streets of Tombstone, Libby drew back inside and leaned against the padded wood next to the window. *I'll just stay right here and ask to buy a ticket to take me back to Benson.* She waited while Marcella and Horace got out. Horace seemed elated to have finally arrived. He began reading the flyers pasted to the windows of the hotel. China Mary slipped down the steps and scurried away.

Cotter was last to leave. After he gathered his books and his gloves and scarf, he said politely, "Are you coming, Miss Campbell?"

She looked at him. What was he going to do in this place? She dared to glance out the window. As near as she could tell, they were in front of the Cosmopolitan Hotel. Along the wide street stood several other hotels and rooming houses. Brown's Hotel, The Grand, The American Lodging House. Several restaurants and saloons sported ornate façades. On the corner of Fifth and Allen Street, a sign read, "The Occidental Saloon," and nearby to it, "The Alhambra," and the "Oriental Saloon." Another sign said, "Tivoli Gardens." There were other kinds of establishments, purveyors of ready-made furniture and goods, such as P. W. Smith and Company, and McKean and Knight's store on the corner of Allen and Sixth. Part of Smith's store looked like it was reserved for the Pima County Bank. A sign for The Rescue Hook and Ladder Company hung on a small building marked "Engine Company #1." So, the town was at least equipped to take care of fires, Libby thought. She knew they had learned the hard way, though. Cotter had read her a newspaper article about how sixty-six businesses in Tombstone had burned to the ground on June 22 of the past year, and how the tough people of the territory had rebuilt everything within a few months.

Miss Campbell? How strange that Cotter now addressed her so formally. It was awkward for him to be bent over in the coach for so long, but Libby realized he was waiting for her.

"Are you coming?" he asked.

How is Cotter, pure as the driven snow, going to survive in this town? Libby wondered. If he was here, perhaps she could try it. "Sure," she said, and put out her hand. He took it and pulled her up. The crinoline crackled, and the dress unfolded like the revival of a crumpled paper bag. Grasping Cotter's hand sent a powerful electrical charge through her.

"Be brave," he said. "It's not going to last forever."

She gritted her teeth, silently promising herself that she would hold on to him if nothing else happened here. His gracious manners were the last bastion of civility she could count on.

Her vow became all the more intense when she leaned out at the top step to begin her descent from the coach. The minute she put one foot after another to proceed down into the town, she regretted it. The air in the street hit her like a powerful gas. It was filled with a stench so fetid, she almost couldn't breathe. Garbage and refuse rotted on the boardwalks of the hotels and establishments, and newspaper lay trampled and torn everywhere. Libby read "The Nugget" at the top of some of the front pages. In one filthy gap between two buildings, dogs growled, fighting over a bone.

"Oh," Cotter said, glancing down at her as though interested in her reaction.

She could not speak. She had left a Kansas City mansion whose floors were washed down every day—for this?

"You sure you wanted to come here?" Cotter asked.

"Are *you* sure?" Libby shot back at him.

He stood tall beside her, clean and very out of place in the dusty street. He looked extremely civil against the background of garbage, garish signs, and horses whipping their tails. "It's entirely different for me," he said. "There is work to do here, and I'm here to do that work."

Libby wished she had a mission here too.

After Mr. Phillips untied the luggage and Cotter took his own case down off the rack, he had to help Marcella undo her trunk and place it on the dolly. Horace carried his own valise.

Marcella was still the picture of anticipation. "I am so excited to see Nora! Just turn on Sixth. It's not far. You wouldn't mind, would you?"

Earlier Cotter had told her he had reservations at The American Lodging House, run by Mr. and Mrs. Grant. Libby had no idea what she was going to do—only that she would follow Cotter as long as she could.

The house Nora kept was a handsome two-story Victorian mansion of red brick with a black slate roof, navy-blue porch steps, and pillars of dark green. Libby was not sure of the color combination, but the house seemed sturdy, and the scrappy bushes boasted white flowers. She had never seen flowers growing in January, and come to think of it, she had not seen any live flowers for a very long time.

Horace stayed reservedly standing beside the luggage in the street, but Marcella almost tripped as she hurried up the blue steps, holding her skirts high. At the door, she knocked energetically. "I'm sure there's always somebody here," she said back to the others.

When no one answered, she came back down the steps to stand with Cotter and Libby on the pathway. "I don't know why no one is around," she told them.

But soon they heard the sound of a chain sliding into a lock, and Marcella turned. Whoever had come to the door did not open it very wide. From the dark crack of the door over the chain, a white face peered through.

"Nora? Nora Baron? Is this the house of Nora Baron?" Marcella said loudly. Horace began to pick up the luggage.

The face behind the door scrambled back into the dark, and in the dusky interior of the house a voice faintly called, "Nora!"

And then something happened that Libby would never forget. When the face behind the door disappeared toward the back to fetch Nora, someone else took hold of the knob, undid the chain, and with a swift movement, opened the door wide. Libby stared. It was a man. Very tall, wearing a black stovepipe hat, and wrapped in a large black cloak. She knew him. It was Charles Grenville!

Libby gasped.

When Mr. Grenville saw her standing with Marcella and Cotter, a look of surprise crossed his face, but as he spoke his voice was as steady as ever. "Well, Miss Campbell!" He stepped onto the porch and tipped his hat to Marcella, Cotter, and Horace.

"Mr. Grenville," Marcella gushed. "This is a surprise! Did you know this was my sister's place?"

While Marcella and Charles exchanged pleasantries, Libby tried to quiet her nerves.

"Yes, you told me about Nora, remember?"

"Oh, yes, I did. I remember." Marcella seemed flustered.

As he departed, Charles looked back and tipped his hat to her, and again to the party he had met briefly on the train. "Nice to see you have all arrived safely in Tombstone," he said with a curt bow of his head to everyone. But his eyes pierced Libby. "I'm sure I'll see all of you here in the city from time to time." He nodded, and then suddenly reached out and touched Libby's elbow. "I'll see you soon."

She felt assaulted by his stare.

"Marcella!" A woman who had to be Nora appeared at the door and ran across the porch and down the steps. She rushed forward with her arms spread wide.

"And this is Horace, Nora," Marcella exclaimed.

"Horace!" Nora smiled. "Oh, I'm so glad to see you."

While the two sisters and their brother embraced, Cotter and Libby glanced at one another.

"Did she ask you to stay here?" Cotter said under his breath.

"For a while," Libby said quietly. "She talked me into it. I don't know what I'm doing. I told her she was very nice to give me a place to sleep. Otherwise I could try to get a room at your hotel."

"There was only one room left when I made reservations from the telegraph office in Salem, Massachusetts. I'm not sure there's any room in town." Cotter paused. "Seems to me you need a little time to look around and find out what your options are. Might be okay for a night or two." He took a moment to gaze at the house. In the upper story in the dormer window a white-faced woman looked back at him.

Libby was not naive. Though no one had breathed a word about Nora's manner of earning a successful sustenance, or the probable profession of Marcella Baron, Libby knew more about it than she was willing to admit. Marcella had been kind and very persuasive.

And Libby was "at sea." Here was the only acquaintance who had ever offered her shelter, and even clothing.

When the three siblings turned to walk up the steps, Marcella beckoned to Cotter and Libby. "Come on, you two. Come in for just a visit."

Libby stepped forward, but glanced back and saw Cotter hesitate. "Thank you so much, Marcella, Horace, Nora," he said. "It has been so nice to meet you. But I am anxious to get settled at the lodging house and meet my parishioners."

Libby's blood went cold. *He is leaving me!* She nearly panicked. But she couldn't very well blurt out anything childish. She couldn't seem to form any words in her mouth that would express how abandoned she felt. The realization crowded out the breath in her lungs.

He looked down at her from his great height. "You'll be all right for a few days, Libby, if you hold to your hopes."

Hold to your hopes? Is that really all he could say to her? They had spent so long side by side. Did she even *have* hopes? If so, what were they, really? Had she ever told him anything that resembled a plan she might have conceived for her stay at Tombstone? In a split second of revelation she knew she had been relying with all her heart on the possibility that she could stay close to him and feel protected in his presence.

Unexpected tears blinded her vision, but she forced them away quickly.

"Will you be all right?" Cotter said. There was a pause. She could not really see, but she felt him take her hand. He cradled her small fingers in his huge palm and laid something heavy in it. Of course—her bag of gold.

"Come to my services on Sunday," he said. "I would be honored. The District Courthouse on Fremont Street. Eleven o'clock."

Why didn't you expect this moment, plan for it? Libby berated herself. Nothing could ever erase from her memory the glorious feeling of being under the wings of this gentle man. She thought her heart was breaking, but she would hold it together with the scolding she was giving to herself.

"We'll see you, Cotter." Marcella smiled and moved toward him, her skirts rustling against the wood slats of the boardwalk. "It was such a pleasure to make your acquaintance." She took his hands in both of hers and held them. Unexpectedly she leaned up close to him and kissed his cheek. "Good luck bringing your Bible talk to Tombstone."

He bowed graciously and turned. As he turned, he looked at Libby one last time, then appealed to Marcella. "Take care of our young friend here, will you?"

"Of course we will, won't we, Libby?" she crooned.

Libby watched the tall, light-haired preacher turn and walk away.

Marcella took Libby's arm. "When I first saw you I thought you were his little sister." Her step quickened as she tugged Libby forward. "Nora, I trust we will have room for Horace? And I promised Libby a place to stay for a while."

Nora's eyes flashed. "Of course, of course. She's beautiful, Marcella. She's a very beautiful girl!"

12

Walking into the dim house, Libby could not see clearly for several seconds. Finally, she made out a window draped with panels of exquisitely embroidered Chinese brocade, emitting a shadowy light through tightly gathered purple gauze. A large leather settee sat under the window, decorated with maroon pillows covered in lace. At each end of the settee, a delicate carved table held a lamp with a cut-glass shade trimmed in gold fringe. There were graceful chairs upholstered in maroon velvet, and a loveseat with a carved back of cherrywood. Lace doilies adorned all the plush arms and headrests, and on the mantle of the high marble fireplace.

"Oh, it's lovely, Nora!" Marcella gushed.

"The furniture was shipped from Milan," Nora said proudly. "This is our reception area." She looked back at Horace. "You may be sleeping on our divan here." She laughed. "Unless you want to try the cot in my room."

Once her eyes adapted more fully to the darkness, Libby saw a large sign hanging from the archway that led into the parlor. Part of the wood was badly burned, but the message was readable: "Bless House." A word between "Bless" and "House" had been ravaged by flames. Libby presumed the sign had originally read, "Bless This House."

"We found the sign after the fire last June 22, 1881," Nora explained. "We don't care about the missing word. It still makes sense. We call ourselves Bless House. We are in the business of offering blessings. That is our business."

Now Libby noticed a row of girls standing on the far side of the parlor, near the opening that probably led to the rest of the house. She counted three of them, their white faces rising into focus like petals of roses slowly responding to light.

"And these are a few of our girls." Nora gestured. "Little Gertie—Gertie the Gold Dollar. She's little, like the coin the U.S. Mint makes that's smaller than a dime but worth a dollar." Nora paused and lifted the little woman's chin. "She's smaller than anything we've ever seen, but worth everything." Gertie was tiny, all right, about four feet tall with mousy brown hair piled on the top of her head. That heap resembled a big dropping in a crowded corral, Libby thought.

"And this is Mag. We have a Margarita, but this is Mag." Nora lowered her voice. "Are you all right, Mag, after that visit?"

The girl Mag smiled and nodded. Her black hair framed a beautiful face with a flawless complexion.

After that visit? Libby wondered if she referred to Mr. Grenville.

"Mag is our Irish beauty," Nora added. "She is especially good with visitors. We have new ones in Tombstone all the time."

"You mean Mr. Grenville?" Marcella asked, clearly paying close attention.

"Oh, that one. Is that his name?"

"He rode with us on the train as far as Denver."

"Well, yes, Mag is a sweetheart," Nora went on, ignoring Libby's comment.

Mr. Grenville was a "visitor" here? Libby felt heat under her hair and a grip on her scalp.

"And this is Lizette, our actress. Our flying lady of the Bird Cage."

Lizette was of medium height, with hair pulled into a tight bun at the back of her head to reveal high cheekbones and large, rheumy blue eyes.

"You're dismissed now, girls," Nora declared with a wave of her hand. But as they turned to go, she stopped one of them with a raised hand. "Lizette. Come here, Lizette."

For a moment there was silence in the room as the others left on slippered feet.

"You may be just the one," Nora said to Lizette. She glanced at Libby, standing stock still, shocked, and trying to assess what had happened to her heart when Cotter left her, and when she saw Charles Grenville.

"You wouldn't mind taking Miss Campbell into your attic room, would you, Lizette? You're gone on performance evenings anyway." Nora turned to Libby. "Libby, this is Lizette. She is an actress from Paris. She does an act at the Bird Cage you must all see." Nora smiled. "She flies across the room on invisible wires. It's quite wonderful."

Horace finally got his tongue going. "A bird flyin' over Tombstone? Like a phoenix? Maybe that's why they call it Phoenix, Arizona." Libby could tell he was enjoying his own banter. But his gaze had softened in the low light. "You've got a nest in the attic, eh?" His laugh seemed to catch in his throat.

Nora was watching Lizette, whose eyes were on Horace. "Are you all right with that, Lizette?"

"Oh, yes, ma'am." Lizette curtsied. She smiled at Horace. "I am from Phoenix."

He laughed. "So, you are that bird, making your appearance!"

Libby glanced at his face with its hefty grin. Something almost tangible passed from him to Lizette and back again.

But Lizette's face registered puzzlement—or an unreadable expression.

Horace continued, obviously trying to hold the girl's attention. "If you ain't a dirty bird, maybe you're somethin' like the blue lady from the sky."

"Blue lady?" Marcella said.

"The angel that flew all the way here from Italy! Don't she look like an angel?"

It seemed Marcella wanted to hear the story about the blue lady. Lizette's eyes were also fastened intensely on Horace.

"In 1860 the Pima Indians just north of here greeted Spanish Father Kino like a god. Reason why? A lady dressed in blue stood on a hill with a cross. Told them a white God was coming."

Marcella averted her eyes. "Horse, you were always a story teller." She glanced at him. "But you better be careful about all these stories you tell to these young people."

"That one come from that piece on the wall at the stage stop. Everybody in these parts must know it," Horace protested.

"Yes, that's an old legend around here," Nora said. "The legend of the blue lady."

Lizette didn't say anything, but her glance softened. She smiled coyly at Horace before she turned to Libby. "I'm glad to meet you, Miss Campbell."

"Then take Libby and her little bag upstairs," Nora said to Lizette, then turned to Libby. "Is that all you brought, Miss Campbell?" Libby still had the small cloth bag Marcella had given her with her overalls inside wound into a tight ball, and her gold in the pocket. "Well, now, there are a few rules. Dinner is usually in the afternoon so as not to interfere with the best business hours. We send the laundry to the Chinaman on Toughnut Street." As the girls left, Nora gathered her siblings together, put her arms around them, and took them down the hall.

When Libby stepped on the steep, narrow staircase behind Lizette's ample skirts, she stared at each rung, unsure if she should take the one above it. But she plodded ahead. At least she had a roof over her head. For now. At the top of the stairs, Lizette opened the door, and out gushed a trace of fetid air. It stopped Libby for a moment.

"You can put your bag inside the closet," Lizette said in a friendly tone. "The attic always smells stuffy, even in January. It's lucky you came now, because it's cooler than summer. Land, it's like an oven in the summer." The young woman went to the windows and opened them a crack. "I'll open them wider later on. A breeze starts coming in at about seven or eight o'clock."

Libby placed her bag on the inside of the ragged green curtain that hung over the hollow under the eaves. When she turned, Lizette was pulling up the covers on the unmade bed and plumping the pillows. "We don't have a place to sit except the bed," she said. "And this old dairy box."

Libby hesitated for a moment and then sat on the dairy box, feeling a twinge of homesickness. She knew what kind of house this was, but it had never been said in words she could hear. She wanted to hear the words—to hear the definition of what had happened to her, and to discover what her next move should be, and what might lie ahead.

"Lizette, is this a . . . a house where . . ."

"Yes, Miss Campbell. I thought you knew," the young woman said kindly.

"Please call me Libby."

"Libby, then. I thought Nora had recruited . . ."

Libby shook her head. "No. No, Miss Baron mentioned I could stay here for a while. But there was never a word about . . . I had a suspicion she was into . . . but I did not know for sure. She would never talk about it with me."

"No." Lizette got up from the bed, plumped a couple of pillows against the back wall, and jumped back up on the bed, then leaned against the pillows and straightened her legs out in front of her. "It's hard to talk about, I guess." Lizette must have seen the look of wariness on Libby's face. "It's not bad. We pay Nora for our keep. But we earn as much as we want. We're happy here. We are not forced to work—don't worry. Nora is kind to us. Not like that French count who keeps four other houses on Sixth Street. He's cruel. If each house don't pay a certain amount, he shuts 'em down. And it's sure not like the cribs up north."

"Cribs?"

"There's a row of shacks. They call 'em cribs. The rates is cheaper."

"Oh." Libby had no idea.

"Nora believes in reading books, in education, making ourselves better. She went to school in China." Lizette paused. "Did that sister you came with tell you how her parents were killed when she was a little girl?"

"Yes, Marcella said something."

"The people who burned down their family home sold her and Nora separately to two different places. They lost track of each other. Nora was nine. Some kind Chinese gentleman trained her geisha-style. She's always been busy because she was an oddity in China, bein' English. She heard by some mistake that her sister was smuggled on a boat and sold in San Francisco. A famous Miss Donaldina saved some of them girls from their awful fate. They were treated like animals, packed in boxes. Miss Baron was one of those. Miss Nora suspected her sister came to America, so when she became a head madame in China, she saved up some money and came here to look for her. Neither one of them knew where their little brother was. But now he is back! It's a miracle."

Libby stared at Lizette's slender feet stretched a good eight inches over the side of the bed. Then Libby looked at the window in the attic wall, now open a small crack to the blue sky. She felt strange in this house in Tombstone and wondered if she would ever feel at home again.

"Do you know Mr. Baron?" Lizette asked. "How did Miss Marcella find him?"

"He stole a horse by mistake," Libby replied.

"Oh."

"When he went to get out of the Wyoming Territorial Prison, a notice showed up on a bulletin board in Kansas City. He went home and found his wife had left him. So when Marcella wrote to him at the prison, he decided to come here."

Lizette looked thoughtful. "A wife?"

"No one knows where she went."

"Oh."

Now Libby was brave enough to ask her own questions. "Do you know if anyone here goes to the Episcopal church?"

Lizette raised her eyes. "Are you an Episcopalian?"

Libby hesitated. "Well, no."

"I don't go to church. I was a Baptist when I was a little girl in Phoenix. My little brother and I sang in the children's choir." Lizette paused for what seemed like a long time. "But it's been years since I went through the door of any church. Do you go to church?"

Libby didn't want to reveal too much. "There's a new preacher in town, and yes, I'd like to go on Sunday to hear him. Do you know anybody in the town who might be going to the Episcopal church?"

Lizette paused, and Libby watched her toes reach over and grapple with the toes of the other foot. "Hmm. Yes, I think Sheriff Virgil Earp and his girl Allie go to the Episcopal church. and maybe the brother Morgan and his girl Louisa, too. The Earps all have girls, but I don't think any of them is married." Lizette seemed to add thoughts as she went along. "Louisa Earp is the granddaughter of Sam Houston, who finally saved the Alamo."

Libby knew about the Alamo from Stuyvesant's newspapers. Lizette went on. "I don't know about their brother Wyatt. He has a girl named Mattie, but I haven't seen her with him for a while."

Lizette stopped as though she had finally realized she was doing all the talking. But when Libby was quiet, Lizette continued. "I don't know if they go to church, because they like to hate each other. I think Deputy Wyatt stole the sheriff's girlfriend. Sheriff Behan had this crazy obsession for this pretty actress named Josie. She come with the Shakespeare troupe last year. It seems that Josie took a liking to Wyatt Earp. Mr. Behan got jealous. But that wasn't the first thing he was mad about. He already didn't like Wyatt. He cheated Wyatt out of being elected sheriff. It was the cowboys who elected Mr. Behan. But maybe Mr. Wyatt won anyway when he got the girl.

"One early morning when I was working and still hadn't gone to bed, I looked out the window and I saw Mr. Wyatt riding with this Josie lady down Allen Street. I don't think Wyatt has ever been to church. I know all the churches change preachers all the time. I don't think there's been an Episcopalian preacher since Reverend Mr. Hill preached at Ritchie's Hall."

"Well, there's one now," Libby said, "and I would like to go. You are welcome to come with me on Sunday."

Lizette looked down at her feet and stretched her toes. "I don't know. The talkers always tell you what you're doin' wrong."

Libby wanted to say something, but the words stuck in her throat.

"Nora says what we do is a necessity of life," Lizette declared. "She says we are the most giving of all the creatures on earth. We bless lives. That's why she calls this Blessing House."

"Bless House," Libby corrected her.

13

Cotter had always been focused on the task at hand. And he was focused now. His bags were at the American Lodging House, and he was anxious to see his room, unpack, and prepare for Sunday. They wrote to him that Reverend Hill was gone. They would be holding services "Sunday morning at 11:00 AM in the courthouse, Feb. 5, 1882." Cotter was rifling through texts in his mind—mostly from the New Testament.

He had no idea who would be in attendance to hear his sermon. There might be a handful of old folks honoring their old-time religion in preparation to meet God. There might be no one. The landlord, Mr. Grant, assured Cotter that Mr. Clum, the editor of *The Epitaph,* had notified the town of his presence, and they were delighted to be back in association with the Church of England, "from which some of us fled in our youth and have not seen in this hole of the devil since we come here." The preachers, Mr. Grant said, never lasted more than six months, and you can hardly blame them. "They is often run out in the middle of a brawl."

When Cotter began studying for his sermon, the thoughts of his past, of his schooling in England, of his family's concern for him in the "hog belly of the nation," seemed to fade. Even the transportation he had just suffered at the hands of grimy engineers and shotgun-totin' stage riders was placed on a shelf to be perused later. Cotter had a job to do here in Tombstone, and he knew that attending to it well would serve him for the rest of his life.

But one thing still bothered him. When he turned away, leaving the girl from Kansas City on the steps of Marcella's sister's "rooming house," Cotter felt uneasy. What could he have done? He questioned his responsibility to Libby. She had clung to him that day in the rail yard. She had petitioned for protection, and he had offered it, and probably saved her from the direct confrontation of her pursuer, at least for a time. But now, seeing the girls, and witnessing that pursuer leave Nora's house at the moment they arrived, Cotter wondered what troubles lay over the horizon.

He had talked to the red-feathered Marcella about many things: her escape from the bawdy house in China, her journey to America, and her sister's profitable business. In the course of their conversation, Marcella had asked about Libby and said, "She can stay with me at Nora's house."

"She escaped from an abusive situation in Kansas City," Cotter had told her. "I'd hate to see her caught up in something she does not believe in or is forced to participate in for a living."

"Oh, it's nothing of the kind," Marcella had assured him. "Nora is a businesswoman. She keeps a professional house with strict rules. And one of them is that her girls are never forced to work. There are other jobs in Tombstone. All those silver mines around? It's on a boom right now. One of the girls is an actress, and some of the others work in the laundry. They must pay for their room and board. Sure, it's true most of them give the kind of service Nora knows best. But no, there is never force. That is the devil's tool. Force is slavery."

"But I am so opposed to that kind of activity," Cotter had said, blushing. "And I sense Miss Campbell is also. I'm sorry if I offend you, but all of my life I've been trained in the ways of . . . God."

"Mr. Cotter!" Marcella had protested. "Jesus loved Mary Magdalene. And where did he find her?"

"But she repented. She loved the Lord and forsook her . . ."

"You call it sin," Marcella interrupted. "Nora calls it service to mankind." Marcella had grinned playfully. "Many a committed wife has lived far past her need or desire, yet gives such service to her husband in the name of compassion and love, to bless him."

Uncomfortable with this conversation, Cotter had dropped it. Yet it remained in his memory and needled him now. True service to mankind included the major undertaking of raising a generation of responsible children who would make the world a better place. This "family" enterprise would demand purity, discipline, and excruciating mind-boggling concern for the little ones growing up under the most dedicated example of human character and adherence to spiritual laws. Cotter's own parents had been icons of virtue. His father had agreed to move the entire family to England to avoid the possible romantic attachment that had begun to occur between Cotter and his cousin Frances.

Cousin Frances. The thought of his cousin always caught Cotter broadside. The memories still kindled strong feelings. That first powerful memory was of the moment he followed her walking along the bay.

The yard behind the large old house sloped down to the quay on a velvet lawn to the edge of the black water. Though the water lingered too long at the pier and sometimes stagnated with the seeds and leaves from the brush and trees, it always moved slightly. And at night it always reflected the stars and the moon in ribbons of rippling light.

On that particular night, someone had been sitting upstairs in the library of the bulky Victorian house in Salem, Massachusetts, and the lights from the windows pooled in a checkered pattern of gold on the grass. It was a cool spring, and the lawn was as thick as a bear's fur and rolled down to the water like a rug. Cotter always remembered the lamps in the library because along with the stars they gave enough light to make it easy to take his cousin's hand and lead her to the boathouse. When he started to untie the boat, the plank to the pier creaked. The boat rocked, and the tide began to suck at it until it looked like it would slip away.

"Let's not go to the boat," Frances whispered, always apprehensive about taking risks. Through all of their childhood years, she had been the voice of caution. Yet she always followed Cotter to the limits of his judgment. There was the time they gathered the baby geese from the raspberry bushes and the mother goose vented such fury the cousins ran into the brambles, which prickled for days. At another time they stole bread from his mother's larder, and she had not allowed Cotter to come to dinner that night. There had been the time he and Frances climbed the pear tree and its branches had predictably tossed him to the ground.

At thirteen he was a tall, leggy kid. He'd been bigger than other babies from birth. He did not remember being a big baby. But as he grew up he always felt too big, or too quick for whatever mischief was at hand. At twelve he was over five and three-quarters feet tall, pushing his head of coarse dishwater-blond hair through his hat as though he were sprouting like a bean plant.

After Cotter loosed the bobbing craft, he held fast to the mooring. Even though it slipped through his fingers, he assured Frances, "No, it will be all right. If we can't get in the boat now, we'll sit on the pier and wait until the waves wash it back to us." He did not let go of the slippery rope, but the prospect of success looked dim. The craft was about twenty feet from the pier, and he could not seem to bring it closer.

The reflection of the moon rippled below them, and the wind in the trees added a plaintive backdrop for the two renegade cousins trying to match wits with the water.

"Do you know what I'd like to do?" Cotter had told Frances. "I'd like to sail this out of the bay and around the cape and go on a journey across the ocean. You'd come, wouldn't you?"

Frances, at age twelve, had a sixth sense about his grandiose schemes. She laughed. "You have an imagination, Cotter. If you don't watch out, the imagination hobgoblin will get you."

He tried to tickle her. She had laughed many times before. This time she wriggled free of his fingers and slapped his hands. "No!" she said. And she was serious.

"Well, then, I'll marry you," Cotter declared.

She screwed her nose and moved an inch or two away from him to scoff, "You know cousins don't marry."

"We'll make an exception. Come on, Frances. You don't have to do it tonight. Just say that when the time's right you'll come around the world with me."

For a while there was a comfortable quiet. Both of them sat with their shoes skimming the water, the murmur of the bay so silent it could barely be heard.

"Sure," she said breathlessly, so that the roll of the waves against the shore nearly engulfed the sound.

But it was enough. Cotter did not move. He had learned to take what he could get from her. She was not inclined to make a lot of words, and he was not fond of a lot of words anyway. So he sat dead still, pondering the bay, the moon. He had never been so aware of Frances's presence. He wanted to nestle close to her and breathe the scent of her light-bronze hair, as feather soft as flower petals. He had never before been quite so close when the world was this motionless.

Then he scooted closer and dared to reach his hand out to hers. He picked it up and held her fingers loosely. Welling with emotion, he leaned over and kissed her lightly on the cheek.

Frances drew her hand to the spot on her face where she had been kissed. She lowered her eyes. "That's the first time anyone has kissed me."

Neither of them moved. She waited—possibly for the angels to begin singing in the garden. Then she raised her pink hand with the fingers spread apart. "I won't tell," she whispered. The light from the water flickered mirror-like in her eyes. "You can count on me."

He knew he could. Nothing was ever said about the incident at the pier, but his heart remembered. In that moment he heard a familiar hum he had never understood until now. It seemed to have become part of a melody that had lingered with him all of his life. Yet coursing through the melody was another familiar sound nagging at him like the screech of a key on metal: *Cousins don't marry.*

Breathlessly, Frances rose from the pier. "I'd better go," she said. And with the taffeta of her skirts rustling, she began to walk quickly back to the house.

Cotter heard her feet in the grass, but he could not tell if she was crying or laughing, or if she was too surprised to know her own feelings. He certainly had no clue to his own feelings— why he had suddenly reached out to hold her hand, and plant a kiss on her cheek. He stayed on the pier for a moment, reeling with bewilderment.

From then on it was the incident at the pier that seemed to inform every event of his life. The worry of his parents over the possible inappropriate courtship prompted his father to move the family to England, where Cotter eventually graduated from Trinity College at Cambridge with a law degree. But it was in England that he knocked the ball out of the park, breaking the window of the Episcopal chancellery. It was there he met the kind cardinal who employed him to pay for it, and then converted him to the Church of England, where he decided to study for the priesthood. And finally it was a very rich miner from Tombstone, Grafton Abbott, who wanted to marry Frances and invited Cotter to fill the empty post as pastor of St. Paul's Episcopal Church in Tombstone—even before Cotter had graduated with his theological degree. Cotter's superiors at the theological school said it was a wonderful opportunity for him.

14

Cotter unpacked his shirts and laid them out. There were only a couple of hangers in the bulky wardrobe at the foot of his bed. He knew he was probably indulging himself in memory, and that he should be disciplining his mind to make a list of things he wanted to talk about on Sunday. But in this new room, bare of much besides a quilt and a blue porcelain basin and pitcher on the counterpane, he felt a sudden longing for his Massachusetts home.

At that last family dinner at Frances's house, both families had sat at the long table in the dining room. Cotter's mother's sister, Aunt Sadie, had made place cards of white lace on paper surrounded by paper roses. Cotter sat across from Frances and their special guest, Grafton Abbott, who sat next to her. Cotter's aunt had festooned the bank of French windows behind them with yards and yards of white chambray. But there was not enough curtain to obscure the brilliant afternoon light, so Frances and Grafton were a blur to Cotter, silhouettes on the other side of the table.

"What's the name of the mine you own in Arizona?" Aunt Sadie was asking.

"The Empire Mine," Grafton said.

"Silver or gold?" Papa wondered.

"There is so much silver in Tombstone, it will be many years before all of it will be extracted." Grafton picked up the silver salt shaker. "Nobody believed Ed Schieffelin, not even his own brother."

And it seemed nobody believed Cotter's aspirations, either. His father had been gracious but distant when he first told him he was changing loyalty from the Unitarian Church to study for the Episcopalian priesthood. The stern man had been even more bewildered when Cotter announced that Grafton Abbott, also an Episcopalian, had procured a post for him in Tombstone, Arizona, even though Cotter had a year of school left before he would graduate. Entering the foyer of the house one night, Cotter overheard his father in the lamplight of the living room tell his mother, "Wendell may hurt for a while, but it is best. The arrangement will give Frances and Grafton the opportunity to make the marriage work out."

The light from the French windows vaulted like fire into Cotter's eyes. The blurred Frances and Grafton leaned toward one another for some shared words Cotter would never hear.

"All the money in the world did not solve Ed Schieffelin's hunger for life," Abbott continued, cutting his pork. "He left wealth, his marriage, everything his fortune gave him, to go back into the hills by himself to search as he had done before. It was the search itself he treasured. He instructed his family to bury him in his old prospector clothes with his shovel and pick."

"Did they?" Aunt Sadie wanted to know.

"They did."

All Cotter wanted was Frances by his side. In wealth, in poverty. His heart broke when he left the house, fearing she would marry Grafton. She would be gone from Cotter forever—at least in this life. He said goodbye with a handshake.

"You'll do just fine in Tombstone," Grafton told him.

The dusky light that filtered through the curtain fell on the Bible on Cotter's bed. He must pick up the book, collect his thoughts, and compose his sermon. But the yearning in his broken heart held him back for a time. When he finally studied the text, he stopped at the words "If ye have faith as a grain of mustard seed . . ." He gazed out of the window. Perhaps he would be with Frances after this life.

As the sun set, the sky in the distance changed hues a level at a time, staining ladders of stars the color of slate. Cotter remembered when he went back to the house with the hurt raging in his heart. Their gardener, Toby, was cutting off the droopy roses and placing them gently in the wheelbarrow with the heads all at the top, perfectly aligned. The dead blossoms looked like small corpses being buried together.

"Toby, do you believe in life after this one?" Cotter had asked.

"Sure do," Toby said without blinking.

"How do you know?"

"After the Civil War, when my uncle got his freedom, he built a hut in the Catskills for his wife and baby daughter. But he couldn't find work close by, so during the week he had to leave the mother and daughter alone.

"It was a dry summer, and after powerful winds came and sucked up the moisture out of the leaves, there was a forest fire, with tongues of flame so high they licked that house up like it was molasses candy. When my uncle came back to the house, it was gone."

"Did the mother escape?" Cotter asked.

"Uncle Cass found her bones charred and black, and her little necklace still hangin' on a piece of skull. But the cradle where the baby was had been turned upside down and its rockers black as coal."

"What happened to the baby?"

"Evidently the wolves took her. But no one knew that until years later," Toby said. "My uncle told us that many nights he would wake to a whisper and see his wife standin' in the room, all wraithlike and white, her robes flowing. She told him she could not go to God until Uncle Cass found their child."

"Did he ever find her?"

"He spent eight years searching for her, in both summer and winter. And then one cold January he found a little girl shivering in a bank of snow. Her leg was broken. She looked at him with wild eyes out from under a sheaf of matted hair. When he drew near, she bared her teeth and hissed like a wild animal. He waited until she calmed down, then slipped his arms under her to carry her. She fought him at first, but he took her to his house, gave her a splint, and soaked her wound in whiskey. She got well, but as soon as he left for work one day, she disappeared."

Toby was quiet.

"Is that the end of the story?" Cotter asked.

"The mother's spirit never came back into my uncle's room again."

Cotter moved the chair to his small table and opened his scriptures. The light in his candle began to sputter. He found himself in the third chapter of John: ". . . whosoever believeth in him should not perish, but have everlasting life . . . but he that believeth not is condemned already." Was this Cotter's text for Sunday? He blew out the candle and knelt at his bed. "Dear Holy Father, I pray that I may become thy servant. May I speak the words thou wouldst have me speak—to convince the hearts of the people to turn to thee. In the name of thy Holy Son Jesus Christ, amen."

15

Libby couldn't sleep that first night at Bless House. The day's events hung in the periphery of her memory like Chinese lanterns swinging in the wind. Each moment seemed to retain its life as though blinking alternately from one to the other like fireflies: the trek to Nora's; the shock of seeing Charles Grenville exit Bless House; Lizette; the attic room; and finally the sound of the crystal bell that called everyone to the dining room. Suddenly, in a swarm, a throng of girls descended upon the main floor, rushing from hallways and stairways. Some of them were dressed in silk formal pajamas and embroidered kimonos, others in their skirts over crinoline petticoats. A few of them were clad in revealing silk shifts that fell just short of embarrassment. Libby did not look at the necklines, or the shapes of their bodies under the soft fabric. She kept her eyes on their faces and smiled.

Nora stood at the head of the table as the girls seated themselves. She had kept empty places at her left and right for her brother and sister. She gestured to Libby to take the chair to Marcella's right. Lizette sat on the other side of Libby.

The girls did not dare come late to the dinner hour, but there was no rule against pleasant banter, so the level of noise was almost deafening, including giggles and whispers about items of jewelry or shoes purchased at the new luxury department stores blossoming all over Tombstone.

The girls chattered incessantly until Horace appeared. Lizette was a little late, and Horace followed close behind. His male voice startled all of them into quiet. They had seen many men in the house, but not at the dinner table. "Nora says you perform at the Bird Cage," he said to Lizette. "Now that's something I'd like to see. Are you on tonight?"

Lizette presented a smile to him that Libby thought would look appropriate on a show poster. "Not really. I'm in the chorus. Big Minnie Bignon is on tonight. Two hundred thirty pounds in pink tights."

"You don't say?" Horace grinned, coloring up like a boiled lobster. From the look in his eye, Libby knew he was devising one of his bizarre stories. "That must be some colossal sight."

Lizette giggled demurely.

"Big as Bertoli's mother," Horace murmured.

There was a long pause until Marcella spoke up. "Who was Bertoli's mother?"

"He sculptured her into the Statue of Liberty." Horace grinned. "That *is* huge!"

The girls seemed stunned into silence.

"Anybody here climbed up them stairs in Bertoli's mother? Anybody wonder what's under all that garb? Maybe two hundred tons in pink tights?" Horace broke into a guffaw.

The girls giggled and began chatting again. Nora smiled benignly at her brother's laughter. "I see you are well entertained by the master storyteller."

Nora, dressed in a flowing navy-blue skirt and white ruffled blouse under her fitted jacket, wore pearls in her hair. She looked regal—at the top of her game. When she hit the side of her glass with her knife, there was sudden quiet. Even the Chinese cook and his wife and daughter stopped banging pots and pans. "I would like you to meet my family," Nora said. "Some of you knew I had a brother and sister. They are finally here! Horace and Marcella. And Libby is also new to the house. We want to welcome them with open arms." She smiled generously, and the girls broke into applause.

Horace nodded with aplomb, like the big ham he was. "If you can't remember 'Horace,' just call me Horse. Yes, just call me Horse. You ladies may wonder how long a gentleman pure as the driven snow can last in an establishment such as yours. Well, I am here to be your brother. You have never had a brother. I am your bastion of protection, your overseer, your fan."

He puffed out his chest like a rooster and raised his right finger to the chandelier. "I did *not* steal that horse. I borrowed it to save the life of my sick wife. I paid my price with eight months of the most depraved existence on earth, and when I returned to my home, I discovered my wife was gone."

The girls were riveted to his speech.

"But I am a married man, and will be married until I die." He glanced briefly at Lizette, who blinked. "I just need . . ."

No one moved.

Horace cleared his throat. "But we won't go into what I need at the moment. The question is . . ." When he went on, it was with pomp and circumstance. "Are you ready to drink to me, your 'horse' of a different color, to the flying Lizette, and to the Statue of Liberty in pink tights?" He reached for his glass of lemonade. "What is this?" He stopped and examined the yellow liquid. Lizette giggled again, above the hush. "Well, you know, a fella has to be careful about yellow water. I learned a lot of facts from reading those books in a half-lit cell over barley meal. In the 1300s the cure for the plague was to drink a cup of your own urine twice a day."

There was a collective gasp, but Horace did not miss a beat. "You ain't been out makin' collections, have you, Nora?" Breaking into laughter, he stood, held his glass out over the table, and quaffed it with ceremony.

Libby saw the surprise on the faces around her. She was not sure she would survive very long here. Perhaps not because of Nora's girls, the clientele, or the pressure to participate, but because of Horace's unsettling stories and subjects of conversation.

Later, in the attic bed, Libby could not sleep. While the lima-bean soup hadn't sat in her stomach with any particular grace, she decided it was the extraordinary revelations of the environment that kept her mind awake. She could not help playing over and over again in her mind some of Horace's stories, the chatter of the girls, the shock of finding Grenville on the premises that day. But the most pressing image of all was Cotter walking away.

Libby must have dozed, because at 2:00 in the morning, by Lizette's little clock on the table, she heard movement in the stairwell and heard the attic door open. The shadowy figure lit a candle, and Libby recognized the silhouette of her roommate in the quivering light. She sat up quickly from the bed.

"Oh, did I wake you?" Lizette asked. "I didn't want to wake you. I tried to be quiet."

"No, no." Libby stretched her arms and legs. "I don't think I've been asleep yet. So much has happened, I keep thinking . . ."

"Ha," Lizette said from the dark. "That can be a problem. What you thinkin' about?"

Libby hesitated. If she had not been just half awake, she would never have said anything about what had constantly been on her mind. "The preacher who came here with me. He took the train all the way from Massachusetts. I was wondering how long it will take him to go all the way back."

"You want to go back with him?" Lizette had cut to the chase.

Libby changed the subject. "How were the pink tights?"

"If you want to know the truth," Lizette said with a giggle, "there's a seam just about to erupt in 'em. But it hasn't broke open yet. I don't know if anybody else noticed it, but I'm in the chorus just behind Minnie. If it ever does break open all the way, I will see a sight to match Horse's wildest dreams."

Libby laughed. "He's a dreamer, all right."

Lizette leaned over to peel off her stockings. When they were in her hands, she turned to Libby, her face toward her in the candlelight. "Is it true you was traveling all day in the same coach as Horace and Marcella?"

Libby stayed quiet for a beat, then said, "You are a little bit interested in that Horace, aren't you?"

"I just wondered." Lizette drew her feet up on the bed and began to rub the pain out of them. "Yeah," she said with a smile. "But I didn't know until dinner that he still feels married."

Libby turned over under the sheet and faced the wall. She wondered what she could say about Horace that would be kind, or even true. She had to think hard, because although he had told story after story, they had all been jokes or factual anomalies out of those books he had pored over while he was in the penitentiary. He had not talked about his marriage much. "You know, Lizette, I didn't hear him talk about his wife often." In fact, Libby had been surprised he shared it with the girls at the dinner. "I don't think he is looking for her."

"There is just something . . . something unusually wonderful . . . about a man who is . . . faithful." Lizette's words dropped off.

"I guess you see enough of the other kind," Libby said, drowsy enough now to sleep the rest of the morning.

But Lizette went on. "You were with Marcella a long time." She paused. "Did she tell you their story?"

"She wouldn't talk about it," Libby murmured.

"Nora remembered everything," Lizette said. "Everything."

And now Libby heard some of it for the first time.

They lived in a paper house, Lizette explained. As Christian missionaries from England, they chose a small, insignificant hovel in the poorest section of Peking. It was their call from God to quietly, clandestinely bring his word to the humble ones who would listen.

The street, only a few rods from a highway, was a narrow dirt pathway flanked by many other cramped and broken paper houses, sitting haphazardly along shallow gutters strewn with rice paper, rotting cabbages, and angry chickens pecking for a bit of discarded rice.

The children remembered that the chickens looked naked. The fowl had lost many of their feathers to predatory dogs and cats who had stripped them so thoroughly they looked embarrassingly bare. Their father joked it would be easy to dunk one of those birds into boiling water without preparation, and vòila—chicken stew!

When he wasn't opining on local culinary delights, the father, Pastor Holomon Baron, had his nose in his Bible, while the mother, Pauline, sat by the light of an opening in the paper wall, sewing together scraps of goods to add length to the children's clothes.

For six years Holomon Baron had saved half of all the money he earned from his patronage in Exeter to take the word of God to China. It was all he had lived for, dreamed about, believed in, since he had entered the priesthood.

The children would never forget what he had repeatedly taught them: "God wants us to take his word to the far corners of the world." Before every meal, and at every evening before they were tucked into bed, their mother and father knelt with them in prayer. "Dear Heavenly Father, we promise we will spread thy gospel abroad. Please keep us safe under thy watchful care." It was a message that later resonated as an unanswered prayer. It kept all of them from ever thinking of going to church for the rest of their lives.

For a year and a few months, the missionary family found success in China. Because most of the people could not read, Holomon and Pauline, who studied Mandarin day and night, read and translated for them. "There is a man born two thousand years ago who was crucified to save all of us," Holomon explained to them. "Have you ever heard of Jesus Christ?"

Some of the younger people had learned some of the facts of history from their schools. But they had no idea that this Christ had taught mankind to love one another and to bear each other's burdens, and that every human being who would pay attention to the teachings of Jesus in the scriptures would know how to live every day of their lives.

Because the Barons had come to a neighborhood of hardworking families who could barely put a little rice on the table, they won the love and attention of many humble souls.

"There are universal rules," Holomon told the people. "Universal rules like 'If you save the rainwater you will have water to drink.'" The rules were not difficult, he assured them. But they demanded careful adherence. "Keep the Sabbath Day holy, pay one-tenth of your increase for tithes, keep yourself holy and unspotted from the world, and obey the words of Jesus Christ. As difficult as your life may seem sometimes, you will ultimately find yourself lifted by his grace. Keep the commandments and joy will come to you, just as the day comes after the night."

At first there were four rooms in the little Baron house. But when more and more people began to gather to hear God's words, Holomon carefully removed the inside wall of the two front rooms to accommodate the crowd.

For several months of Sundays, people lined up in a queue outside the house, waiting to find a spot to sit on the wooden slats of the floor. When some of the boards began to separate and cry out like strangled birds, Holomon started looking around the suburbs of Peking for larger accommodations.

Someone must have said something. None of the Barons would ever know who it was, or why they would be so cruel as to inform hostile forces. But on one Sunday morning just before dawn—several hours before it was time for the congregation to gather—three large men, huge black shadows against the sun, walked up to the house. Fearsome warriors, they wore black braids hanging down the middle of their glistening backs and wielded the blades of their scimitars unsheathed and reflecting the sparkle of the full moon. Without warning, they marched into the house and tore away the door.

When the floorboards creaked, Holomon sat up suddenly from his bedding and said, "Run, children, run—through the window. Hide under the house."

Marcella, Nora, and Horace had nothing on their backs but their nightclothes. They did not wait one moment to gather anything. They were used to their father's commands. But they had never heard the urgency of his voice as they heard it now. They slipped through the paper window and crawled through the stilts to huddle beneath the floor of the house. Suddenly from above came the most terrifying screams the children had ever heard from their mother's mouth. Their father's cry was cut off with a thump and a gurgle. And then the mother's shrieks were silenced. The children clutched each other in utter terror, sobbing.

"Quiet, they'll hear you," Marcella said.

But little Horace could not curb his fearful wails.

Above them they heard a jabbing blade and the heavy thump of a heel. Soon there was a yawning hole through the sagging floorboards, and a face peering into the darkness with black eyes. "Go 'round," the man yelled to one of the others in the Mandarin all of the children had learned to speak. And before any of them could comprehend what had happened, they saw another pair of beady eyes appeared at the edge of the foundation. All three men had surrounded the house and were poking under it with long knives, now dripping with blood.

"Hunh hunh hunh," the largest of the Chinese police repeated like an animal drooling over its prey. The knives could not reach them. But the smallest of the men lowered himself to the ground and crawled toward them on his stomach. "Get out, get out," he grunted in Mandarin. And there was nothing else the children could do.

"Nora said she had thought of running to one of the neighbors who had been baptized in a pool of water on a nearby hog farm," Lizette said quietly. "But Marcella said no. It was dangerous to irritate the men further."

Libby, fascinated by the story, clutched her pillow with a tense grip. "What happened to them?"

But it seemed Lizette's voice was becoming weaker.

And then what happened? Libby wanted to know. *What happened to the children?* But the purple sky outside the attic window was now fading into dawn.

"What happened then, Lizette?"

"I'll tell you later," came the weak reply. Lizette was lying on the other edge of the bed, crumpling her pillow under her ear. "I'll tell you later. I'm tired, Libby." Her last words were muffled. "They were sold to pleasure houses where they were carefully trained . . ." But the terrible words ended in silence.

Libby tried to process all she had heard until she finally drifted off to a troubled sleep.

16

Cotter's letter of instructions said his first sermon was to be on Sunday, February 5, in the courthouse at 11:00 AM. *Why the courthouse?* he wondered. The host at the American Lodging House told him, "The city fathers thought there would be no other hall big enough to hold all of the curious Tombstoners who would want to hear what the new pastor has to say."

Daunted at the gravity of his responsibility, Cotter walked the streets hoping to find the council people who had made his arrangements. He wanted to introduce himself to them and thank them. As he passed people in the street, they stepped out of his way to let him by, smiling and waving greetings. A couple of them bowed from the waist, honoring the man of the cloth, not really concerned which cloth he wore.

The newspaper man John Clum, who ran *The Epitaph*, had an honest face sporting a small black beard that hung on his chin like a coconut. His busy hands kept the long fingers moving amid his papers and instruments of editorial expertise. He smiled. "I'm glad to see you, Reverend Cotter."

Cotter was in the process of opening his mouth to say he was not a reverend yet, that he had one more year. But John Clum kept going. "Just give me a little about your background. I've heard you studied at Cambridge. We'll put a notice in *The*

Epitaph that you're here. And your first sermon will be . . ." He held his pen over a blinding sheet of white paper.

"February 5th, 11:00 AM at the courthouse. I will make it short enough that no one will miss lunch."

"Ha! You mean breakfast." John Clum laughed. "It's not Tombstone for nothin'. The people around here are half dead until noon. And when they wake up to their gamin' they're still half dead, drinkin' until four in the morning. Two halves make one whole." He laughed at his joke.

Cotter responded with a grin. He had seen the crowds in the saloons in his walks down Allen Street in broad daylight.

"You've had a glimpse, I take it, of the glut of gamblers we manage to jam into our dozen or more saloons in this town?"

Cotter liked Clum. He seemed straightforward and honorable. "I've seen a few." Cotter laughed. "I was hoping I might find an opportunity to make at least a small difference in this town. That's why I'm here."

"Others have tried," John Clum murmured. He lowered his pen and fastened clear eyes on Cotter. "You know about the factions that divide this city? The men who try to enforce the law, and the cowboys who make their living helping themselves to other peoples' livestock?"

"I know some of it," Cotter said. "I'm not sure I can . . ."

"It's a problem that's been goin' on for a hundred years." Clum pushed at the table and leaned back in his chair. "You heard of the shootin' spree?"

"I did."

"The Earp brothers have been tryin' to keep guns out of town. So many factors contributed to the deaths. In some ways it was an unfortunate accident. The Earps had the loyalty of that hothead Doc Holliday. The tubercular dentist saved Wyatt's life once in Dodge City. But he is a feisty one. And when he saw that kid Bill Clanton draw he was quicker than a fly in a teapot."

"Have they settled their differences?"

"Not yet, I fear," John Clum replied. "It's become an excuse for the cowboys to murder for what they see is their revenge. An unidentified group shot and crippled the U.S. Deputy brother Virgil Earp on December 28th." Clum stopped and jammed his thumbs into the fob pockets on his vest. "Sheriff John Behan made a weak effort to pursue the aggressors." He paused. "But without success, and for a reason, I suspect." His sentences seemed halting. "Behan is a friend to the cowboys. So, rather than rest upon us, justice seems to fly over Tombstone."

Cotter was quiet for a moment.

"Not many people around here seem to be too interested in religion," John Clum said, taking up what Cotter had already guessed. "But it would help if they were."

Cotter was about to say he would do his best, when he caught sight of an image in one of the clippings on Clum's bulletin board. A pitcher on the ball green was leaning back into a powerful pitch.

"You interested in baseball?" John Clum sat farther back in his chair as though assessing Cotter. "You look like you could handle a bat."

Cotter was all ears now.

"You're from Massachusetts. Ever heard of George Staples Rice?"

Cotter responded negatively with a shake of his head.

"Civil engineer from Massachusetts who established the reduction plant at the Stonewall Mine on the San Pedro River. Been here two years. Organized a hotshot baseball team, the San Pedro Boys. I hear tell he's looking for a team to play them."

"I've played a lot of baseball," Cotter said.

John Clum leaned forward. "I think we're going to see some good things from you, Mr. Wendell Cotter. Glad you stopped by."

Cotter knew everything that had happened to him in the last decade started with baseball. His parents had interrupted a promising baseball career with their journey to England. And Cotter had never forgotten it. He was thirteen years old when he overheard his father murmur to his mother words that sounded suspiciously like "Frances" and "Wendell." He very clearly heard, "It's time we left Salem." In meetings for several weeks, the financier finally came home one night and suddenly announced to Mother Melinda that the Bank of England wished to hire him for a few years. He promised her it would be good for all of them.

But the news hurt Cotter, and the years that followed were painful ones. His father's employment was important, of course, but Cotter knew one of the main reasons for the transfer was to separate him from Frances. And to make it most difficult, he had to leave his home just when he had begun to make a name for himself among his classmates as a better-than-average ball player.

Years later, when all of his memories were difficult to grasp, Cotter still remembered climbing aboard the huge ship with his mother, father, two brothers, and three-year-old sister. He would never forget hearing the wash of the waves as the ocean sucked them away from the Boston Harbor. A pain in his ribs marked the last vision of Frances and her family standing with the other families waving them away. Cotter ached to see them turning away and disappearing into the collage of the city's shipyards. The tears in his eyes had scrambled the view of the great houses climbing the terraces of land.

The groaning of the ship, the rolling of the waves, the sickness, the close quarters of the family as they bounced their way across the ocean—all of these images floated somewhere in Cotter's mind, along with the Unitarian Church meetings his father insisted they attend. Two or three other families met with them on the Sunday deck, once in a drizzle of rain.

In London they set up housekeeping in a quiet section of the busy city on a street between two roundabouts, which only occasionally saw a collision of surreys. It was not the street, or the horse cars, or the banking partnership that loomed most in Cotter's mind. It was the quiet. They knew no one. They were foreigners. It was as though they had woven themselves into a cocoon. But from their isolation came family unity. The family grew close. In London, Cotter's mother began telling them stories about their early childhoods.

For the first time Cotter could remember, she talked about his birth. In May 1857, with only a midwife and her sister Luella present, Sadie was screaming when her sister Luella broke into the hymn "Rock of Ages." Luella continued to sing as the adults poked and pinched the little red-faced boy. "He is as strong as a little mule, slipping into life with those doubled fists and a hearty cry," the midwife exclaimed.

Years later Cotter learned that when his cousin Frances was born, her father had hired a midwife who had come from a long line of ancestral witches. The hawk-nosed woman had leaned over the afterbirth and wrapped the child in a cloth so tight there was little room to breathe. "She don't know which end is up yet, but you can learn her fast." Cotter was almost two. When he reached for the crying baby cousin, the midwife sat him on a chair beside the bed and put Frances in his arms. Cotter held his cousin without moving. Those who were present said the light in the windows began to shimmer over them in sunbeams thick with dust.

After they had settled into a routine, Cotter enrolled at Cheltenham School. And on the very first day of the five years of his attendance, he made the error that put him on course for the rest of his life.

He could see the ball field from the road when the surrey stopped at the chancellery. "They must play ball here," he said.

"Baseball comes after studies," his mother replied gently. As they stopped to get out at the steps of the school, Cotter saw a group of boys running to the diamond with their coach. Cotter's blood practically jumped out of his veins. He saw himself running in the field with the boys, his hair flying in the wind. His hands tested the bat in his imagination.

"All right," his wise mother said. "Go hit a few balls while I talk to the registrar. It will take some time, and I'll call you."

He raced to the field. The boys and the coach welcomed him. When it was Cotter's turn at bat, he hit the ball so hard it catapulted out of the park, flew at an unprecedented speed, and hit the glass of the chancellery window. The sound of the impact detonated like a bomb in his ears. The chime of the splinters crumbling into the Church offices stung him with fear. The boys standing around him were struck with awe.

A boy who would become Cotter's best friend said, "I'd swear a long streak if it wasn't against the commandments." The team's coach was a little dog-faced enthusiast whose mouth fell open when he saw the power of Cotter's first home run. In one or two days he put the boy on all of the teams. Baseball and soccer were Cotter's favorites, although he tried everything, including hockey. What surprised him most was that he loved school and began to make excellent grades, particularly in math and science.

For the first time he could remember, his father encouraged him with constant praise. "With your ability you'll be a candidate for Cambridge, my son."

Cotter raised his head at the dinner table to accept his father's words with graciousness. But he did not smile.

"With talent like yours you can take over the London banking operations without a lick of any extra training. We could set you up right away."

Silent, Cotter buttered his roll and glanced at his little brother Roland and baby sister Dulse. Mother Melinda looked askance through her curls, listening patiently, also glowing with pride, although Cotter knew she was well aware he wanted eventually to return to Massachusetts.

Cotter's father also knew this. Cotter had shown him in subtle ways that his hopes did not include becoming a financier. He was so relieved one day to hear his father make the special announcement, "When you graduate from Cheltenham we'll all go back to Salem for our summer vacation." This simple statement motivated Cotter for the next five years.

For a while the coach and the chancellor had not said anything about the broken window. But after a few days of success on the ball field, Cotter received a request to see the Episcopalian Reverend Achison, a tall, thin man topped by a head of white hair. When the reverend brought the boy into his vast catacomb of offices, he turned the electric lights up on the massive lengths of book shelves lined with rows and rows of books. Cotter could not help but gasp. The reverend turned to him with surprise. The gentle, white-headed cleric smiled.

Embarrassed and frightened to learn how much money it would cost his father, or him, to replace the window, Cotter remained silent while the reverend spoke. When he asked about the family, Cotter told him they were Unitarian, but had not found a chapel in London yet.

"Do you believe in one God? The God of us all?"

"Y–yes," Cotter stammered.

"Do you believe in keeping the Sabbath Day holy?"

"Yes, sir."

For a moment the reverend seemed to be thoughtful. "I believe you are a boy of principles," he said quietly.

Cotter could not speak, but he was paying attention. "I think this might be . . . is this about the window, sir?"

Reverend Achison smiled. Cotter's heart beat faster.

"It's not the first time a window has been broken," the reverend said slowly, placing his palms together.

Cotter felt very hot in the chair across the desk from the reverend. At all times Cotter was clearly aware of his surroundings, as though the hundreds and hundreds of books were leaning toward him to whisper messages he could not understand.

"We will fix the window," the reverend continued.

Cotter felt air go into his lungs, as though he had not breathed for several hours.

"All we ask of you is that you come to the chancellery for a period of time. Perhaps just for a month or two, so that you may perform tasks until the amount of payment for the window has been reached."

There was a long silence.

"Is that all right with you, young Mr. Cotter?"

"Yes, sir." Cotter envisioned cleaning the windows, sweeping the floors, polishing the reverend's shoes. He was not sure how this would play out against his father's strict insistence on home study hours, and their Unitarian set of mind.

"Please take this note to your parents." The kindly reverend gave Cotter a sealed envelope. He imagined it would explain what had happened. He imagined it was a form letter the likes of which hundreds had been printed and doled out to the masses of boys who had broken chancellery windows. "And we'll see you tomorrow afternoon, after your ball games are over."

"Yes, sir," Cotter said.

Sweeping the maze of stone floors in the rectory and its adjoining chapels brought him into close contact with the men who directed the Church of England. Almost every day Reverend Achison greeted him with a genuine smile. When Cotter approached his father with the reverend's invitation to come to church, his father turned around in his desk chair and tipped the shade of the lamp down so it would not glare in Cotter's eyes.

"Your reverend friend knows how to get the right payment from a boy who breaks windows," Mr. Cotter said.

"They talk about their church," Cotter replied. "I wouldn't get baptized or anything, but should I go?" He was not sure what to expect from his father.

"Wendell . . ." his father began. And Cotter settled in, understanding that this was the tone of his father's voice that prefaced a teaching moment. "Son, you know we have been Unitarian."

"Yes, Father."

"And you know what Unitarians stand for?"

"I think I know, Father. Unity."

"Yes, Son." Mr. Cotter leaned back in his chair and put his thumbs in the little pockets of his vest. "Yes, Son. Unity of all mankind. While for centuries religions have divided men, our hope and prayer is that all human beings will be united in the knowledge that we are all children of God." He smiled. "Don't we look alike? We all have two arms and two hands, two legs, two feet. We breathe, eat, love, work, have families. We are more alike than we are different."

"I know. But . . ." Cotter shifted in his chair.

"We have not found a Unitarian chapel near here in London. I know that." After a pause, Mr. Cotter went on. "If I were not a

Unitarian I would recommend another religion to you, because I believe all people worship in truth. It is the nourishment of God's word on the Sabbath that civilizes us all." He stopped, taking an emphatic breath of air. "Yes, if you wish to attend your friend's church, I shall give you my blessing."

It was not what Cotter expected to hear from his father, this benign reaction of tolerance and unexpected freedom. He had thought his father wanted the family to stay together to worship But they had been together in the home every day since their arrival, and their worship had been at every meal and kneeling at the foot of the children's beds in prayer. There were no chapels, leaflets, or pamphlets. They read from the Bible.

"Thank you, Father," Cotter said. "Thank you very much."

17

It was Sunday morning at Bless House, February 5, 1882. Libby woke at about 9:00 and tiptoed around the room, hoping not to awaken Lizette. When Libby picked up her dress, which Marcella had given to her, she held it to the light. It was looking worn. Lizette was right—Libby needed to go shopping. But she hadn't wanted to get out her gold just yet. There were prying eyes about that she did not trust. She had been staying alert for other residential possibilities.

"Are you going somewhere?" Lizette's voice sounded like gravel.

"Yes, to the meeting at the courthouse. Do you want to go?"

"Not really." Lizette turned her head to the wall. "I worked until 2:00."

Libby knew that. She hesitated to ask any more questions, but she needed one more answer. "Do you know if anyone at the house goes to church?"

"Mag goes. She's second floor, second door to the left. She's usually up for breakfast."

Elegant, clear-eyed Mag. Libby remembered her that first night at dinner, eating her rice pudding with a tiny demitasse spoon. Mag, a taciturn beauty, watched everyone else without entering into their games. Ever since seeing her with Charles

Grenville that first day, Libby avoided her. She wondered if she would ever forget the image of Mag standing in the doorway as he left, his boots thumping across the painted planks, his cape billowing. An unexplainable anger at both of them had surged through Libby in that moment. She supposed Grenville was a grown man with the needs of every other man. But it had sent a chill into her neck, as real as though a cuff of ice-cold steel had locked around her throat. She stood, not moving, a thousand questions crowding her brain. Where did Mag come from? What brought her to Tombstone? How could she dare go to church?

There were at least eight doors on the second floor, all closed. Libby knew why there were so many little rooms. Lizette had explained that the odd-numbered rooms were designated for clientele, and those who were working used them. The even-numbered rooms were where the girls shared lodging, as Lizette was currently sharing with Libby. "We wash the sheets once a week whether they need it or not."

She waited a moment before she tapped on the door marked #2. When she heard someone stirring about, she whispered, "Mag." But there was no answer. "Mag, it's Libby. Are you up?" She tapped harder this time and the door opened a crack, revealing half of Mag's white face, the blue eyes. "Lizette told me you go to church. I'd like to go this morning."

The reserved Mag just looked at her. But just before Libby was ready to repeat or retreat, the young woman opened the door wide. "Come in," she whispered. "Talk softly, because Hetty sleeps light." Libby saw two other girls sprawled on the bed and floor. "They come here because it's noisy in their rooms."

Libby zipped her lips.

"Sure, I'll go with you," Mag said very quietly. "You want to hear the new preacher's sermon?"

"Yes," Libby whispered, keeping an eye on the two sleepers. Mag was almost ready. She threw a gauzy white scarf around her neck over the puffed sleeves of the pale green chambray. After they slipped out of the room and shut the door, she put more sound into her words. "Percy Thompson is excited that the new man plays baseball." *Percy Thompson?* There was an unspoken code in the darkness of the profession to stay quiet about the clientele, so Libby was surprised to hear a name. The underlying business of who showed up at Bless House was an underground maze of connections. "He might organize a baseball team to play the San Pedro Boys."

"Do you watch the games?" Libby asked.

"I love the games." Mag drew her gloves over her long fingers. On the way down the hall past the kitchen, she ducked into the food cupboard, took two slices of bread, and gave one to Libby. She pulled out the cheese. The cooks did not work on Sunday, so the girls would cook on that day.

"The Wangs are Christians from China," Mag said. "I see them at the Baptist church. But they will probably be at the courthouse today out of curiosity."

Libby also took a slice of cheese from under a glass dome. Mag carefully opened the door to the back and slipped through.

"How did you find out about the new preacher?"

"There's a buzz about him," Mag replied. "He's only twenty-four years old." She drew the scarf over her hair when a gust of wind blew a dirt devil in the dust of Fifth Street. "I saw him that day you came. He's handsome, smart, and a great ball player."

That day I came, Libby thought. She wanted to approach Mag about Charles Grenville again, but she held herself back. She hugged the tops of her arms from the morning chill of the desert in February. Fortunately, the courthouse was only a few blocks away.

"I'm glad you came," Mag said. "I usually have to go alone."

Libby was surprised Mag would go to church with her. *There must be more to her than I thought.*

When they approached the courthouse fifteen minutes early, Libby noticed a particular group of men and women standing in a circle near the entrance. It looked like an enclave of show people entertaining each other. The tall man in the center raised his arms in the position of a fake gun. And when he said "Bang," the women in their white bonnets and lawn dresses laughed heartily.

"The Earps," Mag said.

Libby stared. The Earp brothers were already a legend in Tombstone, and a popular topic of conversation at Bless House. When they gathered in the front room to gossip, the girls beat to death topics ranging from the court's decision to let the lawmen go, to Wyatt's affair with the actress Josie Marcus, and the cowboys' attempted murder of Deputy Marshal Virgil Earp. Over custard and checkers, Libby learned what happened.

It started when the Earps went after the cowboys for rebranding some government mules from Fort Huachaca. "Them mules wandered on our property," Tom McLaury said. But the Earps insisted on adherence to the law. They asked the McLaurys to bring the mules in, but they didn't.

Conservative lawmen like Wyatt and Virgil Earp became unpopular often because they did their jobs "too well." At least too precisely for those who liked to "bend" a little. And the cowboys bent the law all over the place.

"The cowboys get away with murder," Nora had said.

Libby learned about the tragic shooting in which the county sheriff, Mr. White, was killed by Curly Bill Brocius. *Curly Bill Brocius?* Libby wondered. Was he the one who smelled like a barnyard and crushed Marcella's dress, the one Libby wore, on the coach ride down from Benson? Evidently Curly Bill thought the sheriff was ready to shoot, so it was deemed self-defense. Libby remembered that gossip session at Bless House. And Gertie, who was usually quiet, said something that sounded like she had served him.

When Sheriff White died, the cowboys elected Charlie Shibell by giving the chickens and pigs the vote. Shibell appointed John Behan in Wyatt's place. Behan had promised to hire Wyatt, but broke his promise. So both Wyatt and Virgil decided to resign.

The Earps were now out of office. So they invested in water and mines. However, when problems arose, Behan still wanted the Earps to ride with the posses to enforce the law. One such posse, on March 15, 1881, went after the parties who robbed a stagecoach and killed the driver and one of the passengers. The cowboys blamed Doc Holliday for the robbery because one of the robbers was Doc's friend Bill Leonard. But the only one the posse picked up was Luther King, who let his mouth flap open and gave the names of every man who participated. They were all "cowboys." Sheriff Behan dilly dallied, and perhaps out of fear never arrested or indicted the others. And poor Luther King. After he told on them, the cowboys killed him on the spot!

"Does Sheriff Behan get paid by those cowboys?" one of the girls had asked. "It seemed he lets them get by with murder."

"Behan hates Wyatt Earp because of Josie Marcus."

Another girl piped up, "Josie is Sheriff Behan's girl."

"Not anymore," Ruby Jarett said emphatically. And she ought to have known, for Behan had been visiting her for the last few weeks. "Josie is sweet on Wyatt Earp. But it's supposed to be a secret."

It was Sunday, time for Cotter's first sermon. When he woke, he shook his head out of a bad dream, then lay still for a few minutes to allow his mind to climb up from the darkness. He listened to the sounds of the street, the distant conversations of the all-night gamblers, the drunks finding their way out of the saloons—the Cosmopolitan, the Alhambra—the clunk of a boot in the stirrup, the muted slap of a rein on a horse's neck, the clop of hooves on the gravel, an occasional croak of a wagon wheel.

This morning it seemed Cotter was repeating that first bad experience he had many years before in Salem, Massachusetts when his dreams took a dismal turn. As then, he woke today in a cold sweat. His pillow and the back of his pajamas were drenched and clammy. In his half-consciousness, he tried to piece together the essence of this morning's nightmare. He had been standing on the driver's box of the stagecoach, trying to give his Sunday sermon to a crowd of hundreds of masked men gathered below him. They stood motionless, like tombstones, their eyes glazed, their faces dark with beards, their skin leathery from the sun. Cotter had begun to yell, but nothing he said to them made a difference in their faces. With frozen glares, they kept both hands on the barrels of the pistols that glittered in the holsters on their belts.

Cotter drew the curtains of the room aside, grateful for the dawn. He had wrinkled his best white collar in packing. He took it out and looked at it. This morning it would be more visible than it had ever been. There was no hiding now. He wet the collar with some water from his shaving cup and pulled on the cloth, hoping to straighten it out.

He was afraid, but he did not want to give in to fear. He had spent more than sixty hours thinking about this morning's critical speech without actually deciding upon a text. But he also knew the words he would say were not as important as the spirit in which he would say them. He was a foreigner in the midst of a community torn by hatred and careless behavior. Every peril that had ever been mentioned in the scriptures was normal behavior in this place. In his mind Cotter recited verses from the second epistle of Timothy: "For men shall be lovers of their own selves, covetous, boasters, proud, blasphemers, disobedient to parents, unthankful, unholy, without natural affection, truce breakers, false accusers . . . despisers of those that are good, traitors, heady, highminded, lovers of pleasures more than lovers of God."

Cotter could find all of those sins here in Tombstone. Yet the townsfolk were also human beings. And if in a kindly manner he gave the message Jesus Christ wished him to deliver, his sermon might be at least somewhat effective.

It was 9:00 AM. A pork sandwich from last night's dinner at the Alhambra sat heavily in Cotter's stomach. Food was the last thing he wanted this morning. He would perform this critical sermon in an attitude of fasting and prayer. He took time dressing, trying to calm his hands, which sometimes shook if he fasted or felt nervous. When he finally came to his scriptures, the pages fluttered to the subject of his recent thoughts, the second epistle of Timothy. Cotter's eyes went to chapter 1, verse 7—"For God hath not given us the spirit of fear, but of power, and of love, and of a sound mind."

Cotter drew back, feeling the light in the room. That passage . . . that was his message. That was the text he must offer to these frightened people, badgered by opposing forces of evil.

The gall of those who ambushed the sheriff and shot him in the night, thinking to avenge the deaths of the gunfight! Virgil Earp would now be crippled for life. Yes, the Earps had taken violent steps to clear up a plethora of threats made against them. But as far as Cotter could tell, the gunfight had exploded between two armed groups in the quick-draw style of the Old West. Still, he knew their activities must evolve into something more peaceful. Solving the problems of the world at the advantageous end of a gun or blade must someday give way to civil talk, honorable concern, and a listening ear for something resembling the kind of society Jesus Christ gave his life to achieve.

18

For 10:45 in the morning, the street was crowded. People were still coming as Libby and Mag approached the steps where the Earps stood in a haphazard circle. At the top of the steps was an impressive man flapping away the flies with his handkerchief.

"That one is Wyatt," Mag whispered.

At the bottom of the steps, one of the women happened to glance toward Mag and Libby as they drew closer. "Mag!" she cried out.

"Louisa!" Mag hurried her step.

"So good to see you," Louisa said.

"Louisa, this is Libby. Libby, this is Louisa Houston Earp. She stays with Morgan. We were friends in Texas. Her grandfather is Sam Houston, who led the forces that finally defeated the Mexicans at the Alamo."

Libby wasn't paying much attention to the history. But her gaze was riveted upon Louisa, who was what Libby called "regal." Her blond hair framed a face with well-proportioned cheeks and full, rosy lips. She wore a white ruffled blouse that cradled her jaw like the petals of a lily.

"Louisa is here with Morgan. And Allie, who is Virgil's girl," Mag continued. Libby noticed that Louisa and Allie dressed like the girls at Bless House.

She was impressed most by the man standing alone at the top of the steps, swatting away the flies. Mag whispered in Libby's ear, "Wyatt also has a girl, Mattie, but she hardly ever comes out to anything."

As Mag continued with Louisa, she included Morgan. "Morgan, let me introduce you to Libby Campbell. She just got here from Kansas City."

He tapped the ashes from his cigar onto the pavement and stomped out the embers. "Welcome to Tombstone, Miss Campbell."

"Thank you." Libby could barely speak.

Louisa filled up the empty space. "Good to see you, Mag."

By now Allie had turned toward them.

"And this is Allie . . . well, Alvira," Mag said.

Allie was smaller, and sweet-faced. Her thick, straight brows emphasized her large eyes. She had the look of a child who had just been denied a second piece of blueberry pie. When Libby extended her hand for a handshake and felt the cool grip, she feared she might crush this tiny woman's fingers, which were loose and soft like the stems of dandelions.

"This is Virgil," Mag said. "And Wyatt Earp."

"Kansas, eh?" Virgil's grin was practically hidden under his huge black mustache. "Kansas City to Bless House?"

"Yes, sir." Libby felt suddenly far away, as though she were looking down from a great distance upon a group of actors who had just played a world-shaking drama upon the stage.

"This is a church meeting, you know," Wyatt Earp chimed in. He was tall and wiry with a steely look in his gray-blue eyes. His light brown hair was longer than that of the others and curled across his broad brow.

"She knows. She come down on the train with Mr. Cotter," Mag informed them.

"Is that right?" Virgil said. "Well, you oughta know what kind of a Sunday treat this town is in for."

"I think . . . a good one." Libby looked up and smiled, overcome to be standing with the three murderers of the gunfight at the OK Corral. But as mesmerized as she was by the brothers' charm, she felt Wyatt's comment about Bless House needed some amendment. She was not going to allow a momentary shyness to cause any misrepresentation of her character.

"My stay at Bless House is temporary," she explained, surprised at the sudden emphasis in her own voice. "I'm looking for a job. If you know of anything . . ."

From the top of the steps, Wyatt Earp gazed down at Libby. Putting his hands under the flaps of his coat, a movement that briefly revealed his firearms, he pulled back and gave a distant grin.

Mag spoke up. "Wyatt and Virgil both have interest in the Occidental. They need waitresses from time to time."

"Might be, might be," he said in a low drawl that Libby barely heard.

Just then the doors to the courthouse were thrown open.

"We'll see what this new preacher has to tell us," Morgan said. He took Louisa's gloved hand and walked up the steps past Virgil and Wyatt, leading her forward.

But Virgil, the ex-marshal of Tombstone, was still at his post, and still expressing an interest in Libby. "The people at Bless House don't much come to church . . . perhaps with the exception of Mag here," he said. "So why you?"

"I'm only a guest there, Mr. Earp," Libby said firmly.

"Hmm. Well, we're glad to meet you, I'm sure. And if ever you are in need of help, let us know."

As the lawman drew away from her, he took his Allie by the hand. Libby could see it was his left hand. The right one dangled by his side, a useless limb in his coat sleeve. The girls at the house had told her the doctor ordered the damaged arm to be amputated, but Virgil would not allow it. There were rumors that the cowboys Frank Stilwell, Johnny Ringo, and Ike Clanton, among a host of others, had joined the gang for avenging the death of the McLowrys and Billy Clanton at the OK Corral. But no one had been apprehended so far. The wounded lawman walked with Allie and the others into the courthouse.

Libby stood behind with Mag, watching the churchgoers. Many of them were probably curiosity-seeking miners or shopkeepers, but, dressed in Sunday clothes, they streamed past into the courthouse, looking eager for what they might hear.

Libby was ready to go in, but Mag did not move. For a moment the morning light seemed to darken as though a cloud passed overhead. Libby had started forward when Mag clutched her arm. "Wait, Libby." She searched the crowd, and her eyes narrowed into slits. "I can't believe what I am seeing. Is that . . ."

Libby turned to follow Mag's gaze. In the distance surrounded by the crowd, there was no mistaking the dark head above all the other heads, the knit brows on the earnest face, the black cloak. Charles Grenville! Libby felt a jolt and looked at Mag, wondering why he had not been seen among the clients at Bless House since that first day. Libby would observe before she asked any questions.

"That's Charles, all right," Mag said. "I wondered if we'd see him at this meeting this morning. He told me he'd met this Mr. Cotter."

Uncomfortable with Grenville's paramour standing at her side, Libby wanted to shut her eyes and hurry into the courthouse. If there was anyone she did not want to run into, it was Grenville. She had almost forgotten she had stolen Stuyvesant's gold, that Grenville had followed her all the way here to the "hog belly" of the West, that he had accosted her in the train and would likely press her unremittingly for the gold from now until she coughed it up and sent it back to his wicked employer. Since Grenville knew where she was, she was shocked he had not come to harass her yet.

Libby stopped in her tracks, unable to speak a word, but Mag offered some answers as to why he had not appeared at Bless House again. "He's helping Mayor Clum at *The Epitaph* office and doing legal work for miners on the side," she said. "He's an attorney. He's been busy . . . but . . ."

But what? Libby felt the world's vexations waiting to burst upon her like a thunderstorm. She could not tell anyone about the gold or Grenville's fervent quest to pin her to a wall.

She turned and would not glance at him, hoping he would not catch her eye. And at that moment the assistant pastor began to call out over the crowd, his voice equipped with that piercing sound that carries over noise. "There are still seats in the front," he cried. "Try to find a place. Mr. Cotter will be here soon. Try to leave a path for him."

Libby watched the Earps take their seats. She was still interested in what was going on, but something shimmered in her vision like the corona of light that appears when a person chances to look at the sun. She hadn't expected to see Charles Grenville in the massive hoard of this congregation. And now beside her, introducing her to the Earps, coming to church as though nothing on earth could possibly stop her, was Mag. Libby was pretty sure Grenville knew Mag intimately.

After Libby followed her through the courthouse door, two of the deacons gently guided them to the right side of the aisle. "He's coming up the steps now," one of them whispered. "There's no time to find a seat at the moment." Libby backed up as far as she could, and Mag placed a hand on her arm. They were blocking the view of the people seated on the benches behind them, but it couldn't be helped.

There he was. Libby had not seen him since he had walked away from her over a week ago. She drew a quick breath. He had not changed. He was the same man who had shielded her from danger in the Kansas City railroad station. Wendell Cotter looked convincing, dynamic. His light hair fell loosely over his brow. His collar was blinding white, like a rim of porcelain framing the smooth-shaven chin, the perfect cheeks, his ears flat against his regal head.

When he stepped close to her, Libby let his name out of her mouth with a cry. The name that had been cooped up inside her like a trapped bird flapping to get out had now simply escaped.

He stopped. As though unnerved, he turned swiftly in the aisle and caught her eye. That may have been all the contact she needed to fill her hunger, but the miracle was that he stopped. When he recognized her, he turned to her.

"Libby! You came."

"Yes, I'm so excited to hear you today."

He tucked his Bible under his arm and took both of her hands in his. She held her breath.

"Are you all right?" he asked softly. "I've been concerned about you."

"Yes, yes. I'm fine."

"Are you safe?" He paused. "In that house?"

Libby gave a brief laugh. "Yes. Yes, I'm fine."

"I'm worried about the kind of job you might find . . ." Cotter did not finish, but caught a glance at the huge crowd. "I will be in touch," he said quickly and turned to the aisle.

He was gone.

19

All the praise heaped upon the new preacher in Tombstone—
his demeanor, his sermon that struck at their hearts, all of the
complimentary articles in both *The Epitaph* and *The Nugget,*
all of the chatter along Allen Street, the curiosity of the girls
at Bless House who began to berate themselves for missing
Sunday's event—all of it swept over Libby's consciousness like
tidewater on an empty beach. She heard it, but it had little effect
on a consciousness already alive with feeling. Seeing him win
over the crowd with his powerful sermon had done something
to her heart. She lay awake in the morning thinking about him
while Lizette slept.

During her time in Bless House, she had asked as many
questions as she dared about the places in town where she
might find employment. When Marcella announced that she
and Horace were taking a shopping trip to town on Monday,
Libby discreetly inquired if she might go with them. She was
a little shy to explore the town by herself and was thinking of
finding work that would pay for her room and board, and would
Marcella mind if she came along?

Marcella's face froze as she heard Libby's plea. It was a
surprised look bordering on disappointment. Libby knew Marcella
had wanted to recruit her for employment at Bless House. But it

was her sister Nora's policy that if a girl would rather pay board and room, that was acceptable. Of course the other profession made more money. But Libby had money—though it had so far stayed securely untouched in the leather sack, wrapped in one of her panties in her coat pocket. She was loath to get it out, to flaunt it, to let anyone know about it. The memory of Charles Grenville's aggression floated about her like a mist of fear. She would rather wash dishes a hundred years than come under the condemnation of the attorney who knew everything about her.

Once in town, she would look for Wyatt, for Virgil, for Morgan, for anyone who might put in a good word for her at the establishments they frequented. She was determined to face reality's demands, but before she took that difficult step, she allowed herself time in the mornings to ponder, to review what it was that had happened to her so suddenly. Or was it really sudden?

On Monday morning, after hearing the amazing sermon in the courthouse, Libby allowed her thoughts to rest on the touch of Cotter's grasp. He had tucked the Bible under his arm and taken both of her hands in his. His eyes sparkled. The expression on his face was one of love and concern. She had known she had strong feelings for him, but not like this—not so completely with all of the fibers of her body alive with hope.

She knew she might be imagining something that did not or should not exist, yet her thoughts were so consuming she could not help herself. Love had always evaded her. But the care Libby felt from Cotter dredged up memories as vague as dreams that seemed to be carved in water—shimmering marks like the ripples in a stream.

Her mother had always been her refuge. But now it may be true that the love of a gentle man had really happened. Did Libby have any authentic memories of her father? Was it true that once he held her close against his breast after a tiny, broken bird had died? And when she fell into the muddy slough at the fair, and after the boy down the street had ripped the sash on her white dress? She thought she could remember that her father had whispered to her, "You will be a beautiful young lady, and you must stay pure and lovely for the day you meet that noble and kind young man who will care for you as I care for you."

She remembered bending forward, caught in her mother's arms, and reaching out with both hands to lean on the satin edge of the big box where her father lay still and gray. She did not understand death, not then. Dry-eyed she turned away and buried her face in her mother's shawl. When her mother put her down, the edge of the shawl that brushed her arm was wet with her mother's tears.

Thursday bloomed bright and promising. When Libby bounded down the stairs, she saw Marcella and Horace waiting in the foyer. Horace looked elegant in a hound's-tooth coat. Libby thought he resembled a checkerboard.

"You ready to go, Libby?"

She was more than ready. "Where did you get the new coat, Horace?"

"Some cowboy was so excited about the services at Bless House that he left it," Horace replied.

"Nice of you to let me come along," Libby said.

"Oh, it's no bother," Marcella crooned. "Horace has to see if his money came into the bank. I'd like to visit the dress shop. Otherwise, we're free to investigate the town with you."

As they left, Horace broke into a ditty he learned in prison from a French fellow serving time for killing his father with a frying pan.

Oh, no, Libby thought. *We're going to be listening to Horace all day.* But when she heard the words of the song she felt some laughter warming her inside.

Oh Marie Antoinette
Was a feisty brunette
But don't whistle
Don't whistle
Or suffer regret.
Marie Antoinette
Marie Antoinette

The second verse expounded the historical fact that a woman once whistled at Marie Antoinette in a crowd and was sentenced to prison for fifty years.

Marie Augustin
Dared to whistle, and then
She whistled herself
Right into the pen.
For fifty long years
She won't whistle again.

"It's a true story." Horace winked at Libby. She wasn't sure.

At the bank, she stood in line behind Horace and Marcella, waiting patiently, as a cloud filled the room. She felt the shadow as surely as if shades had been drawn, or a pall had dropped behind her. Someone large was standing very close, practically breathing down her neck. She imagined herself turning around and staring rudely at whoever it was. But that would be uncomfortable. She turned just far enough to look at the floor behind her, where she saw the shiny black toes of huge boots. She knew who it was without seeing his face. Charles Grenville.

"Yes, it's me, Elizabeth Campbell." His voice sounded wintry, maybe raspy from a throat recovering from a cold, yet deep and frightening, nevertheless. "Out and about, are you?"

She spun around and saw him staring her down just as he had done in the train that afternoon. It made her feel off-balance.

"Horace has money coming," she murmured, knowing her excuse for being at the bank was flimsy.

"Coming, going. And yours will be going," Grenville quipped.

The old fear prickled her, but she looked straight into his face and cocked her head. "Are you still trying to get Mr. Stuyvesant's gold, when I figure it's not even a pinch of what he owes me?"

"Oh, he owes you more than a pinch?"

There was a small twitch in Charles's mouth that Libby barely caught. He was laughing at her! Anger simmered up inside of her. Yes, Stuyvesant owed her more than the gold she took. She knew the rates now. As a live-in at the brothel, she was well aware of the amount Stuyvesant should have paid her, but never would. What she took was a pittance. Besides, except for a few pennies she spent on the journey, it was still intact. And unless Charles wanted to rifle through her things in the attic at Bless House, he would never find it.

He was staring at her with a twinkle in his eye. "So, how are things working out for you at Bless House?"

She bristled. "It's not what you think."

"What do I think?" He was still mocking her.

"I'm looking for a position today."

"Oh, you're looking for a position. What position are you best suited for, Miss Libby Campbell?"

Her face went hot as the anger boiled and rose to the top.

At that point, Horace and Marcella finished their transaction at the teller's window and turned around to exit the building. When Marcella recognized Grenville, she turned all smiles and sweetness. Horace registered a puzzled look.

"Oh, Charles!" Marcella gushed, putting out her gloved hand. "I heard you were working for Mr. Clum at *The Epitaph.*"

"Yes, I'm striving for an impressive epitaph." He grinned. "I'm getting in practice to write on my own tombstone."

Marcella laughed. "It's so good to see you!" She glanced at Horace, who was so much shorter than Grenville that he would probably get a crook in his neck from looking at him.

"This is my brother, Horace. I told you about him on the train," Marcella said.

Grenville politely shook hands with Horace.

"You the same Grenville, the attorney?"

"My reputation has preceded me?"

Horace glanced at Marcella and then at Libby, seeming unsure as to how enthusiastic he should be about the imposing figure before him.

Grenville nodded and smiled, performing all of the social grace required for the situation, then turned toward the bank teller. "Nice to see you, ladies. And to meet you, Mr. Baron." Grenville nodded graciously. "If you'll excuse me, I have some business to attend to."

A mysterious warmth left Libby, who still fumed. She had stronger feelings for this man than for anyone she had ever known. An strange urge came over her—a desire to speak out, to stay in the bank for a few more minutes to chastise him.

She hadn't finished with him. That was it. When he turned to the teller, Libby concentrated on pushing away the anger and the disappointment of missing the opportunity to lash out.

"Huh!" Horace huffed. "That fella is a real dandy. And tall! No need for Louis Fourteen's elevator shoes."

Marcella was smiling. "Let's find a job for Libby now."

Most of the shops were just opening. As the trio tramped up and down Allen Street, more shopkeepers began to unlock their doors and drag their brooms out to the boardwalk. Some retailers stopped sweeping to say hello. Others came out just to take a deep breath of the morning air. The early hours were perhaps the only time the atmosphere wasn't polluted by the noise and smoke from the gold mills.

Because Horace had finally received his savings from his Wyoming bank, he wanted to stop at J. Myers and Brothers at the corner of Fifth and Allen to buy a pair of trousers. He had been amused by the ads in both *The Nugget* and *The Epitaph*, posting poetry in the shape of pants. "Just note the grace of every line, where quality and style combine."

"Anybody that can write poetry like that ought to be able to fit you in a pair of pants. Both legs ought to be the same length, eh?" Horace laughed.

Marcella wanted to visit a dress shop on Fremont Street. While Horace was in the haberdasher's, she pulled Libby into Mrs. Addie Borland's foyer, encouraging her to get a new dress. But Libby was determined to get a job first. Lizette had lent her a couple of frocks, and there was a pile of used dresses at Bless House. Libby felt anxious about wasting time. If the truth were known, she hoped to see Cotter somewhere on the street. That was her first desire, though she would be happy to see any of the Earps who had been so kind at the courthouse. When they offered her help to get employment, she wondered if they really meant it.

She stood at the window of Mrs. Borland's Garments and Alterations while Marcella was measured. Looking across the street, Libby saw two buildings with clearly marked signs. One was Fly's Photograph Studio, and the other the OK Corral. So this was the spot of the famous gunfight! She stared.

Mrs. Borland knew immediately what Libby was interested in. "I was sitting at my window when I saw those five men opposite my house just standing in the street there," the seamstress offered, with a row of pins in her mouth. "They were leaning against that small house west of Fly's, and one of them was holding a horse by its reins. Four men came down the street toward them. A man with a long coat walked up to the man with the horse and put a pistol to his stomach and then stepped back about three feet. I could see everything from that window."

Libby stared at the boardwalk across the street as she listened to Mrs. Borland's account. The woman was tall and thin like a crane, with a sallow face. When she leaned over Marcella's hem, she looked like a starving monk in an attitude of prayer.

"Then the shooting commenced. I don't know which party fired first—it was impossible to tell. I could see both parties, but no one in particular. I did not know the man with the long coat until somebody told me later it was Doc Holliday."

Libby squinted her eyes, trying to reconstruct the gunfight in her imagination.

"Move this way a little," Mrs. Borland told Marcella as she took a few pins from her mouth.

"I'm used to keeping close to the corset," Marcella said.

As Mrs. Borland continued pinning, she also continued talking. "Later, the inquest asked me if any of the cowboys threw up their hands, but they did not. I saw that they did not throw up their hands. That was a big point Ike Clanton wanted to make in the trial—that the deputies were shooting those men while their hands were in the air.

"I testified at the trial that their hands were not in the air, because they weren't. Both sides just started shooting, and it terrified me so much I got up and went into my back room. I just heard later that Bill Clanton and the McLowry brothers were all three killed, but not until they shot holes in Morgan and Virgil and Doc Holliday. Nobody really cared about them robber cowboys, but on the day the mortician put those three bodies in the window, all hell broke loose. You don't see three people you know lying there pasty-faced in their coffins and not feel a tug of sympathy for them."

Mrs. Borland stood up and took a couple of pins from her mouth. Marcella turned to face her. "So everybody was shot. What did Mr. Clanton want?"

"Clanton ran away from the fight. He didn't even see it. But he swears the deputies murdered these three boys. He brought his lawyer brother all the way from back east to fight the case. But I saw everything, and no hands came up. Clanton paid somebody to say their hands was up, but the judge listened to my testimony. They may have had their arms up earlier. But in the corral my eyes didn't deceive me. They never raised their arms."

"Did Mr. Clanton's lawyer accept the verdict?" Marcella asked.

Mrs. Borland went over to a dresser drawer to retrieve more pins. With the pins in her mouth, she was a bit handicapped to answer. There was a pause for a moment while she came to tug at Marcella's corset strings. "You know, you have a high bosom. Not many women can boast of a high bosom."

"My mother," Marcella said.

Mrs. Borland took up where she left off. "Mr. Clanton's lawyer, his brother, hightailed it back to his home in the East."

Marcella gasped as the corset went tighter. "What about Mr. Clanton?"

"His cronies tried to kill Virgil at the end of December. Mr. Earp was shot in the side and is now paralyzed. Can't use his arm. No one knows who did it, but we all suspect Clanton is involved. And Sheriff Behan is a coward. He is caught between. He knows the law should do something, but he also has to live with those cowboys. Plus he hates Wyatt for dallying behind everyone's back with his girl, that pretty actress Josie Marcus.

Sometimes I think that fake lawman, Johnny Behan is getting paid under the table for not apprehending those stage robbers."

"I heard there were more stage robberies than ours." Marcella sucked up her breath again. "That was a fearful crime we suffered on the way from Benson."

"There's something evil and sinister about what's going on around here," the seamstress went on. "There's a group of prominent men like Ike Clanton who seem to threaten the peace of this town, and you don't know going up and down the road who's honest and who's not. Mr. Cotter can calm us down every Sunday and tell us not to be afraid. He makes a good sermon, but it don't always apply in the middle of the week."

Libby saw the light in the street move the shadows away from the boardwalk. She felt the top of her head prickle. Mr. Cotter? Mrs. Borland must have heard Cotter's sermon. She turned, wanting to pursue that subject.

But Mrs. Borland obviously had other ideas running through her head. "Did you want to be fitted too, missy?" She tugged one last time at the measuring tape around Marcella's waist, removed it, and walked over to Libby.

"Oh, no, thank you, ma'am," she said as pleasantly as she could. "I am not spending any of my savings until I can find a position."

"She's wanting to work somewhere," Marcella added. "You don't know of any openings, do you?"

Mrs. Borland stopped a few feet from Libby. "You're wanting a job then, little lady?" She removed a couple of pins from her mouth and sized up the girl before her. "Sure you just don't want to be measured?" She cocked her head. "You're a pretty little thing."

"No, I'll wait, Mrs. Borland. Thank you very much." Libby took the compliment with pleasure.

For several seconds the woman seemed to be thinking, or checking the ceiling for some inspiration. And while Marcella was putting herself back together, Mrs. Borland came up with an idea. "I do know Mr. Campbell at the Campbell and Hatch saloon was looking for a pretty girl. You mind serving pool and poker players?"

Libby wanted to wait for Cotter, or Wyatt and Morgan. But she knew her chances for employment were slim with the rush of newcomers moving into the town. "Campbell?" she said.

"That's my name. Libby Campbell."

"Well, it's a fit then." Mrs. Borland, who was used to fitting things together, seemed duly amazed and gave a large smile. "I know Mr. Hatch, and I'll send a note over with you if you'd like."

"Oh, I would appreciate that very much," Libby said. "Thank you."

While they waited for Addie Borland to write the note, Marcella came to the window and stood for a few moments to look with Libby. "It's hard to believe that just a few months ago there was a gunfight in that corral across the street," Marcella mused. "It seems it's unsettled everybody here in this town. No one knows how to stop the mayhem."

Even Cotter seemed powerless. Obviously, Libby thought, the sermon he gave on putting away your fears seemed to be just a Sunday thing. She wanted him to make a difference here because she knew that's what he wanted. But if what Mrs. Borland had told Marcella was true, there was still a storm brewing.

Marcella wanted to visit the millinery and told Libby to just duck into the Campbell and Hatch Saloon by herself. She thought it might give her a better chance than if a whole bunch of people were hanging around.

20

Libby opened the door to the Campbell and Hatch Saloon. The shiny surface of the polished cherrywood floor reflected the crystal bobs in the chandeliers above. She imagined stepping on it would be like walking on sunlit red water. In the back of the room, two flanking windows shed light on the ornate pool table in the alcove. Impressed by the high ceilings and the luxurious, mottled light-blue walls, Libby sighed as a heaviness lifted from her. When she closed the door behind her, the crowded streets of Tombstone seemed instantly far away. Card players at several tables were conversing quietly, and Libby could hear the taps of the sticks as other men hit the wooden balls across the felt.

A clean-cut man in a white shirt, a bow tie, blue suspenders, brown trousers, and navy-blue armbands came out from behind the bar to greet her. He wore his dark hair slicked down with a wide part in the middle. He smiled pleasantly. "Welcome! My name is Bob Hatch. What can I do for you?"

Libby had expected dense smoke and drunken brawling, but everything seemed well ordered and even friendly.

"And you are . . ." Mr. Hatch went on.

"I'm Libby Campbell . . ."

"Campbell? That's the name of my partner!" He paused and looked askance at her. "You're not related to him by any chance?"

"Oh, no. I don't think so. I'm from Kansas City, just arrived a couple of week ago. Mrs. Borland . . ."

Hatch blinked. "You know Mrs. Borland?"

"She told me to tell you she thought I ought to try for the waitress position," Libby finally got out. "She said you have an opening for a girl to help with customers and cleaning." Libby paused. "And I'd be very good, sir . . . Mr. Hatch, sir."

He was the kind of person whose face was totally open, and he lit up now with an even greater welcome and surprise in his eyes. "Why, yes, young lady, Miss Campbell. I need someone right away. When can you start?"

"As soon as you need me, sir."

"Today?"

Libby held herself steady. "Today would be fine!" If she had truly found a position, it would be the beginning of a new life for her. She felt buoyant and almost flustered. "What can I do for you today, Mr. Hatch?"

The light blue walls seemed to represent sky. If she were privileged to work here, the place would resemble heaven.

"I need someone to remove the glassware from the cabinet and wash the shelves," Bob Hatch explained.

Libby unwound her scarf and removed her wrap. Glancing at the pictures hanging on the wall, she saw a large military insignia.

Hatch followed her gaze. "We're a patriotic bunch. I served the Union in the Civil War. You'll get to know Mr. Campbell and myself. We're a respectable outfit here."

"I am very grateful to you for this opportunity," Libby said. "Do you have an apron?"

Bob Hatch stopped for a moment to look at her. "Well, I like that get-right-to-it attitude! I think I'm lucky today." He reached under the counter on the bar and brought out a clean white apron.

Libby took the apron and opened it up. Just as she had found the ties and tied it on, a shadow crossed the doorway. When she glanced at the two tall men who entered, gearing herself up for her first customers, she did a double take. The man in front was Morgan Earp. She knew the mustache, the lean neck and cheeks. He wore a white shirt and dark tie. She wasn't sure how she recognized him, or how he recognized her. His eyes were fastened on her as she tied the apron behind her back.

"Well, hello. Aren't you the girl from Kansas?"

"Meet Libby Campbell," Bob Hatch said to Morgan. "She's our new gal now. Did you know Ella left?"

"Yes. Well, hello again, Miss Campbell. So you found a position on your own, did you?"

"Yes, sir."

"Congratulations."

She smoothed the apron with her hands and smiled. It was at that moment she noticed the man who came up behind Morgan, half hidden during Morgan's greeting. He had been focused on Bob Hatch's pool table, but now he emerged, his face clearly visible, his rough two-week beard unable to serve as a disguise. It was Charles Grenville.

"Oh, Mr. Grenville," Bob Hatch said at last. "Nice to see you, sir. I guess you know Morgan Wyatt. This is Miss Campbell."

Grenville's brows were so black they looked like two storms about to sweep up his dark eyes. His glare struck Libby's nerves.

"I know Miss Campbell," he said simply, but his gaze said more.

Libby froze. Everything in her body tightened like the strings of a violin. She felt the blood drain from her face.

Bob moved toward an unoccupied table in the middle of the room. "Are we having drinks?" He gestured toward the other tables deep into poker or faro. "Or would you like to join one of the other games?"

"This is fine," Morgan said. "My brothers will be here this afternoon." Morgan and Grenville sat down.

Bob turned to Libby and said quietly, "This will be your first service. Make sure the glasses are clean—pour just to here. Do it right and you'll get a tip. Morgan is always generous. I don't know much about the other fellow."

But Libby did, and at the moment she was grateful to be in a room full of people. If she'd had a choice, she would rather have served a chain gang than Charles Grenville. She stood by Morgan's chair, as far from danger as she could.

"Bob knows. Same pint," Morgan said.

Libby raised her eyes to take Grenville's order, still irritated he would have the nerve to follow her all the way to Tombstone. She felt the gold was hers, and she hadn't even spent any of it yet, except the railway ticket, and lunch at The Owl and the Pussy Cat.

His eyes flashed something she did not understand. "So, you're a working girl, Miss Campbell? Congratulations. I guess you no longer need much gold."

The words stung her. She glanced at Morgan, but he was watching a game of pool at the back table. As Libby waited for Grenville to order his drink, he addressed the deputy sheriff. "Do you often have fugitives from other states come to hide in Tombstone?" Grenville articulated each word. Libby thought it was because he did not want her to miss one.

Morgan turned from the game and leaned back in his chair. "We're pretty nearly all outsiders. And new outsiders are all over the place. We can't keep up with them." He cocked his head and grinned. "You're an outsider. How do we know you're not hiding some crime you committed?"

Libby barely held back a gasp. Her mother had said Grenville killed a woman working in her garden during a deer hunt. Somehow, Libby forced herself to say, "May I take your order, sir?"

It was no surprise to her when Grenville continued to play her to Morgan. "You're a deputy. How do you discover what's going on?" He turned to Libby. "For example, this adorable-looking girl right here? She looks innocent, and as honest as the day is long. But how do you know she's not a thief who kited a handful of gold coins from someone's fortune and came here incognito to hide it?"

Morgan glanced at Libby and laughed, his eyes twinkling. "If she had a handful of gold, I doubt she'd be cartin' drinks back and forth. That is, if she can actually cart 'em back and forth. Haven't seen nothin' yet."

Morgan was one of the best-looking men she had ever seen. There was a wave in his ash-brown hair, and a curl in his mustache. Wyatt was good-looking too in his way. The only one of the brothers who looked a little used up was Virgil, who was a little hefty in the jowls. She had noticed that his expansive cheeks were rough with chicken-pox scars. But Morgan, like his brother Wyatt, was slender and tall, and his cheeks were clean shaven.

It would be so easy to say, "Anything for you, Mr. Grenville," but the words wouldn't come. Libby turned away. But she did manage to add, "By the time you decide, Mr. Grenville, I'll have Mr. Wyatt taken care of."

She thought she said it in a pleasant voice, but some anger must have seeped through. The animated Mr. Grenville put his great big boots in her way and grabbed her by the wrist. The strength of his smooth hands startled her. "Not so fast!" he said, the look in his eyes sending chills into her neck. "What do you have to run from?" Grenville asked, then turned to Morgan. "You gonna arrest this girl, Deputy Earp?

Libby's head burned with panic, but Morgan laughed again. "You got some evidence against her? Sure, I'll arrest her and put her to work shinin' my shoes."

"You ready for that, Libby Campbell?" Grenville said stoically, a challenge roiling beneath the surface.

Struck dumb, Libby stood staring at him.

He pulled back as though realizing he had pushed her too hard. "All right, bring me a ginger ale, no ice."

Keeping her anger inside, she grasped the rag tied to her apron and flipped it through her fingers, then headed to the bar like a horse free of its saddle. She hated to be in a situation where someone tried to control her. Grenville posed a definite threat. She resented how he had always managed to force the hot coals of anger in her memory to ignite like so much gunpowder, to threaten to burst into some ignoble fire. He had twisted her like this rag on the belt of her apron.

At the bar, Bob smiled at her and said kindly, "Don't let them get up your dander. They're just teasin' ya."

But there was more than just teasing with Grenville. His look drove some unfamiliar feeling through Libby, heart and limb.

When the tray was almost full, Bob showed her which glasses carried which drinks, and let her pour from the decanters.

At one point he raised his eyes to the doorway, and Libby said to herself, *Oh, no. More of that teasin'*, but when she turned and saw who it was, she caught her breath. She couldn't believe it. The large shadow blocking the light, the heavy shoulders, the hair burnished by the sun, was Cotter.

She hurried to place the napkins on the tray, the olives on the wooden toothpicks.

Cotter was standing at the table where Grenville and Morgan sat. Libby stared, her feet unmoving. Bob came up behind her. "Oh, I forgot baseball practice was today at 4:00." He glanced at Libby. "Do you think you could take care of things around here for a couple of hours?"

Without hesitating, she said, "Sure." *How handy to have someone in the saloon just in time for baseball practice.*

"Bob! Hello," Cotter said. "Yes, I've come to collect you."

"I'll be just a minute," Bob Hatch called out from the room behind the bar.

Cotter seemed huge standing over the table. The white collar set off his tan neck.

"Sit down." Morgan pulled a chair out with his boot. "You been makin' the rounds again?"

Grenville cocked his head. "You been gettin' any takers?"

"On building the church, or on the baseball team?"

Grenville chuckled. "Well, both. You hit me up for fifty bucks last time for the church."

"And I appreciated that, Charles. We had enough to pay Clum's architect friend to draw up a plan."

"Well, you tried to get me to play on that baseball team, too, Reverend. By the way, I never saw anybody hit it out of the park like you did. I couldn't do that. You probably don't want me on your team."

"Sure you don't want to be a star outfielder?" Cotter made an expansive, imaginary banner with his hands. "Charles Grenville, outfielder of the year."

Grenville leaned his head back and laughed. He turned to Morgan. "You seen this man hit the ball?"

"I haven't," Morgan said.

"He's amazing. Told us he broke the chancellery window in England and met the pope."

"Not the pope." Cotter grinned, his hands slipping into his pockets. "Close . . ."

Nobody noticed Libby waiting patiently behind Cotter's back with the loaded tray still in her hands. She hadn't moved much since the preacher's shadow appeared in the doorway. He hadn't seen her yet, and she was not sure she wanted him to know she was there. She hesitated to interrupt the conversation. But it wasn't long before Morgan looked around Cotter's arm and caught sight of her.

"Here she comes!" Morgan said. "Good." Libby held the tray high. "Do you want to lower it just a little?" He reached for his drink. "You always have to train the new girls until they catch on."

New girls? When Libby lowered the tray, she felt a blush heat up her cheeks. Cotter moved back out of her way a step and searched her face. "Libby! Libby Campbell, it's you!"

"Sit down, Cotter. Have a drink."

He did not hear Grenville's invitation or chose to ignore it.

"Amazing. I didn't expect to see you . . ." Cotter paused as if catching his breath. "Are you working here now?"

She was tongue-tied. The preacher affected her more than she wanted to admit.

"You found a job on your own? Good for you!"

"Yes. She came down from Kansas City on the same train we both took here," Grenville told Morgan. "She's landed a job already and is aiming to get rich now."

Oh, please! Libby prayed silently. *Please don't mention the gold.* Miraculously, he didn't. She placed the ginger ale in front of Grenville and pulled the tray away from the table.

Cotter still stood. "Libby, I'm proud of you. Good for you."

She wanted to open her mouth but felt foolish. "I saw your sermon . . ." she began. "You did a remarkable job."

He smiled. With his hands in his pockets, he looked like a boy clutching a mouse in his fist. "I had a lot of help," he stammered and glanced up to the heavens. "Are you going to stay here in Tombstone indefinitely?"

She yearned to say, "I'll stay here as long as you're here." But of course she could not say that. "I don't want to miss any of your sermons, Cotter." She tried to keep it light. But she would like to have followed him from saloon to saloon, soliciting funds for the new church he was constructing, and she would gladly tag along with him to the ball field.

"Well, I'll be giving more than a few of them." Cotter smiled.

At that point Bob Hatch came out from the bar in his athletic trousers, white shirt, and baseball cap. "I'm ready, Cotter—ready to hit a few homers."

Cotter turned to the men at the table. "Good to see you folks. I'll be around pestering you for funds again. Maybe at the Alhambra? Or the Continental?"

"We'll see you Sunday for one of those rip-roaring, slap-dash discourses you're preachin'." Grenville lifted his palm.

"Take care of yourselves," Cotter said in parting. "Don't let those cowboys get you, Mr. Earp."

Morgan raised his hand in goodbye.

Still at the table, the men ordered more drinks. When Libby turned from the bar with the tray in her hands, she glanced out the window and saw two figures coming toward the door. She felt nervous without Bob there. But as party came under the skylight, Libby noticed one of them was a woman dressed in flowery maroon, edged with black lace. It was Marcella with Horace.

"Miss Campbell!" Marcella said brightly, taking in the tray, the apron.

Libby set the drinks down. "Marcella, Horace, hello!"

"We've been every place along Allen Street looking for you," Marcella said. "Finally we ran into Cotter and he told us you were here. And you found a job!"

"No, she just stopped in and stole an apron." Horace was still being himself.

"Yes, I did," Libby answered Marcella with a big smile.

"I'm so impressed, Libby. How wonderful! Good for you! Well, I hope we still see you from time to time."

Libby tucked the tray under her arm. "There was something I wanted to ask you about . . . if it was all right if I stayed at Bless House for a while longer. I'll pay for the room."

Marcella beamed, but before she could speak, a handful of men entered the saloon. The afternoon sun had suddenly faded, and a desultory gloom seeped through the curtains. A gust of wind rose up and blew an old paper box up off the road like a skittery hen, and when the box hit the hitching post in front, it slapped it hard with the sound of a gunshot.

"Well, who are you, girlie?" the front man crooned.

"Welcome to Hatch and Campbell's," Libby said.

Marcella and Horace said goodbye and left to finish shopping. The older man was dressed in a natty wool suit coat, a striped tie of bright red and blue, and a tight black vest and trousers. He looked like one of the wealthy men who frequented the town businesses. He seemed familiar, and Libby wondered if he had been a visitor at Bless House.

She glanced at the table where Grenville and Earp sat. Alert now, they watched the three men with bright-eyed stares.

"You're new here," the man stated.

Libby tried to smile. When she lowered her eyes she saw three pairs of cowboy boots, some of them caked with dust.

"Well, we'll have whiskey," the man declared. Suddenly, he saw Grenville and Morgan Earp, and his eyes stopped.

"Hello, Ike Clanton." Morgan crumpled his napkin and pushed back his chair. Grenville also began to get up.

"Earps everywhere," Ike murmured. "Can't get away from the Earps."

"We just been at the Alhambra and the Continental. Wyatt was in one, and Virgil in the other," said one of the cowboys, a scrappy-looking hombre with graying hair that stuck straight up from under his hat.

"Maybe they're trying to protect the town from desperados like you, Johnny Ringo," Morgan addressed the wizened cowboy.

Ringo stiffened.

"And desperados like you, you barefaced gunslinger," Ike Clanton retorted. He knit his brows and said in a different tone, "But the law is in the hands of a bunch of murderers, ain't it? And it seems there ain't nothin' nobody can do about it. You boys are in charge, and murderin' is your game."

Nervous, Libby stood back. It looked like both Morgan and Charles were going to get out fast. But there would be nothing she could do. She was in charge here while Bob was gone.

"You're leavin' like a coward?" Ike slurred his words. "Can't take the truth?"

"You'd better watch it, Ike," Morgan said.

Ike Clanton sneered. "You'll get it in the neck."

Johnny Ringo put up his hands. "I'd have nothin' to do with it. Ask Stilwell here. I ain't guilty. Tell 'em, Frank."

The third man hadn't spoken yet. He was a slight, wiry, baby-faced cowboy with a perpetual half-grin, and his thumbs in his belt loops. "Yeah? Is this court or somethin'?"

"It's somethin'," Ike growled. "Somethin' you don't want to have nothin' to do with."

"I second it," Ringo said.

Morgan was standing now. He turned to Grenville and said, "Let's go find Wyatt."

Grenville hesitated. "I'll be along in a few minutes." He was looking straight at Libby, who felt the gaze up and down her spine.

Morgan left money on the table. "You did good, miss. Don't let these fellows give you dirt."

Libby saw the most hateful look cross Mr. Clanton's face.

When she glanced at Grenville, his eyes were fastened on the cowboys, who stumped about arranging the chairs at the empty table. They scraped the legs across the plank floor with no thought for the earsplitting noise they raised. Once seated, the men leaned over, hunched together, and began talking so low no one could know what they were discussing.

Grenville did not speak to them, but sauntered to the pool table where two players wielded their cue sticks in a thick cloud of smoke. He had his hands in his pockets and edged along a table where some other players were hard at poker.

Before Libby approached the cowboys, she found she was looking toward Grenville. She caught herself. He was probably more dangerous than these rough men in clothes that reeked of dust and manure. Yet somehow he seemed safer, probably because he had been with Morgan. Or was it because of his strength and imperial force of character? Something about him heartened her. For some reason, she was praying he would stay in the saloon, and he did.

"Can I get you something?" she asked the man in the black suit, glancing toward Charles Grenville.

"Whiskeys," Clanton said, then sat in the chair Morgan had vacated. "Give Ringo and Stilwell one round on me."

Libby walked toward the bar. As she ducked behind the counter to pick up the glasses, she felt a shadow over her.

"Need some help?"

She did not have to guess who was behind her. When she raised her head she was face-to-face with Charles Grenville. She felt confused but suddenly grateful. In that moment the image that crossed her mind was of the tall Charles Grenville, Stuyvesant's accountant, picking up apples in the snow. It was a vision as clear as if it were happening now: the moon glossy on the snow with a dazzling sheen, the music of the carolers in front of the porch. Libby's mother was dressed in her red knit shawl, and the wide muslin skirt she still wore in her grave. *My beloved mother.* She held the basket of apples in her arms until the angry master tipped them into the ice, breaking up the moonlight into a thousand shards. And it was Grenville who leaned over them, his tall frame, the flowing tails of his overcoat, the hat he let fall for a brief moment into the snow. It was Grenville who picked up most of the apples. Libby thought she could look through him at that moment.

"Has the cat got your tongue?" He took the glasses from her fingers and set them on the tray. "You're off somewhere."

"I was . . . I was remembering Christmas a year ago. You picked up the apples in the snow.

Grenville stood tall now. "You remember that, do you?"

"My mother. . ." Libby hesitated. "My mother died." She glanced at his face. It had gone pale.

"Your mother . . ."

Libby was not sure what he would have said, because he glanced at the table and nodded at some gesture of impatience from his friends.

"Here, let me pour that," he said. "I didn't like the way they looked at you."

She was speechless. Grenville took hold of the decanter. She was not imagining his hands—they were real. His fingers were long and white, tapered at the ends like the colored wax candles she had seen in the windows at Hibbard, Spencer and Bartlett just this morning. It seemed years ago, yet it was just this morning with Marcella and Horace. Horace had laughed at the colored candles. "In 1491, a Swiss court sentenced a chicken to death for laying a brightly colored egg," he had reported.

Something lifted in her heart. "Thank you, Mr. Grenville. You don't need to . . ." But she did not finish. He took the tray to Ike Clanton, Johnny Ringo, and Frederick Bode. By now they sat away from the table, leaning back in their chairs, their voices relaxed, even strident.

"It was my shot got Virgil," Frederick Bode was saying.

Libby froze at the brazen confession.

Grenville paid no attention. He set the tray on the edge of the table and nodded to Libby to deliver the drinks. She did so, trying to steady herself. The men did not notice her. It was as if she were absent—a wraith or a spirit without substance. She was glad.

When the customers laid down their money, Libby took it up and folded the bills into her apron pocket. Grenville followed her back to the till in the pantry.

"You see? Easy as falling off a bridge."

He seemed to watch every move she made. "Mr. Grenville, you don't trust me."

He smiled. "Charles to you. Should I?"

"Yes, you should." Only a few moments ago she would have screamed at him. But everything seemed different now. Even the afternoon light flooding the floor had turned the color of magenta. The dust in the beams had become luminous like splinters of silver.

21

During that week, suffering with the onset of some sniffles, Cotter was determined to keep an interview appointment with Mr. Clum of *The Epitaph*. Though he gargled saltwater for his throat, his eyes were weepy when he came into the newspaper office. He hoped Mr. Clum would not notice.

But Mr. John Clum was pretty savvy. He took one look at Cotter and, after a warm welcome, asked, "You been to Nellie Cashman's place yet?"

"I'm sorry. I think the stress has finally taken its toll." Cotter paused. "Nellie Cashman?"

"She has a tea that puts the starch right back in you," Mr. Clum said. "I visit her restaurant every chance I can get. She serves good food and takes care of the sniffles around here."

That was the first Cotter had heard of Nellie Cashman. "Thank you, Mr. Clum, I'll have to see about her."

"John to you."

Cotter smiled and nodded his head.

"I was not able to hear your sermon, Mr. Cotter," Clum continued. "I'm usually with the Presbyterians. But you have become the talk of the town. People are buzzing about your powerful messages, and the baseball team you're putting together to beat George Rice's San Pedro Boys."

Cotter grinned. "Yes, we plan to do that soon."

"I admire you for dedicating yourself to Christian causes," Clum said. "I was studying divinity at Rutgers College until the rheumatic fever took me down and I was sent home."

When he first met the preacher he was to replace, Cotter asked him about some of the pillars of the community he should meet. John Clum, editor of *The Epitaph*, past owner of the *Arizona Citizen*, was one of them. Once a highly successful Indian agent, he transported the Apaches north to their reservation in San Carlos, and taught them agriculture.

"I heard of your exploits as an Indian agent," Cotter said.

John Clum moved nervously in his chair. "That was hardly heroic. I was working for the government." He was a sallow-cheeked man with a straight nose, heavy brows, a thick mustache, and now a slight blush. "I did teach them to farm." Clum paused. "But then the government chose the most God-forsaken desert for them to live in, and force-herded them by the thousands."

"All reports are that you did a good job."

"Thank you, Mr. Cotter," Clum murmured. He was quiet for a moment, as though in deep thought about what he did to the Indians to make way for the Americans. Then, seeming to find the present again, he looked up and smiled. "Who's interviewing whom here, Mr. Cotter? You've been kind to show an interest, but when we met briefly the other day, I had a specific reason for asking you to drop in."

"Any way I can help," Cotter said.

"There's an element in town. And *The Nugget* . . ." When Clum said the word "Nugget," his lip curled slightly.

"Yes, I know," Cotter said. "I'm well aware that *The Nugget* is the voice of the opposition."

John Clum paused, then raised his head and looked Cotter in the eye. "Have you ever seen such division?" With a reflective expression he gazed at the windows across the room. "I've known the editor Harry Woods since he was the right hand man at the *Tucson Record* for the Nugget's founder, Artemus Fay. He's been here since Fay built their office building." Clum paused. "He's not a bad man. But have you known people who gravitate to the side of loose principles simply because of comradeship?"

Cotter nodded. "That's the way it happens, sir. Popular, charming, unprincipled people win over regular folk and offer friendship. You're a stick-in-the-mud if you don't join in."

Clum leaned back in his chair and grinned at Cotter. "You don't seem to be a stick-in-the-mud."

He laughed. "It depends on who's doing the assessment."

Clum took a breath and settled down to business. "There are two factions in town."

Cotter nodded.

"Right now, Harry Woods is spinning everything against the lawmakers." John Clum leaned forward, his elbows on his knees, as though he wished to confide something in secret. "I think he's afraid. He doesn't want to offend the cowboys. I think he's in their camp. Yet that faction is willing to murder, and it's frightening the populace."

Cotter listened attentively.

"They tried to murder Virgil Wyatt. Managed to shoot him in the right side and destroy the use of his arm." Clum looked down, drew his brows together. "But what's next?" He paused briefly. "I have hired Charles Grenville to write some text about the political situation. I believe what is most needed is a return to principles. I am asking some of the pastors and church people if they would please write a small announcement for the newspaper, encapsulating the sermon they will be giving on Sunday. It might help to remind all of us to attend to the words of the Lord."

So that was the request. Cotter was pleased to hear it. He saw in Clum that would-be divinity student who could blush if someone gave him a compliment.

"Do you think you could bring me a summary of your weekly sermon for each Thursday's paper?"

"Certainly, certainly," Cotter replied. "I would be happy to do that, John." He found Clum to be a kindred spirit and was honored to be asked to help with such a project. And he had to admit he thought the publicity might bring more people into his congregation, and as a result more donations—which would be helpful in building the church he was determined to build. "I will gladly write about my sermon for your newspaper. And I will pray for the success of *The Epitaph.*" Cotter paused. "It takes courage to stand up for the right. Believe me, I know all about that."

Clum did not ask more questions, but stood and put his hands into his pockets. "You're a good man, Wendell Cotter. And I appreciate your willingness to offer your services to Tombstone at a time that is particularly critical for our citizens."

Cotter stood also, hat in hand.

Clum continued. "It is a dangerous time when dishonorable men are willing to steal for economic advantage, and then defy those who are appointed by the law to keep the peace."

"I did notice that after more than a month of deliberation, Judge Wells Spicer ruled in favor of the Earps and John Holliday."

Clum walked toward the windows with his hands in his pockets and began reciting as though he had memorized the most important words the judge had uttered, a practice that was implemented to give him comfort under the storm clouds that still seemed to hang over them. "'When we consider this is frontier country, often with lawlessness and disregard for human life, there is naturally the fear and feeling of insecurity that exists in the presence of bad, desperate and reckless men who have been a terror to the country, who discourage capital and enterprise and make threats against the work of the officers of the law. So, considering the many threats that have been made against the Earps, I can attach no criminality . . .'"

Clum's pause gave an opening for Cotter's reply. "If that is the verdict, I suppose we must ask, Can it be upheld by everyone?"

Clum turned to look at him. "That's the question, Cotter. That's the question." Suddenly his expression turned to fear. "And . . . it's not over yet, Mr. Cotter. It's not over yet."

22

After becoming acquainted with his congregation, Cotter was ready to begin his fund-raising rounds. He had already seen Nellie Cashman's hotel, though he had never entered it. Perhaps he had never tried because someone had told him she was a staunch Catholic and a fund raiser in her own right who had just finished efforts to build the Catholic church at Safford and Sixth. Probably, after building one church, she would not be interested in building another.

When Cotter approached the hotel with its plain sign posted in front—"Nellie Cashman's Hotel"—he noticed flowering bushes sprouting blossoms well before the anticipated spring. Behind the hotel and restaurant, he saw an extensive garden, and a small house with a steep roof and red door. Two young boys were splitting firewood in a wide patch of dirt in front of the house.

Cotter entered the restaurant on the main floor, and a girl about eleven years old, dressed in a maid's uniform and white cap, came forward to greet him. "Hello. Would you like to be seated?"

He was at once impressed with the interior of the place. Neat tables with white cloths were decorated with small silver vases of tiny white blossoms tied with green ribbon. He hadn't thought he'd get lunch yet. It was early. "Well . . . ah . . . er," he stammered. "I was hoping I could talk to Miss Cashman. Is she here?"

A look of disappointment crossed the girl's face. But she was either naturally positive, or well trained. "No, she's across the way with my mother." The girl smiled generously. "Over there." She pointed. "Very close. My aunt and my mother just purchased the American Hotel, and they are looking to do a little remodeling."

"Your aunt is Nellie Cashman?"

"Yes, sir. We live in the little house behind this hotel. My father died last year, and Aunt Nellie took us in."

It was more information than Cotter really needed, but he allowed the child her piece. He walked to the door that still stood partially open behind him and peered down the street. "Thank you so much," he said.

The young girl gave a polite curtsy. "If you ever come back this way, we are happy to serve lunch. Both Aunt Nellie and my mother, Frances, are wonderful cooks, and they will see that you get a meal fit for a king."

"Frances?" The name suddenly burst from Cotter's mouth.

"Yes," the girl said. "Frances is my mother. When my father died, all five of us children, three girls and two boys, came to help Aunt Nellie with her hotel. My older sister Lottie is the cook today. She can fix you a meal fit for a king."

Now the child's ramblings seemed to be rote from a speech she had been trained to give.

"I appreciate your invitation," Cotter said gently. "You make a lovely hostess, but I am really not interested today. Perhaps some other time."

The American Hotel was not far. When he drew close, he saw two women on both ends of a large signboard, one teetering on the second rung of a ladder, the other on the boardwalk, attempting to lift the sign high enough to hook its chain under the eaves. Cotter hurried forward and asked the women, "May I help you with that?"

"Oh, just in time, thank you," the one on the ladder said.

A man coming from the other direction rushed over and took the sign out of the hands of the woman on the street. Cotter climbed the ladder. He was tall enough to hook the chain on one end with ease. When he got down from the ladder, he moved it to the other end, climbed up, and hooked that chain also. The sign read, "Nellie Cashman's American Hotel."

"I just bought this place," one of the women declared.

The other man looked up and grinned. "Trust you, spunky Nellie Cashman. You're never daunted, are you? Buildin' a church, a hospital, and now redoin' the American Hotel."

Cotter recognized the man. It was Wyatt Earp.

Wyatt spoke to Cotter. "I heard your sermon, Reverend Cotter. I must say you know how to strike to the heart."

"I've heard about that amazing sermon," Nellie said. "We're Catholic. But I've been tempted to find out what you're doing to stir people up over there!" She glanced at her sister, Frances, who smiled.

"I understand," Cotter replied.

"We don't pay much attention to which church we go to," Nellie said. "Just that we get there. We're all God's children. Once a week we ought to go to hear his words. I'm glad you're building a church."

"I've heard of your fund-raising experience. Thought you might have some suggestions."

Nellie tipped her head. "Sure, I could help." She was a regal woman with a clear complexion and soulful blue eyes. Cotter read once that she had nursed men in mining camps from Pioche to Virginia City. When she heard of miners stricken with scurvy in the frozen north, she organized a party of six men who took fifteen hundred pounds of supplies up Telegraph Creek and nursed the sick miners back to health. She owned Delmonico's Restaurant in Tucson, and with her friend Jenny Smith had opened up a fruit and provision store in Tombstone. When Frances and her children arrived at the death of their husband and father, Nellie converted the Russ House to a hotel where the family stayed in back. It was obvious she was not sitting on her laurels, for she had just purchased the American Hotel.

"Wyatt, you sure you ought to be out and about on the streets?" Nellie asked with a pleasant lilt to her voice. "You have some dangerous enemies stalking about."

He laughed. "Just doin' my job. My enemies know I've served my time in jail. For nothing, I might add." Not many people knew he had once been in jail as a brash young ruffian.

Nellie seemed small when she looked up at him. "You're always doing your job. But sometimes it gets you in trouble."

"If we're doing the Lord's work we have nothin' to fear. Isn't that right, Reverend Cotter?"

At that moment Cotter sneezed. After he apologized, he got to the point. "I heard you could brew some strong tea, Miss Cashman."

She laughed. "I'll get you some tea, Reverend, if you'll help me with some tables. My sister and I can't budge 'em."

Wyatt followed them into the new hotel, and the four of them moved furniture and swept away dust and grime. Nellie set a pot of water on a stove in back, and sent Frances to the other hotel for the tea. When the sister returned, she was wrestling with two of her little ones and carrying bags of crullers and fried dough. All six of them sat down at a table, and Cotter drank a hot drink that made him feel cleaned out from head to toe.

"I was willing to go to jail because I knew I was right," Wyatt told Cotter over the steamy cup. "Laws are made to protect the innocent from the harm that greedy unscrupulous creatures may inflict upon them. And there must be people of courage to uphold the law. I was doing my job."

"There are courts to make decisions," Frances said.

"And Judge Spicer made the decision in our favor," Wyatt added.

Nellie asked, "Should it have been taken care of before the deaths happened?"

"I wasn't wise," Wyatt drawled. "Remember, we tried to indict them for stealing the government mules. They never returned the mules. And what's more, they bragged and laughed about it."

Cotter listened with interest.

"I'll admit I wanted to arrest the men who robbed Wells Fargo, so I'd win the election," Wyatt said. "And I knew Clanton had an idea where they were. I promised him all the reward money if he'd tell. Yeah, it was a lousy deal." Wyatt leaned back on his chair and grinned sheepishly. "And my party got voted out by a bunch of pigs and chickens."

"Risky," Nellie said, starting to pour more tea.

"If I hadn't been searching for information about the reward, no one would have known. But Clanton asked me to find out if they'd give the reward for a dead man. They would. But somebody leaked that it was me who asked. His cronies suspected he was ready to rat on 'em, and they threatened his life. He blamed the leak on me, and hated me for it. Later somebody else found all the Wells Fargo robbers killed anyway."

"The adage is 'Don't deal with criminals,'" Nellie said almost under her breath.

"Now they're calling us deputies criminals. They almost took Virgil's life."

"How are Allie and Virgil doing?" Nellie asked.

"Can't use his right arm. Allie helps."

"Morgan and Louisa? Holliday?"

"All good. And deputized once more."

Nellie rose from the table and began to clear the tea cups. "I think they're still after you," she murmured. "I still think you're taking a chance to be out on the streets."

"It's a risky business, all right."

In a short time, the tea had warmed Cotter's entire head. He thought he ought to be going. "Thank you so much, Nellie."

"Drop by any time," she said. "If you need names of good donors I can fill you in."

"Is your team playin' the San Pedro boys?" Wyatt changed the subject when Cotter stood up to go.

"March 13th. You ought to join us!" Cotter said.

Wyatt looked across the table and the children in Frances's lap. He slipped his thumbs into his waistcoat. "Too much goin' on in Tombstone. A twenty-four-hour job."

"Good luck." Cotter tipped his imaginary hat. "I feel much better, Nellie. Thank you so much for the tea."

"A lemon would help you too," she said.

"Nellie can fix almost anything, can't you, Nellie?"

"Or I can try to prevent you from things I can't fix."

"I know. Like death." Wyatt was still leaning back in his chair, the front two legs off the floor.

"Like death," Nellie repeated.

Cotter felt a strange tension as he left the hotel.

The effects of the tea had worn off by the time he reached the lodging house. He asked Mrs. Grant if she had a lemon he could buy, or if she might brew some hot water for him.

"I'm sorry. I don't have a lemon," she said. "But I'll be happy to bring you some hot water."

"I'm coming down with the sniffles. It would help very much."

As he turned to go upstairs, she raised her hand to stop him. "Mr. Cotter, wait. We received a post for you this morning." She shuffled the papers on her desk, and when she found the envelope, she picked it up and held it to the light. She peered over her glasses to read the return address. "Salem, Massachusetts. Isn't that where you're from?"

"Yes!" Cotter answered, his heartbeat quickening. "Thank you!" He had sent a couple of quick notes giving the news and mentioning his address. But so far no answer had made its way to Tombstone. This would be the first he heard from his family for a long time. He took the envelope and glanced at the handwriting. It was a letter from Frances! His heart turned over.

He carried the letter to his room but did not open it at once. He took off his vestments and collar, put on his warm pajamas, and wrapped himself in his robe. As he slipped under the covers of his bed, he noted there was just enough afternoon light through the shutters to illuminate the text.

Dear Cotter,

I received your letter saying you arrived the last of January and have already given them good words about Jesus Christ. Those people are so fortunate to have you with them to help raise funds to build a chapel. I know you will do what the Lord wants you to do. You have always loved Him and tried hard to live His commandments.

Last week two young men came to our door and said they were working for Jesus Christ. They said He had not forgotten us, and to prove it they had a book He wanted us to read. They said, "Do you think God, who loves His children, would leave them without speaking to them often?" They said to read what Jesus says now to us.

Mother told them that so few people could live what Jesus taught in the New Testament, that we didn't need more. But she promised to read the book on a trip to Boston with Father. Before she went I was curious and read about a young man whose father, Lehi, took his family away when Nebuchadnezzar destroyed Jerusalem. I thought of you when you told me how Tombstone was divided. This story reminded me of your city—half good, half wicked. I didn't want you to suffer the destruction of your city. I didn't get very far into the book when Mother took it and left it by mistake in the hotel.

There isn't much other news here. Your father is suffering from gout this winter, and your brother is graduating. There is not a day that goes by that all of us don't think of you. When the mothers get together to knit and mend, I hear them talking about things they remember. For one thing, you always hit the ball out of the park. Remember when your little sister cried because a big dog came up to her? You took her in your arms and carried her to the house. Remember when I fell in the water at the quay? I will never forget that you saved my life, Cotter. And when your parents scolded you, you honored their request never to go down there again.

I think about you every day. You're my hero. When I sing the hymns in the choir, I remember you, and I feel close to God. He is watching over all of us.

Love,
Frances

Cotter read the letter over and over again. His heart beat so hard he was not sure it was from the joy he felt, or from the fever. When he heard the knock on his door, he let Mrs. Grant in with the hot water. "If there is anything else I can do, let me know," she said.

After he drank the warm water, he was dozing when he heard someone at his bedroom door. The knock, which didn't sound like Mrs. Grant's, wakened him from a vivid dream. In a stupor, Cotter had been walking among the tombstones in the graveyard at the top of the hill. It was barely dawn. A sharp light over the distant mountains sent a ray of sun like a knife into his eyes, almost blinding him. But he was aware that a crowd of people moved about him, men and women in gauzy shrouds, or draped in embroidered robes and colorful feathers. Some had top hats. Some of them wore headdresses made of beaten gold.

Soon it became evident that all of these people were looking to him for some kind of direction. They put out their hands, yet he knew they were not begging for food, but for some kind of information. They were asking for signs to show them which path they should take out of the graveyard. The dream was so real, Cotter shook his head to get back to reality.

The knock sounded again, just a slight tap on the door. He heard a voice. "Cotter, are you there?" He stumbled out of his bedding, pulled the belt of his robe around his waist, and tied it. He answered the door. It was not Mrs. Grant. It was Libby Campbell. When he saw her, his immediate thought was how small she looked standing in the narrow hallway, her face white like some budding flower. "Libby!"

"I heard you were sick. I brought you this." She held a lemon in the palm of her hand. "Mrs. Grant sent her son to Bless House. It's close by. He said you needed a lemon, and we had one."

Cotter heard her rambling like the chatter of a stream he had expected to hear running through his dream. His focus was on her face. He had not remembered how beautiful she was.

"I loved your sermon," Libby said. "I miss seeing you." There was a pause. "May I come in?"

Cotter felt tongue-tied. It wouldn't really be proper to invite her into his room, though he trusted it would be no more than a friendly visit.

"I won't stay very long." Libby cast curious eyes across the carpet, the table at his bedside, the shuttered window.

Taken aback, he said, "Well, yes, yes," and moved to let her enter. "I was proud of you for getting a job with the Hatch and Campbell Pool Parlor." He paused. "And I thank you for the lemon." He tightened the belt on his robe. "Would you like to sit?" He offered his only chair, and Libby took it. She sat down hard on it, flouncing her skirts, as though she had a right to park on his premises. He remembered how she had found him at the Kansas City Railway Station. Though it had been several weeks now, she had not changed much. He was aware of the sweet memory of her laying her head on his shoulder while she slept.

"I wanted to tell you something," she stammered.

Cotter felt a little uncomfortable in his bathrobe. There was a long pause. "What is it, Libby?"

She looked away from him toward his table, toward the open Bible, the scattered papers, the quill pen. "How many hours do you spend each day studying or writing?"

"About four," Cotter said kindly. When she gazed at his open scriptures, he added, "I spend much of my time trying to get to know people around here—to discover if there is anybody willing to donate funds to build our chapel."

"I know. When you sit down to study, how do you choose what you're going to talk about?"

Cotter gazed at her when her eyes were diverted. This was not what she had come to say. "I listen," he stated.

She raised her eyes at the simple answer. "You listen? What do you hear?"

He was reluctant to get into religious subjects with just anyone. He had felt that same hesitation on the long journey from Kansas City to Arizona. Libby had seemed to be miles away from the serious studies he made, of his continued quest for understanding what work he would next be called to do. There was so much opposition, so many ungodly obstacles in the world, but especially in Tombstone. He knew it was his mission to challenge some of the cataclysmic obstacles if he could—to stop the missiles wheeling toward them like dangerous meteors or asteroids, capable of destroying so much that was good.

"Libby," he said. "This is not really what you wanted to talk about . . . is it?"

She moved nervously in the chair.

"Are you doing all right at Bless House?"

She squirmed. "Yes. I'm doing all right."

"It's not the kind of place I had hoped you would find to make your home."

"Horace says we can just shut our eyes. He tells true stories all the time. He says shutting them is better than scooping them out. Ivan the Terrible cut out the eyes of his architect after he drew the palace, so the man couldn't build one for anyone else." Libby smiled for the first time during the visit.

"Horace." Cotter laughed, shaking his head.

"Why don't you go ahead and take some of your lemon?" She surprised him, changing the subject.

He got up from the bed, found his pocket knife on the dresser, and cut the lemon in half. "I'd offer you some, but it's pretty sour." He laughed.

"It's hard to tell someone he saved your life," Libby said. He stopped squeezing the lemon into the water, now cool in his cup. "Is that what you came to tell me?"

Tears rimmed her eyes. "You saved my life, Cotter." The statement was bright with caring, yet fraught with heavier meanings.

Cotter's chest tightened. "Libby, I didn't save your life. You did." He seemed to feel her tears in his own eyes. "You were the one who had the courage to break away, to run to the railroad station in Kansas City. And you chose to come to me rather than anyone else—say Marcella, or some other man."

Libby wiped a tear from her eye, obviously trying to smile. "You were wearing the white collar." She indicated it by a throat-cutting gesture.

"And if I influenced you in any way, it's because you allowed me to influence you. You chose to listen to me read for hours in the New Testament, warning against the crimes in Tombstone, like gambling and drinking and dishonesty."

"But I was a thief. I stole Mr. Stuyvesant's gold."

Libby's sudden burst seemed to change the atmosphere in the room. Outside the windows a slow *tap-tap-tap* became a spatter of rain. For a moment, Cotter could not assimilate her confession.

She finally broke the silence. "It's raining."

He knit his brows. "I wanted to tell you it was all right. You were desperate, but . . ."

"But of course it was wrong," she said. "And his accountant followed me all the way here to charge me with the crime."

"Mr. Grenville?" Cotter said.

She nodded, wiping the tears from her other cheek.

Cotter had heard rumors about Charles Grenville. "But he's had plenty of chances to turn you in, and he hasn't done it yet. I've heard he's not only been working with John Clum on *The*

Epitaph, but has also volunteered on the water committee, and he's been prospecting on the San Pedro every spare chance he gets. They say he's running from some crime he committed."

Libby thought of the story her mother had told her about Mr. Grenville and the hunting accident when he shot a woman he thought was a deer.

The rain began in earnest now, punching the shutters with a clattering barrage of water music. From his place on the bed, Cotter leaned forward, almost touching her knee. "Libby, you've made some good decisions. Now you must continue to make them." He paused. "Have you really thought about what it is that you want?"

Libby clasped her hands in her lap and raised her feet to the first rung of the chair. "Do you know who Nellie Cashman is?"

"Yes, I do. I met her today. She just bought the American Hotel."

"I want to be like Nellie. If she can do prospecting . . . I . . ." Libby glanced to the windows toward the rain. "There's a rumor that a girl at Bless House named Mag just had one of her clients pay her half a million dollars in return for a small loan she made so he could stake out a claim. He struck it rich. So now Mag doesn't have to stay at Bless House anymore. She can leave Tombstone any day, go somewhere, and be a lady."

"That's nice." Cotter smiled. "But it's just lucky money. It has a way of disappearing fast. Is that your greatest wish, to be a rich lady?"

Libby's eyes softened. "Cotter." Her voice wavered. "What I wish most of all is to be good like you. I wish I could always be close enough to hear you talk about God so that I would always be a better person." She seemed nervous.

Well aware of her yearning, Cotter fought his own desire to reach for her, bring her into his arms, and comfort her.

"I wanted to come here to tell you that I knew the gold wasn't mine. All I spent of it was my ticket. And that potato at The Owl and the Pussy Cat Café. But I . . ." Libby stopped. "I wanted to give it to God. I wanted you to have it to build the church."

A nerve went cold in Cotter's neck. He could see the love in her eyes, and not entirely for God. "Libby, it's not necessary."

"No, no. I've thought about it a thousand times. I want you to have it to build the church."

"But shouldn't you return it to Mr. Stuyvesant? It's really his. Mr. Grenville knows you still have it. And I suppose he has promised Mr. Stuyvesant to follow you and pay it back."

As Libby stared at Cotter, her words rang in his head: *"I wish I could always be close enough to hear you talk about God. You saved my life."*

She did not look away from him, though her eyes filled with tears again. In the silence, the tears began to spill down her cheeks. She moved forward in the chair. It seemed nothing he could say or do to salve her hunger would be appropriate at this time.

"No, Cotter. No. You must accept my offering." When she leaned forward in the chair so close to him, he could not hold back, but stood, pulled her up, and put his hands gently on her shoulders.

At first she just leaned into him, her cheek resting against his robe. But when she reached her arm around his neck, she held him so fast he almost felt dizzy. "I miss you, Cotter."

She reached close to his face, and he pulled back. "No, dear Libby. Please know that I appreciate and love you as God loves you. But we can't . . . it would be wrong." Cotter disentangled her arms from his neck. "Let's calm down. We'll think about the gift to the chapel. But we must be sensible here."

"I love you, Cotter."

"And I love you, Libby. But just not the way you might hope it would be. I need to be careful. I am a man on a mission. I have work to do. I am here to build a church and entice a group of wayward souls to believe in the saving power of Jesus Christ. And then I must return to Massachusetts and graduate from the seminary so that I can teach in a university, or found a boys' school, or do whatever God calls upon me to do."

Her tears still flowed. "Would you please take me with you, Cotter? Oh, I would give anything to be where you are going."

"Libby dear." His heart felt constrained, as though she had launched a lasso around it and tugged it tight. "Let's just be patient and see what will come of this. All right?" When he gently pushed her away from him, it was all he could do to hold on to his emotions. "I cannot promise you anything," he stammered.

"Oh, I love you so much, and when I walk in the city I pray you will be around every corner in every shop. In every crowd I look for you."

"Libby, let's just be patient. If it's God's will for us to be together, that's what will happen. All right? Please don't count on anything now." He pressed her arms. "I'm coming down with the sniffles. You don't want to get that close to me." He tried to smile.

Libby pulled out of his arms. As suddenly as she had wept, the tears dried up, and she brushed both cheeks with the backs of her hands. "Cotter, forgive me. I've missed you so much. We have been through so much together." She forced a smile. "There, now you know. Just know you changed my life. I have no desire to join the Bless House activities. I don't care how much money they make, or how much they 'bless' the resident miners. But when you read to me about virtue, about purity, about the love of Jesus Christ, it touched my heart and changed my life." She gathered her skirts around her and turned toward the door. "And I just wanted you to know that." She paused, smiling, probably to let him know she had recovered. "And I really did want to offer you the gold."

She was going. The warmth, the sunshine illuminating the room, was leaving. "That was very generous of you, Libby. I just think we ought to ponder it for a while."

"Get your health under control. Drink the lemon," she said cheerily, and she was gone.

It was no longer raining, and the air shimmered with pure silver light. The streets of Tombstone had been washed clean. Little rivulets of rainwater slid through patterns in the dust that made filigree of the road.

Seeing Cotter again filled Libby with joy. She had been forward, but it had allowed her to be close to him. The embrace, as brief as it was, opened the gates to emotions she had never felt before.

She knew she was prone to hear what she wanted to hear. On her walk back to Bless House, she decided she would remember his words forever: "If it's right to be together, that's what will happen." Of course it was right. She loved him. She knew what love was now. It was drawing close to heaven, keeping yourself pure, holding a place in your heart for someone you could admire forever—someone kind, gentle, and honorable. Someone so good you could trust him with your life.

Libby soared as she walked, because she knew in her heart that things would work out if she would just have faith as a mustard seed. In Sunday's sermon Cotter had talked about faith: "If you keep your faith, heaven will offer its treasures to you. If you stand at the door and knock, it will open to you."

She saw the streets of Tombstone now as pathways paved with silver. She would see him again. Someday, if it was right—and she felt it was—they would be together. He understood there was a possibility. His love was overwhelming, so beautiful and pure, she would never forget this moment as long as she lived.

It didn't seem right now to walk back to Bless House where "love" was a commodity to be bought and sold. But Libby's things were in the closet of that upstairs room. She did love the girls, and Marcella, Horace, and their businesslike sister, Nora. Libby's heart swelled with love for all the world at this moment. This almost overwhelming joy came from being loved by a righteous man. He loved her. He had put his arm around her and held her close. He was so good. He would never make promises he could not keep. His words "If it's right for us" played over and over again in her mind. She would wait forever for such a moment to repeat itself in her life again.

As she turned the corner on Third Street, Libby could see the red-brick Bless House rising above the shorter wooden structures of the block. Its dark roof still shimmered from the rain, sparkling like diamonds. A few men were coming or going from the place. But as she began down the street she saw a man and a woman standing at the bottom of the porch steps. She stopped. It was Charles Grenville with Mag.

Having just been in the orbit of a pure, noble man, Libby felt angry to witness a man who would think nothing of standing out in the street with his paramour. Libby's bitterness caught her by surprise. A stab of pain cut her in the ribs. Embarrassed, and not wanting to be seen now, she made an about-face to back-track, to take the long way around the block.

She fought against her disgust. Grenville was nothing like Cotter. Grenville was a philanderer. A man like every other man, feasting upon the needs of his flesh.

23

By the time Libby got around the block, Charles and Mag were gone. But this time several girls and their clients stood on the walkway in front of Bless House, as though they had been anxious to breathe the clear air once the sun broke through the March clouds. After the rain, the horizon looked sharp. The Huachuca Mountains were like microscopic teeth of a worn knife. The contrast of the hills against the blue sky was startling through the dancing light and the blinding sun.

Libby recognized some of the girls on the porch. They surrounded Mag, laughing, asking questions, some of them cheering. When Libby walked forward, Lizette, on the opposite side of the circle, caught sight of her and came around to greet her. "Where have you been, Libby? We've been having a special party to celebrate Mag's good luck!"

Mag's good luck? Was this about the rumor that a man had left her a fortune? Or perhaps she and Charles were engaged to be married. A sharp pain slammed into Libby's ribs. Not very many girls in the brothels became wives and mothers. But it did happen. And it was good fortune. "A party?" she said.

"Yes. There's still cake, and Nora cut medallions of lamb. It's long after lunchtime—you must be starved. There's still a lot left. Come on."

"No, I'm fine," Libby said. She had just been nourished by the warmth of Cotter's embrace, and she would bask in it as long as she could. Perhaps she would never need food, or even embraces, in all the rest of her life. Still reeling from being so close, from sharing his breath, from hearing his words, all she wanted to do was to lie down on her bed in the attic and absorb what had happened to her, and what it meant for her future.

"Are you sure?" Lizette said.

Libby tried to walk through the gathering to get to the door. She barely glanced at the lucky Mag in the circle of celebrants. But in that moment she caught Mag's eyes and quickly turned away. She had not planned on revealing the hatred, the disgust, the anger she felt at the moment toward the young woman. When Libby could not seem to get past Lizette, she decided to discover the cause of the revelry. "Is she engaged?"

"Oh, no!" Lizette gushed. "The rumor came true. She loaned money to stake a claim and was promised half if it struck gold. And it did! Now Mag is worth more than a hundred thousand dollars. She can leave Bless House and go back east to her family!" Lizette's eyes grew large and bright. "Oh, I wish all of us could be so lucky! We can't stop talking about it." She cocked her head toward the door. "Some are still inside exulting over this blessing that came to Bless House." She turned in a pirouette.

Libby didn't see how this was a particular blessing to Bless House. But she couldn't get a word in edgewise.

"Mag Chambers, the lucky woman, was married, you know," Lizette continued. "Her husband died. She had a baby girl her mother is raising." Lizette sighed. "But now she can go back to her home, raise her baby daughter, and give her everything. Or maybe she can get married, settle down, and have a family." The last part was said longingly.

Libby stopped. Did all of these girls really want to settle down and have a family? Evidently so, the way they were carrying on about Mag's luck. Mag Chambers? In the time Libby had been at Bless House she had never heard Mag's last name. She had never overheard any gossip about Mag having a baby daughter somewhere.

Libby wanted to hate Mag for giving herself up to the clients she "blessed" at Bless House. Then a fleeting thought crossed Libby's mind. Was it possible Mag would talk Charles Grenville into going back east with her? Libby glanced back at the fortunate woman. It certainly was a cause for celebration, that someone at Bless House received half of a lucky miner's fortune. How incredible!

For a brief moment Libby felt jealous. But she checked herself, remembering her mother's instructions when she complained about Stuyvesant's wealth. "'Thou shalt not covet' is one of the ten commandments," her mother told her many times. "Jealousy leads to an ugly tendency in yourself that will dry you up into an angry old person. No. You must always be happy for the good fortune of others." Her mother had always spoken kindly of everyone. Sometimes, sitting on Libby's bed, her mother had stretched out her hand and stroked her daughter's hair. Since her mother's death, Libby had only memories to live with.

A miracle happened as she turned from the celebrants on the walkway and crossed the Bless House threshold. She could smell her mother's perfume! Trying to recover from her surprise, she stopped and leaned against the doorjamb of the foyer, when she heard a burst of laughter from the front room. Some of the party was still in session.

Almost dizzy from all that happened that day, Libby suppressed the memories of the old Bible, its pages torn and blackened from work-worn fingers. She pushed away the admonitions, the soft words of wisdom. Her mother once told her, "To stay free is to keep your mind and heart yearning toward God. You are never a slave to anyone else if you find a purpose in what you do." In that long-ago conversation, Libby had asked her, "Do you find a purpose?" Her mother had been quiet for several seconds, tangling her fingers in Libby's small hand. "My purpose is to lead you to happiness, Libby Campbell. And that means obedience to God's word."

Hesitant to break into the crowd, Libby stayed behind the archway. But she could see Horace telling one of his stories. "Well, mankind . . ." She couldn't hear well, so stole a glance at the circle seated in the stuffed furniture. There were about seven or eight girls draped across the arms of the settee, seated on pillows, or leaning on the backs of the wing chairs. They were all listening raptly. Marcella and Nora sat around the table. "No one was allowed to disagree with the king. Right in front of the children, they forced the father to sit up to the fire. They tied his feet together on a stick and pushed him feet first into the flames. His legs were burnt stubs right up to the groin before he stopped screaming and finally passed out. They carved up the wife and babies like pot roast."

Horace looked up when he saw Libby at the door. "Well, hello, Libby Campbell, you're welcome to join us."

"Come on in, Libby," Marcella said.

Nora, used to playing hostess, rose from her chair and approached Libby. "We missed you, honey. I'm sorry there's no lamb left, but we still have bread and cheese, and roasted peanuts."

"Oh, no thank you," she said. "I'm so tired."

"How is work at the Hatch and Campbell Saloon?" Marcella asked. She had a controlled look as if Libby might be judging all of them in the revelry of their profession.

"You must be tired," Nora said.

"You'd make triple the money staying here in this business," Marcella offered.

"I know that . . ."

"We know. To each his own," Nora said gently. "We're not judgmental around here. You're perfectly welcome to stay with us. We've had other girls move on. It's to be admired." Probably realizing Libby was not going into the kitchen, Nora grabbed a chair. "We're all working girls, aren't we?" She sat down on the crinolines that fluffed up around her with a noisy puff of air.

The girls smiled and cheered quietly. Horace laughed. "When the working girls of Mongolia got sick with the plague, they tied them to huge wooden catapults and snapped them over the walls to fly into the city of Caffa to give the disease to their enemies."

"Please excuse me." Libby tried to nod graciously at Horace's entertainment. "I'll be in the attic if you need me. Tell Lizette."

"Oh, she's out there celebrating. None of us can believe Mag's good luck."

"Yes, isn't that something, Libby," Horace exclaimed. "You too ought to have a knight in shining armor come along and finance you. Or—" he began to pontificate "—stumble on them gold plates that young fella in Vermont found several decades ago! I just heard about that at the post office. Wasn't that something! Gold plates with writings from ancient native folks, translated into English and circulating around the Americas and converting the Indian people to Jesus Christ."

Marcella glanced at her brother warily.

"I told you about that Blue Lady. No question the Indians saw her. Well, the story on these plates is that Jews come over at Nebuchadnezzar's destruction of Jerusalem and mixed with the Indians. And what do you know? Right after he died, Jesus Christ appeared on American soil!" Horace stopped and looked at Libby as if making sure she was listening. "Maybe it was

Jesus had something to do with instructing them flying nuns. He made that first trip over here, anyway."

Marcella leaned forward with a pleading look at her sister, Nora. But of course Nora couldn't stop him. No one could.

Horace hadn't finished. "Besides bein' gold, them plates must be powerful. Mrs. Pinnegar at the Continental Hotel said her folks read the translation of it, and it was nothing short of amazing."

Nora ignored Marcella's plea, and the discussion of the golden plates. "I don't think Mag is really lucky," she mused. "I think it's her character to be compassionate. She's financed a couple of other prospectors. She just got what she deserved this time."

"Luck is relative," Horace said, unable to give up his place in the spotlight. "The Greek playwright Philemon was lucky that he could earn his living being funny. But then he died laughing at one of his own jokes." The girls giggled. "It all depends on your point of view. Lucky Louis XIV thought it was a lucky moment when he designed the guillotine. But then his own head rolled out from under it."

Libby nodded and smiled, then slipped away to the stairs.

Even with the cool rain on the roof, the attic felt like a furnace. Now the sun was sinking across the sky into the Huachuca Mountains, but when she opened the windows, a cool breeze skimmed her cheek.

She took off her hot dress and slipped into the shift Lizette had lent to her. It reminded Libby of the apron her mother made her wear over her dress in the kitchen. It was loose enough to let the cool air slip along her thighs, under her arms, and under her chin. At last, lying on the bed, she could let herself bask in the memory of Cotter's embrace. She held to that warmth. His face loomed large in her vision: the blue eyes, the sensitive mouth, his cheeks only inches away. She had been in his arms. He loved her. She felt it more than any other feeling she had ever experienced.

She saw lights move in the spaces behind her eyes, and luminous shadows turning in the deep blue-black chroma of the universe. She fell into musing. With her eyes closed, she heard a flap of air, as though somewhere wings were making a breeze. She thought she might be imagining Lizette's flights at the Bird Cage Theatre. It reminded her of the blue lady of Horace's stories. This particular tale of his had a hold on her, because she believed it was true. Especially his facts about the Spanish father in Gila County. "His testimony proved there really was a Blue Lady." In Libby's mind's eye she saw her mother standing on the distant hills with the lady in robes as blue as the sky. Horace had said the name of the blue woman was Maria Coronel. She was a nun who ran a convent for twenty-four years in Agreda in the northern section of Old Castile in Spain.

No one—not even the Blue Lady Maria herself—knew how she was transported to the New World, though later she speculated that her spirit must have been united with an angel. Maria recorded the visits she made between 1621 and 1631, but when the Church authorities found out, they burned her journal. In 1650, Friar, Ximenez Samaniego met the Pima Indians whose ancestors saw her. The fearful natives had shot dozens of arrows into her blue robes. But they were unable to kill her.

Libby believed it was true. And Horace also told her about gold plates that said Jesus visited the Indians.

Sometimes, when she gazed out of the attic window toward the mountains, she felt a great yearning to discover the heaven Cotter knew was true. She hung on his words as though they were engraved in gold. If she was pure, she could follow him. Everything about the shield of virtue was true. If you lived with the word of God, you could live without fear.

When she closed her eyes, Libby saw her precious mother's face in the diffuse light.

24

At first, Libby's work at the saloon was challenging and exhausting. But soon it seemed easier and more rewarding. It wasn't long before she began to appreciate Bob Hatch. He was a good employer. Visits by Mr. Campbell, the financier of the saloon, were rare, but when he dropped in on Thursday afternoon, Libby was impressed. Tall and good-looking in his top hat and tails, he smiled pleasantly and took her hand. "I'm sure we must be related somewhere, Miss Campbell. Mr. Hatch tells me you are a hard worker. We feel fortunate you have blessed us with your services."

Anyone so gracious was a pleasure to work for, and when Mr. Campbell turned to go, Libby felt that the two good men who ran the saloon were her friends.

By now she knew many of the customers. And although there were difficult ones, Bob Hatch was good enough to take her into the small kitchen area and whisper some of the details that would help her talk to them.

Libby's favorite customers were the Earps and Doc Holliday, whose ongoing saga with Ike Clanton remained unresolved. There was still controversy about the Earps being used as deputies to keep order in the town. They had definitely resigned their offices on February 2, posting the announcement in *The*

Epitaph. It was plain Ike Clanton wanted them for murder. When Sheriff Behan still wanted to use these "murderers" to keep order in the town, the conflict continued.

On Friday Libby arrived at work and found the saloon crowded. Men stood in groups inside the window, across the entryway, and inside the foyer.

"The Earps and Doc were arrested last night," Bob said. "The news is in the morning paper. Ike Clanton brought new charges outside of this jurisdiction. In Contention, just a few miles away." Bob looked at her. "That tells you something, don't it?" Contention was the name of one of the mines whose ownership was never really clear.

Bob's hair was mussed from ducking under arms and rushing into curtains to get out of the way. "They all came in before work," he said. "I'm glad you're here."

It was almost an hour before the room began to clear out. With the groups moving toward the door, Libby could catch an occasional glimpse of the street, which looked even dustier than when she had arrived.

"Well, it appears the town fathers have noticed the streets need cleaning," one of the men seated at a front table said unexpectedly. Libby turned. It was the man Bob had identified a couple of times as Dr. Goodfellow. He was leaning forward in his chair, his mustache wet from the moisture on his cup. He and another regular customer, George Berry, appeared to be the only ones left in the room. Libby knew the intense George often played pool with the Earps. He seemed particularly sad, as though he had come to the saloon to mourn the arrest and incarceration in Contention.

"It's about time they start that cleaning project," Bob said.

"They let that garbage rot in the street long enough," George Berry added.

Libby had begun to believe the people in Tombstone loved refuse. But there had been news that the council was determined to pick it up. Looking through the haze, she now wondered if stirring it into a murky soup was wise.

"And look what's going on over across the street." Now Bob came up to the window and stood, bringing the edge of his hand to his forehead to filter out the bright light.

Narrowing her eyes to penetrate the haze, Libby saw the stagecoach parked across the way. Two women in huge skirts and feathered hats hovered about, pointing and giving directions to the two men loading and tying trunks and hat boxes onto the back of the vehicle. When Libby focused, she recognized Virgil's Allie, whom she'd seen at Cotter's first sermon. The other woman must have been Wyatt's Mattie, who never left the hotel.

"I was wondering when this would happen." Dr. Goodfellow had risen out of his chair and walked up behind Bob and Libby.

Quite a while ago, Bob had pointed out to her that Mr. Goodfellow was the skillful surgeon who patched up Virgil when he was shot. Luckily, the judge from Contention spared the wounded men, Virgil Earp, Morgan Earp, and Doc Holliday, from serving any time in jail. He simply gave them probation.

Dr. Goodfellow watched the process across the street with as much interest as the others. "Finally those women are out of here. There's so much trouble, I wondered why they stayed this long."

"Why are they arresting the lawmen, when no one has found the shooter who maimed Virgil for life?" Libby asked Bob.

"Everyone believes the Clantons were behind that shooting, and Sheriff Behan did arrest them. But they must have paid some cowboys in Contention to lie. Those prevaricators told a doozy of an alibi—that the Clantons were in Charleston at the time. You cain't get justice if somebody's willing to lie."

Libby went silent, straining to hear the others' conversations. "Yes, that's Wyatt's girl Mattie and Virgil's girl Allie. Wonder where they are goin'," George was saying. "Out of here for sure," Dr. Goodfellow replied. "The Wyatt family lives in Colton, California. I imagine that's where they're headed. They'll take the coach to Tucson, and then the train."

"I thought it would take the pressure off the Earps when they resigned from their office as deputies," George Berry continued as though watching the Earp ladies leave was the end of the good pool games with his favorite opponents. Libby knew George was one of Tombstone's best pool players. He seemed lost today, watching his games fall apart.

Still trying to catch the conversation, Libby heard only a mumble. But it didn't matter. The essence of the situation was that the cowboys hadn't accepted the first trial. A second justice of the peace was now after the Earp brothers, and the women were leaving. Libby fastened her eyes on the ladies who belonged to Wyatt and Virgil.

"They hardly ever show themselves," Bob said.

Libby watched the colorful figures at the coach. They picked up their skirts out of the dust, navigated the steps, and climbed into the velveteen interior. They would go to Benson and take the train west. As the horses stomped, the wheels croaked and the coach lumbered away. Libby watched with hesitation. The haze seemed as opaque as colored glass.

When she turned back to her work, silent questions whirled in her thoughts. Was it murder? What was going on in Tombstone? Something ominous seemed to press down on them, and the thick mist in the street seemed to portend despair.

The afternoon dragged on slowly. Every once in a while, as Libby passed the front window, she wondered how far the stagecoach might have traveled. When the dust settled, she was surprised some of the men who had gathered in the morning were returning—as though there were imagined safety in numbers. Perhaps in the early hour they had found some comfort in a world without justice, and had returned to the warmth they found with each other.

The sun drove a sharp wedge of light into the tops of the tables, stamping them with a silver sheen. A vapor of smoky gauze pervaded the atmosphere. It was at about three in the afternoon that Libby saw the two figures through the glass. A woman in black had stopped on the boardwalk because a child stood in her way. It became a dance. When the woman tried to move forward, the child, wringing her hands, moved in her way.

Finally the two came to the front window of the Campbell and Hatch saloon, and both stood for a moment peering in. The woman's face, now visible against the glass, was no ordinary face. Her deep-set eyes were dusky orbs above her high cheekbones brushed with spots of rouge. She drew away and entered the door. When she crossed the threshold, every man stopped what he was doing, and all conversation in the room ceased. George Berry struck his pool stick to the floor and stood like a stone.

"This child outside . . ." the woman began in a soft, deep voice. "She won't come in. She's Nellie Cashman's niece. She's Frances's daughter. Frances, Nellie's sister who lives in the little house behind Nellie." The sound of her voice was almost hypnotic. "She says her mother is sick. Do you have ice?"

Bob Hatch had not moved. "I can't believe it," he whispered to Libby when she backed behind the bar. "It's Josephine Marcus, Wyatt's other lover."

Josephine Marcus was the actress who first came to Tombstone with a troop of players performing Shakespeare for the mining towns of the Arizona territory. The girls at Bless

House said she went back to California after her debut as a Shakespearean actress. But she returned to Tombstone because she fell in love with the handsome deputy named Wyatt Earp. Now she was determined to win him away from his common-law wife, Mattie. Though the Earp women never seemed to frequent the streets, when their men went to jail they appeared like birds suddenly bursting from their boundaries.

Josephine was clothed completely in black, a veil over her voluminous black hair. Her white face was perched like a ripe fruit in the folds of her mantilla.

"Yes, we have ice," Bob Hatch said, emerging from his spell. "We certainly do have some." He looked at Libby. "Get a canister. Go with the child if need be."

But from behind another table in the back, Dr. Goodfellow came forward so quickly he scraped his chair. "Frances. I know Frances," he offered. "Sure. I'll take the ice."

Libby dished the ice into a canister. Outside the front window, she could see the child still pressing her hands and face up against the glass.

"Libby, you stay here," Dr. Goodfellow insisted. "I'm afraid there may be a breakout of smallpox in Tombstone." He looked tall next to Josephine Marcus. His eyes became slits in his intense face. "I'll go with the child, Miss Marcus. You must have been on your own urgent business."

Josephine smiled vaguely. "Yes, I am. If Judge Spicer can influence the judge in Contention to listen to Wyatt, I . . ." She stopped, perhaps thinking better of revealing every detail of her mission. She looked at Goodfellow with a penetrating gaze. "The world is turning upside down, Doctor."

At some bleak hour in the middle of Sunday morning, Libby woke hearing the voice of Horace, who had begun walking

Lizette home from the Bird Cage. This time he was entertaining her with more of his stories. Libby soon discovered he was talking about Wyatt. What she heard in the gloomy rooms was probably the end of some historical narrative.

"The town wanted a law that residents contain their pigs. Wyatt's job in the streets isn't very popular after he won that legal battle with the town council to let the pigs go free."

Libby heard Lizette giggle.

"Wyatt's brother James, who runs the bowling alley here, got a musket ball in the left shoulder when he fought in the Civil War. Wyatt ran off at seventeen, but his father found out and dragged him home again. I guess the pigs was free, but the boys wasn't. Ha ha."

Libby strained her ears for the next nuggets of gold to fall from Horace's tongue.

"I guess the world's turning inside out like an old stinky sock," he finally said. "Can you imagine incarcerating the men of law for attempting to clean up the town of thieves and killers?"

Lizette replied, but her voice was so quiet, Libby couldn't make out the words.

"Good night, Lizette. Sleep tight," Horace said. Everyone at Bless House knew he had a hankerin' for Lizette. He brought her back to the room with respect and courtesy. All of them knew he had never violated a kind of worshipful reverence he had for the beautiful bird that sailed across the audience at the Bird Cage on a wire.

Lizette was sweet on Horace, too, Libby knew. She smiled when Lizette came in quietly and shut the door. Lizette was careful removing her petticoat and dress when she believed Libby was asleep. Libby closed her eyes and felt warmth and gratitude until the darkness folded over her.

Because she had waited all week for Sunday to come, she woke energized, stirred by the light that crept out of the rose-colored sky. Now it was her turn to be quiet for Lizette, so she prepared everything in order to leave the room only once. As she slipped down to the empty kitchen, Libby felt the Sunday morning quiet of Bless House like a huge weight of heavy air, an almost stifling presence of sharp wind that sometimes seemed cold.

This morning, of course, lucky Mag Chambers was nowhere to be found. She had escaped the vortex of the turning spiral that had sucked all of them in.

Libby knew she was early getting up, but last week's rumors suggested she ought to be ahead of the crowd. Rummaging in the kitchen she found a heel of bread in the bread box, and from under the glass dome she cut off a slice of cheese. On her jaunt to the outhouse she sucked in the morning as though it was the last on earth, inhaling the clear air in each breath. Today she would hear the words Cotter had for all of them—words that would soothe a town suddenly in deep despair, standing not alive like a teeming citadel, but with its monuments shrunken, lying underground like the substance of a grave.

A short two blocks away, when she reached the courthouse, she saw that she was right to come early to hear the new preacher. It was a little more than an hour before the service, and already groups of patrons stood on the steps. Libby stopped at the bench by the street lamp. She might have taken a seat to wait, but most of the space was already filled by a heavy-set woman with a transparent veil floating from a startling purple hat fixed with pheasant wings.

"Hello, dear." The pheasant-hatted woman smiled.

Libby nodded. Though she had come to the bench to stand, she had not wished to intrude.

"I believe there's room for you, sweetheart," the woman said.

Standing nervously at the side of the bench was a man in a gray waistcoat who must have been her husband. He seemed anxious, stepping away and back again. When his wife invited Libby to sit, he nodded to her, but he did not smile.

"Mr. and Mrs. George Parsons," the woman beamed. "And you are . . ."

"Libby Campbell."

"Nice to meet you, Libby Campbell. We heard Mr. Cotter several times. He was wonderful," she continued, unimpeded by her remarkable double chin.

Libby thought she looked like the female version of a pair of mugs Nora had won at a carnival and used at Bless House.

"Have you heard him?"

"Yes, I have," Libby said.

"What do you think of Tombstone's new preacher?

"I think he is very good." Libby tried to control her emotions. "I traveled with him on the train."

The woman leaned forward as though she must examine Libby from a different angle. "Where are you from?"

"From Kansas City."

"Kansas City," the woman exclaimed. "We have a very nice young man from Kansas City working on the water committee. We had a terrible fire last year, you know, and need better water pressure."

Libby smiled politely. She had heard of the fire last year that had burned down the entire city. But she hadn't noticed it, because the city built itself up so quickly.

"You are the young lady working at Campbell and Hatch's?"

How does she know so much? Libby was paying attention now. The woman stopped fidgeting and drew close to Libby, peering into her eyes, perhaps to decipher whether or not she was real.

"Yes," Libby said. "I work at Campbell and Hatch's."

"I've heard of you," Mrs. Parsons said. "I believe the young man on the water committee mentioned you."

Mentioned me? Why? How could that be? And what about her would a man on the water committee have mentioned? She would like to have heard more, but Mrs. Parsons changed the subject. "We have a group of the ladies who are interested in reading books. Are you interested in reading books?"

"I love books." The possibility of another side of Tombstone woke in Libby's mind. She had seen so much gambling, drinking, and fisticuffing, it never occurred to her that somewhere there would be a cute, heavy-set lady in a purple hat who loved books.

"We have a literary society," Mrs. Parsons explained. "And you are welcome to join us."

There was something genuine in her voice that Libby heard and could not dispute. "I'd love to talk about books," she said.

Mrs. Parsons looked up and smiled, and then began to rise from the bench. Mr. Parsons quickly came to her side. Libby was impressed with the husband's classic look, except for his smashed nose. She had heard from the girls that someone influential in the town had a smashed nose from performing some heroic deed in last year's terrible fire.

Glancing at the courthouse, Libby saw what had caught their eye. As the police chief David Neagle opened the courthouse doors, there were hundreds of people gathered in the street. Libby was not close enough to the doors to make it to the front of the chapel, but the Parsons stood with her and protected her from a pressing crowd.

"He's the best pastor this town's ever had," Mr. Parsons murmured as they were carried by the crowd into the foyer.

The good news of the morning was that plans for the new chapel had been given the green light by the council, and they already had enough donations in the coffers to lay the foundation.

In the center of the courtroom, flanked by Mr. and Mrs. Parsons, Libby felt so distant from Cotter that it almost hurt. Too many heads stood between, too much like a boundless sea. Then, to the right and up a few rows near the aisle, she saw the tallest head in the congregation. It was Charles Grenville! And standing next to him on the aisle, as though her new fortune had brought her respectability in this congregation, was Mag Chambers! Libby felt hot.

"Love your enemies, bless them that curse you, do good to them that hate you," Cotter was saying in his expressive voice. *"And pray for them which despitefully use you and persecute you . . ."* Every word was weighty with meaning and emotion. *"That ye may be the children of your father which is in heaven."* Cotter's gaze across the pulpit was resolute, yet comforting. "Hate hurts your own heart. If you have anger or hatred for anyone, the bile acts like a sharp knife that jabs one way and another until your body is cut helter-skelter with pain."

The congregation was absolutely quiet. Libby couldn't take her eyes off Grenville.

"Try love. Love is healing. It soothes you. It makes the world a place of joy."

Monday at the saloon seemed quiet, but on Tuesday an unusual fervor pervaded the atmosphere—like fire crackling along an electric wire. Libby knew something was about to happen when Bob Paul entered the room with Charles Grenville.

Libby hadn't seen him for some time. He had purchased a new suit of clothes. He looked at her, but when she quickly turned away, he sat down at Paul's table with his back to her.

"Glad to see you folks." Bob Hatch nodded from behind the counter.

"Wyatt's let out this morning," Paul called back to Bob. Everyone in the saloon heard him, including Ike Clanton, who was buried in a card game over in the corner by the pool table. As the others entered, Clanton looked up from his game and gave a look that Libby would never forget. Of course Clanton had hoped Wyatt and Doc would stay in jail this time, and now his expectations were dashed. For a moment his face seemed to be a gray-blue color under his hat. He turned back to the game, his mouth working without any sound—at least no sound Libby could hear. His eyes focused straight ahead to the table as though he looked right through it. Suddenly there was an unhealthy calm in the room.

Clearly nervous, Bob Hatch instructed Libby to stay and service the bar while he took the orders himself. When he came back to her, he said, "The judge at Contention evidently decided not to hold a new trial. So that means the Earps are free." Libby fastened her eyes on the group. "The Earps will probably show up any minute," Hatch continued.

He was right. It wasn't more than twenty minutes before the Earps—all three of them, Virgil, Wyatt, and Morgan—came in. And Doc was with them. When Clanton saw Doc and Morgan and Virgil pull their chairs out at Wyatt's table, he made some last awkward moves with his deck of cards. Then, twisting uncomfortably in his chair, he bent over his game as though burying his head. The tension in the room seemed palpable.

Libby was already distressed because Bob Hatch had gone into the back room to gather supplies, and it looked as though she was alone. It was going to be up to her to work the table where Charles Grenville sat with the Earps, Bob Paul, and Doc Holliday. She felt heat under her hair. She did not want to talk to Charles Grenville, but it seemed inevitable. She would take Wyatt's order first and hope Bob Hatch came soon.

The men at the table were deep in conversation. It did not seem to be about the indictment, but the Huachuca Water Company, which, with its pipe project, was already promising such an amazing water pressure that its implementation would ensure that last year's fire would never happen again.

Libby hesitated to break into their conversation. So she waited, feeling like a wallflower. She wanted to acknowledge that Wyatt and Virgil were back. Should she offer Wyatt congratulations? She wanted to tell him she had believed in him and Virgil and Morgan all along. But the words stuck in her throat.

So, the men who had killed the McLowrys and Bill Clanton had been delivered from their second indictment. She felt the burning eyes of Ike behind her. She remembered so clearly that day she saw the silhouette of Josephine Marcus in the window with Nellie's little niece. Josie was looking for Judge Spicer, who had already pronounced the lawmen not guilty last December. If she had found him, she might have begged him to intervene for Wyatt, the man she secretly loved. But it had not really been a secret for some time. Had she reached Judge Spicer? Probably. But no one would ever know for sure.

Libby took the men's orders, leaving Charles Grenville for last. But she never reached him. At the Clanton table in the corner she saw some commotion. Clanton was murmuring to his men. She did not know exactly who all of them were, although she had seen some of them with him before. A wizened Indian with a leather face named Hank was one, and Frank Stilwell another. There was also a "Fred," a very small man with a tattoo on his hand that looked like a garland of roses framing the word *Mother*. And there was another man Libby could have sworn she had seen before. He looked like a beat-up version of that huckster Bill Byers who had occupied the stagecoach when Bob Paul and Charles Grenville accompanied the ladies to Tombstone. They were calling him Bill, but he was not Bill Byers. His hair gave him away. This man was Curly Bill.

Suddenly a dead silence fell over the saloon. Ike let out a loud, guttural rasp from his throat. He pushed his chair back until it scraped across the wood floor with the crack of thunder. At his performance, the others at the table began whispering among themselves. Later, Libby found out two of the men she didn't recognize were Pete Spence and Frederick Bode, and that the wily, bearded one she didn't know was Cruz. After gathering up the coat he had thrown at the back of his chair, Ike pulled it on, one sleeve at a time. Without looking at anyone, he made his way through the saloon like a tornado. Everyone held their breath. Libby had returned with her orders to the counter as they passed her. She heard some nearly unintelligible words as Ike led the others out to the street. There were muted warnings, sounding like "No justice. No justice. I suppose it's all right, if the town wants murderers to enforce the law."

Bob Hatch watched their departure. He had at last come to Wyatt's table sometime between the crack of Ike's chair and the retrieval of his overcoat. A pillar of fear, Libby had not even noticed that she missed Charles Grenville until she saw Bob checking with the entire group. She hurried back with her tray, but Bob had already served Charles.

"So, are you all going?" Bob was asking.

Libby had missed part of the conversation. But when she heard Morgan say, "We rounded up almost a dozen who are willing," she knew something big was fomenting. *A posse, maybe?*

But it did not take long for the situation to become crystal clear. Wyatt drained his glass, then stood up quickly and hit his guns on both sides as though checking to make sure they were there. "Ready, men?"

Libby watched Charles Grenville. He rose with the rest of them. Under the hem of his coat, she could now see the belt and the pearl-handled guns. She was surprised at the firearms. *Well, go and risk getting your pretty clothes dirty, Charles Grenville. Risk getting killed.* The words, even though they were only in her head, made her uneasy. Was she no better than Ike Clanton, wishing ill on her enemies?

The group, including Charles Grenville, clattered out the door and mounted their horses. He had not spoken a word to Libby. A cloud of dust in the morning light followed them as they rode out of town.

When they were gone, she found herself shaking. At the counter, washing cups, she asked Bob, "I thought Wyatt resigned as deputy not long ago."

"He did. But the county sheriff, Mr. Dake, hadn't taken them off the Cochise County list of deputies yet. This is unfinished business. The posse is tracking down the robbers who robbed the stage last January 6th."

So, the elected law enforcement officials had not really accepted the resignation of Wyatt and Morgan Earp, at least not yet. It was well known that Virgil had not resigned, in spite of the note he published in *The Epitaph*. It seemed he was still in service, although his right arm was useless. And the Tombstone sheriff, John Behan, hated the Earps because Wyatt stole his girlfriend Josephine Marcus. There had been no arrests and very little investigation into who was perpetrating the trouble. Everyone, at least everyone Libby knew, had long been aware that the lawmen were only trying to clean up the town. But there was someone they were having a very difficult time keeping under control, and that was Ike Clanton.

After the posse left, the town was on edge as Libby had never seen it before. Even Mrs. Parson's pleasant invitation to attend the literary discussion on Alfred Lord Tennyson did nothing to soothe Libby's anxiety. To be polite, and to meet some of the town's most influential women, she graciously agreed to go to the red Victorian parlor of *The Epitaph* editor's wife, Mrs. Clum, to hear poetry and sip tea. The ladies were very kind to Libby, and she listened with interest while Mrs. Sherman McMasters read some of Tennyson's poetry. She knew Mrs. McMaster's husband was on the posse also, and she admired the calm of this woman. This wife must have been as concerned as everyone else whose husband had gone on a wild goose chase to find criminals who might be hundreds of miles away in the barren desert counting pieces of Wells Fargo gold.

"This is really a poem that should be read when the new year began," Mrs. McMasters explained. "But we are in the middle of such terrible conflict, I thought we were in need of a better day."

When the woman began reading, Libby grew alert. She had heard these lines before.

Ring out wild bells, ring in the new.

Now she remembered how her mother sat near her pillow at night and stroked her hair, sometimes singing her to sleep. She had heard her mother recite these lines! They meant more to Libby now than ever before.

Ring out the thousand wars of old,
Ring in the thousand years of peace.

Now she understood why Mrs. McMasters wanted to read these verses. They would be important for everyone living in a troubled world: women, men, children, the believers, the unbelievers. Across the room, leaning forward to catch the meaning of these special words, was George Parsons, who happened to be the only man present. Now he was nodding from time to time, looking fatherly in spite of his smashed nose. Libby caught the weight of the stanzas that pertained so well to Tombstone.

Ring in the valiant man and free,
The larger heart, the kindlier hand;
Ring out the darkness of the land,
Ring in the Christ that is to be.

Libby wondered if Christ would ever come to bring peace to a world fraught with such trouble and evil. She hoped he would. She was not ready yet to meet the Savior, but she knew Cotter was. And for now, that would be enough for her. She would follow his example. She would never miss any of his lectures or Sunday sermons. Cotter was doing the work of the Lord. And if the preacher did not come to Libby now, he was busy making his preparations for the time when Christ would "ring in" to the earth. Cotter would be there in the front row when the Master, in his shining robes, in perfect glory, would say, "Come, thou good and faithful servant. Well done. Come into my rest."

25

The days and weeks passed, sizzling with the same tension in Tombstone that had been there since Wyatt and Doc Holliday had been named murderers. Gloom had roosted like a black vulture over the town roofs, and now began to blister in the March heat. Libby got through the days performing basic tasks: washing the tablecloths, napkins, and rags; scrubbing down table legs; rubbing the cups dry until they sparkled in the morning sunlight; and gathering up the trash and carrying it in the basket to the large can in the back alley, where the city fathers had finally sent a garbage wagon to clean up the debris.

It was not long before the posse returned without much success. They discovered that the robbers of the January 6th coach had already been incarcerated in a jail in Texas. It seemed Cochise County's Crawley Dake had sent the posse just to "spend tax funds," people lamented. It was rumored they formed the posse with a mind to keep Wyatt and Morgan away from Tombstone, and out of danger. Though the weary travelers took their tables as before, there seemed to be little laughter or chicanery. There was nothing but low voices, lowered heads, whispers of unintelligible words and phrases. Libby attended them all faithfully. Charles Grenville did not come again.

These were the weeks Libby decided to clear her soul of sin. She faithfully attended Cotter's services through all of the trouble, determined to prove herself worthy of him while she waited for him. She promised to be Christlike to everyone. The only one in the world who irritated her was Charles Grenville, and she hadn't seen him for a long time. She spent her spare moments reading the gospel of Matthew in the New Testament, and memorizing Alfred Lord Tennyson's poem "Ring Out, Wild Bells." Even in all of these moments of profound dedication, she still felt she came up lacking. Was it because she still lived at Bless House? She wasn't sure. But she was sure the girls and Horace, with his bits of history, brought her cheer.

For weeks now, Lizette and Penelope had been working on a drama to be performed at Schieffelin Hall. The curtain would rise on *Stolen Kisses* on the Ides of March, and lower the next Saturday, the eighteenth. As the date grew closer, Bless House exploded with activity. Nora took her job as costumer seriously, and conducted it nightly with a mouthful of pins, kneeling before Lizette's gorgeous Victorian blue-green tea dress, finding the perfect length for the hem. In her finale, Lizette was to appear in a white garden faille with a broad-brimmed summer hat laden with bougainvillea. Penelope was the maid in a starched cap and apron bristling with ruffles and bows.

The entire house got into the act, making appropriate comments and cheering Nora, as well as Marcella, who passed her the tape and measuring tools as she worked. *Stolen Kisses* was a shocking public display of affection, Lizette assured them. She danced and pranced in the circle of onlookers with the grace of a summer breeze. "I had to learn a hundred lines," she said with a laugh.

Libby wondered if the play fit into her new life as a penitent. But she loved the excitement of the costuming, the extraordinarily bright lights in the parlor, the giggles, the *ooh*s and the *ah*s.

"You look like a princess!" Little Gertie raved.

Horace was ready with his bit, as usual. "Long as you don't wear no glass slipper."

Marcella shot him a warning look, but he paid no attention and continued with his rendition. "Did you know that the story of Cinderella was an old legend finally written in 1697 by a Frenchman named Charles Perrault, who changed the story by misspelling one French word? The word was *vair,* which means "ermine." *Ermine* slippers. But he misspelled it, wrote it *verre,* which means "glass.""

The room fell quiet, as it often did during Horace's oracles.

"In the old legend they were actually ermine slippers for a princess. Get it? Not glass."

Nobody spoke.

"No princess could wear glass shoes. It would kill her."

"Thank you, Horace," Marcella said. "That was something we really ought to know."

Little Gertie threw her head back and laughed.

"We're having a big weekend," Bob Hatch told Libby on Monday while she was cleaning shelves. He approached with his head down, in almost an apologetic stance. "There's a play this week."

Yes, she knew.

"Play nights are usually more crowded than one person can handle," he said. "I'm afraid we'll need you Wednesday through Saturday for crowds that may come in after the play."

"Of course," Libby said. "I'll come in late."

He turned slightly. "It would probably have to be added on to the full day. I can pay your wages for the extra time."

A full day? "That would be fine," Libby assured him.

At first, she was disappointed that she may not be able to see any of Lizette's star performance in *Stolen Kisses*. But when Libby added up the overtime wages in her head, she felt better. She would be able to pay her total debt to Nora.

The run of the play certainly did bring customers into the Campbell and Hatch Saloon. On opening night, Mr. and Mrs. Clum dropped by after the play to let their friend Bob Hatch know that the Lingard Company had put on an excellent drama. And George Berry came back to play pool after he took his wife home. The Clums didn't stay, but the Bartholomews, the Chapmans, and half a dozen other couples stayed to talk and enjoy refreshments while some of their men played a short game of pool.

"Sometimes the men play pool until the sun comes up," Bob told Libby. She now saw why he was so tired some mornings.

Every night of the performance, enthusiastic groups came into the saloon with glowing reports of the quality of acting in *Stolen Kisses*.

"The star is that little gal who flies across the room at the Bird Cage," George Berry told Morgan. "Very realistic. You get caught up in the bright lights."

On Saturday afternoon, when Libby waited for Morgan and Wyatt to make their orders, she heard Morgan say, "I think we ought to see *Stolen Kisses*. This is closing night. I heard nothing but praise for it. Are you game?"

Wyatt laughed. "Josephine says it's the basest kind of trash."

Morgan drew back. "Maybe because she's not in it."

"Even the title! *Stolen Kisses.*"

"I was thinking of taking Louisa."

"Go. Go if you want to. I know Josie would never cross the threshold of Schieffelin Hall for the Lingard Company.

"But she might like it."

"She's Shakespeare, man. She's high class—been doing her own stolen kisses. And they ain't stolen." Wyatt laughed at his own joke.

"Well, I think Louisa wants to go."

"I'll be here. Probably playin' pool with Bob or George Berry."

Wyatt must have made the rounds to the Continental and the Alhambra. At Campbell and Hatch, Bob had enticed Morgan to play a game of pool with him. It was not long before Morgan and Louisa dropped by. Libby served them again.

"Was the play all right?" Wyatt asked Morgan.

"It was okay," Morgan said without enthusiasm.

"Come, Morgan," Louisa urged. "It was better than okay." She tugged at his coat sleeve.

Bob approached the table. "You ready for that pool game, Morgan?"

"After I take my wife to the hotel," he said. "You ready to turn in, Louisa?"

"I would like a night toddy first." She glanced at him coyly.

For the next half hour Wyatt played George and Bob both. Morgan and Louisa ordered drinks and watched. When Louisa's eyes began to droop, Morgan walked her to the hotel. Within minutes he was back, rubbing his hands together. It was almost midnight. "You ready for defeat, Bob?" he chided.

Bob Hatch grinned. "I've got the time if you got the money."

"It's not your money for much longer," Morgan bantered.

Cue sticks in hand, they moved to the back pool table, while Wyatt stood against the west wall watching the game with his friend George Berry.

"All right. Show me what you got," Bob said.

Morgan was good at pool. He had excellent eyesight and canny judgment. It would be a close match.

Libby picked up the dirty glasses and silverware and heated some water on the small gas burner in the kitchen. All evening she had been picking up scraps of garbage, old newspapers, and cigar butts, until the waste basket was full. She picked it up and made her way past the patrons at the pool table. She noticed the back door was not entirely closed. The glass in the top half of it looked cloudy.

"Can I help you with that?" Wyatt, always the gentleman, rose from a chair he had grabbed to wait out Morgan's game.

"No, thank you," Libby said cheerfully. "I'm used to it."

Wyatt sat back down, leaned back, and tipped the chair until it stood on its back legs.

Because the door was slightly ajar, she kicked it. It opened up to the alley. She had emptied the trash into the large can more than a hundred times. But the night was so black, it startled her. There was almost no light from the sliver of moon overhead.

She paused. She would let her eyes adjust before making her way through the air that seemed as thick as molasses. But as she waited, she felt something. Someone was in the alley, and she thought she heard a quick step on the gravel. Could it have been a cat? But then she saw large, dark shapes moving beyond the trash can. She quickly left the unemptied trash basket on the ground and backed up through the door. She closed the door gently, not wishing to rattle the glass. And when she was inside, she turned to lock it. Hastily she hurried past Wyatt in his tipped chair, past the pool table, and past Morgan and Bob. George Berry was keeping watch on the other side of the room.

In Libby's fright, beads of sweat gathered on her brow. When she went to the bar she stood for a moment with her hands on the counter to catch her breath.

And then it happened. The crack of the shot broke the thick glass in the top of the door. The sound was like nothing Libby had ever heard before in her life. The blast seemed to tear her ears apart and break her nerves wide open.

The scene at the pool table spun like the images of a dervish in the garish lights. Morgan, who had been standing with his back to the door, suddenly lurched as though some force had slapped him in a hearty way on his spine. The cue stick in his hand dropped to the floor, and he pitched forward, his hands clutching the pinewood rail, scratching at the green felt. A rosy smear of blood bloomed in his shirt.

A scream came from George Berry. "We been ambushed!" He was on the floor holding his leg.

Wyatt leaped to his feet so fast, the chair toppled to the floor. He stepped across the shards of glass on the rug and bounded out of the violated door while reaching for his gun. Bob Hatch turned the color of flour paste.

"Goodfellow is at the Alhambra!" George cried out. "Get the doctor!"

Bob looked at Libby. "Go to the Alhambra, Libby, quick. Find Dr. Goodfellow." He rifled through the drawers under the bar and scooped out all of the towels. "We'll staunch the blood. Go, Libby."

She did not waste a moment. She did not grab her shawl. She went bare-faced into the murky street, facing the gaslights with tears in her eyes. She might have asked herself what had happened. But she knew. And the men who had thrust the gun through the glass in the door and shot Morgan in the back were still somewhere out on this street, lurking in the dark. Libby ran. It seemed at any moment her ankles would turn and she would find herself sprawling over the boardwalk, but she ran. The Alhambra was not far. And once through the door she could see Dr. Goodfellow at the first table. It did not register at first that he was with Charles Grenville. It did not matter.

Feeling torn apart, her hair disheveled, she ran through the saloon. "Morgan's been shot," she shouted. Though she believed she had given force to the words, they came through what felt like tears in her throat and seemed to dissipate into a weak din.

Dr. Goodfellow stood up so quickly, the cards in his hand hit the floor in a spray. The other men at the table backed up their chairs. Charles Grenville's face grew white.

"Have you told Morgan's girl, Louisa?" the doctor asked Libby.

By now, Libby was nearly sobbing. Her hair was strung across her face, and she wiped her cheeks with the backs of her hands. "No."

"Then go! She's at the Occidental Hotel."

Grenville stared at Libby. When she turned away from the doctor she had not meant to meet Grenville's gaze, but her eyes had gravitated to his face. His expression made her long to find herself in his protection. She ran out of the Alhambra and down the street to the Occidental. Her hands shook.

In all of her time in Tombstone, she had never walked into this elaborate hotel. And now she was entering it, still in her apron, her cheeks washed with tears and stained with the grime of her hands. "Morgan's shot!" she told the concierge. "At the Campbell and Hatch. Can I tell Louisa?"

"Oh my!" The woman at the desk looked pale. She was a matronly professional dressed in proper black, topped by a white lace collar. She leaned into a room behind her. "Ralph! Please get Mrs. Earp!"

"What is her room? May I please tell her? It's important to hurry," Libby said, surprised she had garnered enough composure to insist on performing the mission herself.

"Room 4." The woman nodded toward the hallway on the first floor.

Libby tore down that hall and knocked furiously. "Louisa, Louisa! It's an emergency. Morgan has been shot!"

When the door opened, the woman's pale face looked drained of blood. "Morgan?" she choked.

"Come with me," Libby said, afraid Louisa was going to faint right there at the door. "Please come with me, Louisa."

The woman put out her hand. Already she had dressed in her nightgown, so she put on a shawl. She hunted about at the door and slipped her feet into a pair of heavy shoes. Looking down on them, Libby knew they belonged to Morgan, which would not make it easy for Louisa to walk in the street.

When Libby took Louisa's hand, the long fingers felt like cold bones. But they were not weak. Louisa's grip was so powerful, Libby felt some pain.

"I had a feeling." Louisa's low voice was grating. "But I can't say it was unusual. I've had the same premonition for months."

The darkness seemed to sweep out of their path. Libby did not let go of Louisa's grip. She held the woman up across the gravel and across the boardwalk, the night breeze blowing the airy nightgown like gauzy moth wings. Libby and Louisa moved as rapidly as they could with Morgan's shoes getting in the way.

"Oh, dear Heaven! Let him live!" Louisa cried. "Ever since the shoot-out at the OK Corral, I have had this premonition."

"Not to worry," Libby said. "Just hurry." Holding Louisa up, she felt like a mother leading a child.

The saloon was crowded. Bob had pulled a rope across the back by the pool table to keep out curious bystanders. George Berry lay panting on the floor, holding a towel to the wound in his leg. One of the patrons knelt beside him.

Morgan lay across the pool table, his belly packed with towels. Louisa ran to him. "Oh, my darling! Morgan! Morgan! Speak to me!"

Bob placed a chair at the side of the pool table. Dr. Goodfellow had opened Morgan's shirt and was cleaning away the blood that still gushed from his flesh.

"Please, Morgan!" Louisa sobbed. "Talk to me!"

The room behind Libby buzzed with worried chatter.

"It will be like Virgil. The wound will heal," Bob Hatch said. But as Dr. Goodfellow gazed at the crowd in the room, his face looked ashen.

"If we could move him to his quarters," Bob was saying.

Dr. Goodfellow shook his head. "Any move would mean an even greater loss of blood. We'll do as much as we can here to stop the bleeding before we try that."

Louisa gripped Morgan's hand. "Breathe, darling, breathe." She stood and leaned over him, pressing her cheek against his brow. "Oh, dear Heaven," she prayed. "Spare his life."

Libby now saw the face of the man kneeling with George Berry. It was Charles Grenville, comforting George and holding the towel against his bloody shin. Libby glanced away.

The air seemed stifling and the quiet heavy, as though the spectators stood in a huge tomb. Louisa's grip visibly tightened on Morgan's hands, and Libby realized she must have felt him slipping away. Louisa wanted to hang onto him and pull him from the web of heaven that seemed to fall over them now. It seemed symbolic that the lights in the saloon began to flicker as they often did when the night grew late.

"Speak to me! Speak to me!" Louisa begged. "Morgan, talk to me!" Her voice was crowded with tears.

When Morgan moved his lips, the room grew dead still. "I've played my last game of pool," he said in a low, gritty monotone. The words were halting.

"Oh, my darling, no! Morgan! Morgan!" Tears coursed down Louisa's cheeks. "Don't leave me!" She addressed him now with what sounded like a scolding. "Morgan! Oh, I can't believe you got mixed up in Wyatt's stupid schemes!"

The front door opened and Wyatt entered, his face tense with pain. "I didn't find them," he said. Virgil emerged from behind him, his paralyzed arm dangling at his side.

"I saw Frank Stilwell at the Oriental. He was in a twit with Frank Bode and the Indian, Hank Swilling. It didn't look good," Howard Lee said. Lee was Bob Hatch's friend—had served on the firefighter committee with him.

"I know who did this," Wyatt Earp said. He scoured the audience until he saw Sheriff Behan. Wyatt stared at Behan with a piercing, gaze—as though he knew his brother's death could be blamed on Behan and his lax law enforcement. Behan had not arrested or indicted one cowboy. Wyatt's face grew pale. When he came to the table, he took Morgan's hand. "Morgan, look at me," he petitioned.

Morgan moved his eyes. His lips did not respond.

"I promise! I promise!" Wyatt almost sobbed. But there was anger in his voice now. "Morgan, do you hear me?"

But Morgan was gone.

26

What came over Tombstone in the next few weeks was like a thick fog—dense as though the town swam through ink. It seemed to float over all of them, to seep into their greetings, to cover them like a pall.

Until much later, no one knew the details of what happened to Wyatt when he led several posses into the Arizona hills. What they did know was that on Monday, March 20, 1882, the townspeople saw Louisa and Wyatt load Morgan's body onto the Wells Fargo coach and cart it down the streets toward the train that would take them all to Tucson and then to Colton, California, where the Earp family would bury Morgan and nurse Virgil back to health. *The Epitaph* said something like "Threatened by unprincipled killers, and allowed by the local law enforcement to go free, these citizens could not be protected. So they have taken the only course open to them: to leave Tombstone. Perhaps forever."

When the news filtered into the town that Frank Stilwell's body had been found on the Tucson railroad tracks at the same time Wyatt saw his brothers off on the train, there seemed to be no secret about what had happened. Wyatt had brought about his own brand of justice. And later, reports also came back that Frederick Bode, Hank Swilling, Ike Clanton, and others known to have mouthed off about their nefarious intentions had also been killed—their bodies found in distant ranches and hills.

No one knew the details. But they did know Sheriff Behan organized a posse to go after the perpetrators who had committed these killings: Wyatt and Virgil Earp.

Bless House continued to chatter and speculate. But Libby was not there often. She continued to work, feeling quiet and sad. Bob tried not to let the tragedy sour his business. He put up a sign in the window—"Half Price Pool." Still, fewer patrons entered the doors of the Campbell and Hatch establishment.

Cotter came once or twice to say how sorry he was that the town's less desirable element had undone the peace in such a manner. Libby was happy to see him, but she had lost some of her hope that he might take her back with him to Massachusetts.

March 18, 1882

My Dearest Frances,

Are you well? I have not received a letter from you in over a week. It may be that the Wells Fargo coach has let us down.

Much has happened since I last wrote to you. On May 12 an old lady by the name of Mrs. Morton dropped an oil lamp, and six buildings on our street burned down. My lodging house was one of them. Luckily I got myself and my things out in time. But I feel so sad for Mr. and Mr. Grant, who just last week made their final mortgage payment! This fire wasn't as bad as the one last year that destroyed whole blocks, but on March 6, the city water committee began a monstrous pipe project bringing water from the Huachuca Mountains, which they promise will give enough pressure to take care of any more fires. It should be ready in June.

The flames didn't touch the bare bones of our church construction, thank heavens. It is far enough west to be out of the way. I wish you could see it! It's going to be beautiful. We had more than enough generous donations, so I ordered stained glass. We'll be in the building in another month, I hope. It should hold over two hundred people. I will be glad, as my congregations seem to be bulging at the courthouse seams. I suppose that's good news.

On May 5th we organized the Tombstone Baseball Association—working with Mr. Rice and the San Pedro Boys, who head our executive committee. But playing with the San Pedro Boys didn't guarantee us any victory over the Tucson boys in Pima County. Tucson whitewashed us good, but we aren't daunted. We'll take them on again.

The town is still nervous about the murder of Morgan Earp. John Behan is such a weak excuse for a sheriff that Wyatt and Virgil have gone out with their own posse to take the law into their own hands. All of us felt safer when we heard reports that they've killed some of these murderers. But wouldn't you know, instead of going after the real culprits, this amazing sheriff Behan has organized a posse to go after Wyatt and Virgil! I will be glad to get back to Massachusetts, where there is a little more civil order. I told the diocese I'd like to come home as soon as the church is built.

I think about you every day, praying you are well and happy. I hope you remember who I am—that fellow on the pier who saved you from drowning in your own petticoats.

I pray for us, Frances. But we know that the heavens are in charge.

Any news from the family? I haven't heard from anyone for a while. Write to me one more time.

I send my fondest thoughts,
W. Cotter

27

Bob Hatch told Libby that having her come to the saloon at night was a comfort to him. He asked her if she would consider working longer hours as a standard practice.

All of Tombstone was in shock after the murder, reeling from the news that Wyatt and Virgil were bent on revenge. And then, on May 16th, before the miracle water system was ready, six buildings burned to the ground on Main Street. The old lady, Mrs. Morton, had dropped her oil lamp onto her carpet.

Bob Hatch told Libby after the fire, "It feels like we're tiptoeing in hell. At least it wasn't like last year when the whole town burnt to ashes. That kind of tragic fire won't happen again when they get them modern wrought-iron pipes from Pennsylvania to bring that water from the three mountain springs to the Miller Canyon Dam and the Tombstone Reservoir. We need that water faster'n them two camps of boys can lay that pipe, I'm thinkin.'"

For a time the citizens of Tombstone held their breath. The city was quiet without the Earps. After the reports that Wyatt and Virgil had killed the murderers, a weight seemed to lift. News filtered back: the Earps were on a ranch, the Earps were in New Mexico, the Earps were in Colorado. The town gave a sigh of relief, except for John Behan who, feeling his ideological oats, organized his own posse to capture the new murderers: Virgil and Wyatt and their friends. But it seemed to be for show. Wyatt escaped. And at some point Josie went with him to California. For the most part—although they missed the Earps—the town began to settle. It had become a virtual "tombstone."

When he felt a little more confident, Bob still kept Libby on an as-needed schedule. But there were many afternoons that he let her go. Like an animal let out of a cage, she exploited her freedom with exuberance—shopping, meeting people, exploring Tombstone. She loved to look in windows for trinkets she could afford. But she seldom purchased anything. There was something about the weight of a thriving community that calmed her nerves: Spangenberg's gun shop, the Leventhall's Clothing Store, Fish Brothers Wagons, the Hibbard, Spencer and Bartlett Company Hardware store, and Lenoir's Furniture Store.

Staying close to the town generated so many second and third encounters, she began to know more of the townspeople. The Earps and their posse were obviously gone, but many friendly souls frequented the streets. There were the proprietors of the shops, the men at the pipe-laying camps, and people relaxing at the saloon after working hours. Many times Libby greeted Constable Kenny and Chief of Police Dave Neagle, who always had a cheerful word for her. Others, such as Mr. Stoddard and Mrs. Smith, the printers *of The Epitaph,* and Mr. Blackburn, the fire chief, tipped their hats as she walked by. Libby also got to know Mr. James McCoy, the financial agent and manager of the Huachuca Water Company, and Hayman Solomon, one of the managers of the Cochise Company Bank.

From time to time she saw her own friends from Bless House: Nora and Marcella buying dresses; Horace and Lizette window shopping, laughing, and enjoying Horace's jokes; Kitty and Cordelia, Gertie and Della following them. Horace might have had great success with any of the Bless House girls, but he had taken a liking to Lizette, the flying bird. Though it seemed he kept arm's length from her, afraid if he touched her she would fly away.

Sometimes, when she was feeling brave on her walks, Libby entered some of the other saloons just to check them out: the Alhambra, the Eagle Brewery, the Oriental, and on Allen Street a festive eating place called Tivoli Gardens, decorated with beautiful live potted trees and flowers lit by electric lamps glowing under an outdoor canvas roof.

But if she ventured into a saloon, she was careful to study the clientele. Once, when she walked into the Alhambra, she heard a voice behind her that seemed to cut her to the bone.

"Libby Campbell!"

When she turned, she realized Charles Grenville stood between her and the door. She tried to duck out, but he moved.

"You're like a little wild animal, aren't you?"

When he stood over her, every nerve in her body seemed to collapse. Certainly, he couldn't still be after the gold. It had been too long, and he knew she was working and paying her way. But whenever she saw him, some anger or guilt or embarrassment still crowded her heart. Libby wanted to scream, to curl her fingers into fists, to run, to forget his face.

"Are you always going to run the opposite direction when you see me?" Grenville grinned.

"I like to run. But walking is just as good, if you don't stand in the doorway," she quipped.

"Ha!" He laughed as though he enjoyed watching her squirm. "Frustrated, are you?" He was still smiling. "Well, you're a feisty one. I'll give that to you."

Again she attempted to duck under his arm.

"You don't stop trying, do you?"

But by some chance and sheer will, she slipped through. And it was in part because another patron had darkened the doorway, and it happened to be someone she knew. "Hello, Mr. McCoy," she said in her strongest voice through Grenville's bulk, and Grenville stepped aside.

When the fire of May 16th raged, Libby heard Charles Grenville's lodging house had burned to the ground. She did not know where he stayed after that. Standing at the construction site on her way across town, she wondered where he lived now. She was acquainted with most of the hotels and boarding houses. She had always thought that someday she would be able to move into one of them, so she had often taken the liberty to walk in, look about, smile, and walk away. The Russ House and the American Hotel, both operated by the respected Nellie Cashman, were perhaps her first choice. But there was Molly Fly's Boarding House, and the Grand, the Cosmopolitan, and the Brown, all first-class lodging places.

In spite of Charles Grenville, Libby still felt sad to see the old places gone. Rumors flew that one of the recently wealthy miners had purchased all of the lots, and now new buildings were going up rapidly. One of the casualties of the fire had been the American Lodging House where Libby had gone to visit Cotter. That devastation mattered to her the most. She could remember every detail of that day she had been in his arms. And now he was helping the workmen build the church. She often thought about walking west into the empty desert to see the stark timbers rising like spikes against the afternoon sun.

Her Sunday walk was the one she looked forward to more than any other. It was quiet, and she could find time to think away from the mayhem at the busy Bless House. After hearing Cotter's sermon, she wanted to think about what he said. She did not always want to face it, but his words on the Sabbath were all she had of him now—the themes out of the gospels, his voice, solemn and sincere. As his popularity increased, as more and more people attended his services, cheered at his baseball games, and demanded his attention to speak at clubs and attend the widows and fatherless, Libby knew he was slipping away from her.

When the fire happened, Cotter's kindness soothed every broken spirit. He spoke of long-suffering. And Libby identified with it. Though there was so much suffering with loss, the goal of every person was to overcome the gravity of pain and march onward. Cotter's speeches gave purpose to many souls. This week, eight days after the fire, he spoke from Galatians, and she listened to every word. *The fruit of the spirit is love, joy, peace, longsuffering, gentleness, goodness, faith, meekness, temperance.* In one sense they were just words. But when they came from Cotter's mouth, Libby knew they carried more weight than words. From his mouth they were expressions of love.

One Sunday afternoon, when it began to rain, she ducked into the dark space between the Tivoli Gardens and a Chinese laundry on Allen Street. Neither building was tall enough to keep the downpour from spattering her hair and her shawl, but it was better than nothing. She backed up against the Tivoli wall and felt it slightly give. Above her, the canvas ceiling was visible. She was about to condemn such construction, when she heard laughter on the street and saw a man pull a woman by the hand into the same space ahead of her. Horace and Lizette.

"Horace!" she cried out. "Lizette!"

"Oh my stars! Miss Libby! You got a dry spot here? Wet feathers, you know. Ha!" He looked at Lizette. They both laughed.

Libby did a double take. And Horace noticed it.

"Your wheels are turnin'. You thinkin' how come I got Miss Lizette by the hand?"

"Well, I . . ." Libby began.

"Wing, Libby. She's a bird, remember. So it's just a wing." He winked at Lizette. But once he had pulled her to safety, he withdrew his hand. "No, I . . ." He bowed his head while the last slivers of rain pummeled them, slipping down from the canvas roof of the Tivoli Gardens. "I got the utmost veneration for Lizette. Nobody I'd rather hold by the hand." He did not look up. "But you know I'm a married man."

"We know that, Horace." Libby smiled. "And I love you for staying pure. Not an easy thing to do. Isn't that right, Lizette?"

She smiled at Libby and turned to smile at Horace. "First man I ever know with enough love to give me that kind of respect."

"Nora says, if someone you love wants something very bad, isn't it respect to give it to them?" Horace declared. "But I say, do you give a little child a diet of candy because they want it very bad?"

The rain didn't last long. Libby could not hear all of Horace's philosophies and historical anecdotes as they left the dark space to walk back to Bless House.

"The sun is coming through." He glanced up. "Hot as a kimono."

"Kimono?" Lizette cocked her head, ready as she always seemed, for another bite at history.

"Remember, I told you about the Japanese exorcist in 1657 who set fire to the evil kimono the little girls wore and burned all of Tokyo?"

"You did," Lizette said. "But you wasn't going to say that story out loud again in Tombstone for fear that fate might hear it."

"Oh, that." Horace grinned. "I was afraid mouthin' off would bring another fire to Tombstone! But we already had it last Friday." He could not stop. "And it weren't much. Burned six buildings. Of course six buildings is six buildings. But we got that water-pipe project just about done now. Gonna have

Marilyn Brown

water pressure strong enough to pump some human being up in the air like a bird."

Lizette clapped. *How nice that Horace has a good audience,* Libby thought.

Approaching Bless House, she thought she could hear the cry of a child. She shook her head from that notion. But as they drew nearer to the porch and saw the front door open, there were voices. Beyond the door in the dark maw of the house, the talking, laughing girls were gathering in the parlor. Libby and Lizette and Horace hesitated on the steps. A couple of the girls suddenly turned and charged out of the crowd toward them.

"He's here! He's here!" Little Gertie called to the others still congregating inside.

"Horace! Horace! Someone's here you want to see. You'll be surprised," Cordelia called to him.

Marcella followed Gertie and Cordelia to the threshold. "Horace! Are we glad to see you! Come in, girls." She nodded to Libby and Lizette.

The trio on the porch stopped. Inside the dark parlor the girls backed up in two flanking lines as though their military experience was second to none. And at the end of the line, as it separated, Libby could see a small, pale face. The face was connected to a tiny body clothed in a worn blue cloak.

"Elvira! Oh, Heaven be praised!" Horace cried out. He ran to the little woman and took her in his arms. He folded her up like a small cloth doll in a ragged cape and shabby shoes. "I've wondered where you were! How did you find me?" He glanced at Nora. She was holding a small baby in her arms. It could not have been Horace's child, for he had been in the penitentiary for nine months and in Tombstone for five. But no one was counting months, or days, or hours now. They were riveted upon Horace

234

holding this tiny woman in his arms. He lowered his face into her mass of tangled hair, then glanced up at Nora again.

"Oh, oh, Elvira, Elvira. And oh, this is your baby!" he cried, reaching out to take the baby.

"She's four months old," Nora said with a smile.

"What an adorable child! Where did you go, Elvira? Why didn't you wait for me? Or contact me? I've been worried about you so."

Elvira had not said a word. Horace had enough words for all of them. Even Lizette continued smiling as he grasped the infant in his arms, held her high in the air, and laughed. The baby giggled. "Oh! She's beautiful!" He counted the baby's digits.

The girls laughed.

"Always ought to check the finters! Queen Elizabeth's mother, Anne Bolyn, was born with eleven of them, you know. What's her name?"

"Clara." Marcella touched the baby's cheek.

"Baby Clara!" Horace rejoiced. "Clara, to make clear the future!"

Elvira stood by, still mute. Libby wondered if she could hear or speak.

Horace gave the baby back to Nora and took Elvira by the shoulders. "Elvira, dear, have they asked you to stay with us in Bless House?"

"We've already got it all planned," Nora said. "She's got one night left and paid for at the Cosmopolitan Hotel."

"Oh, no!" Horace objected. "She should be here tonight."

Nora stayed calm, as though she had restrained her brother's emotional outbursts many times before. "Horace," she said softly, "she came an hour ago. We will need to make space for her, make up her room. She says it will be best if we all go to bring back her things in the morning."

"We can keep the baby here, though," Cordelia gushed. "Says she sleeps all night."

"Then I'll go with them!" Horace announced. But when the words came out of his mouth, he paused and looked warily at Elvira's stiffened frame.

"We've already arranged for the cook to take her back to the hotel," Nora said firmly. "We didn't know where you were."

"She needs to be with her luggage. If we keep the baby here, she'll get a better night's rest. And her room isn't ready yet," Marcella added. "We need your help to make it up."

"Elvira, Elvira." Horace held his wife close. "Oh, Elvira! Tomorrow we'll be a family once again." He ran his hand through her fuzzy hair. "Oh, Elvira, I hope you will be all right."

"And she needs to get herself together, take a long bath without any interruption," Prynne said.

Libby had never seen this kind of activity in Bless House. The girls had a project. Chattering, giggling, plotting, they discussed how they were going to supply Elvira's new quarters with clothing, baby food, bottles.

Strangely, in all of it, Libby could not discern what had happened in the atmosphere. For a moment she thought the sun had gone down. But it was too early for that. There had been that early rain, and perhaps some clouds were pulling across the sky. There was no question that darkness moved through the house—a shadowy weight she could not explain. She looked back toward the door and saw Lizette. The girl still stood by the threshold in an obscure corner, her face in a forced grin.

Libby went to her as soon as she could make her way through the others. "Lizette! Oh, I'm so sorry, Lizette," she whispered. "You needn't have to stay and look." She stood close to the girl in the foyer and urged her to move through the dining room to the attic stairs. Yet she could not protect Lizette from the image of Horace and Elvira in the parlor facing one another, and him reaching out and pulling her into his arms.

"Oh, my darling Elvira!" he was saying. Libby was surprised at his urgency. She heard tears in his voice. "I've worried about you for so long."

Libby took Lizette by the hand and hurried her up the stairs.

When Libby saw the smoke on her way to the saloon in the morning, it resembled what sometimes floated over the city from a refuse fire in a pit. Sometimes garbage fires looked pervasive. Only this one was a little dense. The sun seemed to be struggling through an oblique red haze in the eastern hills, vibrant with more color than usual.

At the saloon, she took out the bucket and rifled through some old rags. The pine soap was so dry she wet it thoroughly with water from the pump, and scrubbed it with a metal scraper to loosen up the slivers.

With Bob late, Libby was alone. So when she heard screaming on the street, she straightened up on her knees, alert, as though she had been stabbed with a knife. The soapy water in the rag trickled to her apron.

"Fire! Fire! The redcap dropped his cigar in the liquor barrel at the Tivoli!"

Libby watched the water in her hands wet her apron, soak her thighs. Fire? Again? Her first thought was that the Tivoli was far enough away that she should wait for Bob. Where was he?

She leaned over with the wet rag in her hands to scrub out the corners under the bar—spots she had cleaned many times before. She rubbed the soapy cloth back and forth on the ooze from spilled beers, whiskey, gin, fruit compote, syrup. It was not pleasant work, but it was rewarded by access to a living. And living was the goal.

Suddenly there came a *whoosh* of wind overhead unlike anything Libby had ever heard. As she stood, the bucket toppled over and the water seeped across the floor. A loud crack sent vibrations into every inch of her body.

Where was Bob? He had never been this late before.

And then it happened. The roof began to beat with a slapping sound. It was fire. Flames from the roofs of the shops next door whisked over the saloon. It took only fifteen minutes for the fire to devour the neighborhood. Above Libby, the coals crumbled and let go of a beam in the ceiling of the saloon, and dropped it into the maw of the smoke and heat. The wood brushed against her brow, and she moved her head away from it. But then she felt the weight of the beam on her legs. She could not move.

It was a vague world she entered, a consciousness outside anything she had ever experienced. She did not see her mother, but she believed an angel spirit stood over her, a warm pillar of light, a tower of strength. And when she grabbed her mother's skirts, Libby felt moisture and knew she had grabbed the soapy rag in her hand. The heat from the walls on the other side of the bar began to beat toward her.

A slurry of voices—cries of horror, chattering, commands, rumbled in the background. And suddenly an excruciating pain tore through her legs.

"She's been hit," a voice said softly.

Though she was half conscious, Libby felt fingers search for a pulse in her wrist.

"She's alive. Hurry!"

Surrounding her were several men tugging, groaning, moving the heavy beam, and shoving aside tables and chairs, while strong arms slipped under her shoulders and legs, lifting her, shifting her. She felt airborne, moving through blackness and flames. On the way out into the street, she heard the doorjambs breaking away from raw walls and then tearing and rocking. Her head fell back. As the smoke seeped into her nostrils, she gasped for air and choked.

"It's all right," her rescuer said. "You'll be safe now."

She stiffened, every nerve jamming in her back. She knew that voice! But when she tried to raise her head she couldn't breathe. "Quiet!" she heard the familiar voice say. It was Charles Grenville.

She leaned back and tried to pull away.

"Libby," he said, "you're hurt. Please . . ."

"Let me go," she said, but her head pounded and she felt blood trickle into her hair. "Mr. Grenville, you don't need to . . ." Her voice hardly made a sound through the sharp pain.

"Libby . . ."

"Charles! What . . ."

"You're hurt, Libby."

"Oh!" Pain pulsed through her legs in stabbing waves that drove her head into his shoulder.

"You're hurt, Libby. Let me carry you."

She fell against his chest. "What?"

Charles did not speak, but his legs moved under her, each foot searching for a hold. There was silence for a time, and then, while he walked with her into the street, she heard his voice from his chest, as though far away.

"Libby Campbell, my little love."

"Where am I?" She felt weak, but the pain that drove her also pressed her to speak.

"I'll take you to Russ House, Nellie's American Hotel. Her brave girls and their buckets have withstood disease, robberies, and fires twice. It's the safest place in town." Charles paused. "I've been there since last week, and there's enough room in my quarters."

With him? The words spun in her head. "What?"

"Quiet, Libby. It will be easier for you."

The walk to the American Hotel produced pain in every nerve. Charles pulled her close, probably trying to minimize her discomfort. She wanted to cry, but pride stopped her. She would not let a weak protest reveal her feelings. And the words she now uttered seemed to come from a resentment she was not sure she still harbored. "What about Mag?"

"Mag?" he returned. "My sister?"

For a moment his voice pounded like a dervish in Libby's brain. The fire raged on the street. And in her head. *His sister?*

"She's gone back to her child in Peoria. As soon as I struck silver—"

"What?"

"Shh. We're almost there. Quiet, Libby. Dr. Goodfellow is around the corner."

"Who?" Charles should have known she wasn't going to keep quiet.

"I'm never taking you back to Bless House. I finally got Mag out of there. It was lucky she funded me on that strike."

"Your strike?"

"Libby, I'm going to take care of you," Grenville announced as though he heard her thoughts. He reached for the doorknob, then kicked at the door.

She was vaguely aware of Nellie and Fanny and the children tossing buckets of water on the roof and walls. The house was still standing away from the raging flames on every side. Charles approached the door, again shifting Libby close around his neck. This time she did not resist. She raised her arms around his head and clung to him.

"I've felt like rescuing you for a long time, Libby Campbell."

The words mingled with the crack of the door, the haze of smoke, the sound of the women's voices as they pumped bucket after bucket of water from the well, and passed each of them to the daughter on the ladder, who in turn passed the water to the girl on the roof, and far above them, the bucket poured its life-giving deliverance from the hell that raged around them.

"You've been a feisty one . . ." Charles didn't finish his words. He stepped across the threshold with her in his arms. She buckled with the pain, but kept her arms around his neck.

As he carried her up the stairs, Libby laid her cheek against his shirt. Still in a daze, she felt herself lowered to a surface that seemed to swallow her up like a heap of feathers. Soon, she felt someone pressing on the bones of her legs. She did not remember what happened after that.

Finally, out of the murky soup of unconsciousness, she woke to a gentle afternoon light that slid in ribbons through one of Nellie Cashman's blinds and illuminated the room in patterns of gold. When Libby stirred, she felt a hovering weight above her. It was Charles Grenville. The same eyes that seemed to accuse her so many times in the past were now only inches away from her face.

"Mr. Grenville!"

"Charles to you, Libby."

"I can't believe . . ."

His tender look caught her off guard. It seemed a light had bloomed inside of her, as though a spark of fire that might have plummeted from the roof of the burning saloon had slipped into her heart.

"You could have died in the smoke." He paused. "I examined your legs. No broken bones. Can you get up and walk?"

Libby wasn't sure, but when he gave her his hand, she took it. "Charles, I . . . can't believe . . ."

Before she raised her head, he tightened his fingers on hers. "Do you remember, I picked up your apples one by one?" he asked. "Well, from the moment I saw you with the apples in your arms, I knew . . ."

She heard his words in a kind of joyous recollection. Taking courage to ignore her sore muscles, she grasped his strong forearm as he brought her to a standing position. For a moment she felt lightheaded and began to collapse. But he brought his arms around her and held her close. As she rested against him, she felt the power of his body, and it breathed life into her heart.

His lips brushed her hair. "Did you know I cared for you?"

She brought her head back to look into his eyes. "How could I?" she said, still weak. "I thought . . ."

"Whatever you thought, forget that . . . and remember this."

Charles tilted her chin and leaned closer. Then he kissed her. He held her so close to him, her feet came off the floor. She dissolved in the moment and responded with every heartbeat of her body.

When he set her feet back down on the floor, she felt unsteady. He turned and reached for a walking stick standing by the bookcase. It had been carefully carved out of a branch from a Joshua tree. "This will help for a while."

She took the stick. It was smooth and polished. "Did you make this?" She tightened her fingers on the knob of the stick, testing her weight against it, then raised it slightly.

"Yes, I worked on it while the assayer was weighing my gold," Charles said. "It's all yours now."

"Your gold is mine now?" She managed to grin.

He leaned his head back and laughed. "All of it, Libby. If you will take it."

Dear Frances,

I think about you every day. Your letters are precious. My prayers are with your mother in her time of trial, and knowing that I will see all of you soon gives me the greatest pleasure of my life.

We finished the church! For our first meeting on Sunday, June 18, the pulpit and stained-glass windows had not yet arrived. For two weeks now we have fashioned a pulpit out of wooden crates, and sat by open windows with nothing between us and God's world. It's invigorating.

But the absence of windows and pulpit has not stopped us from celebrating three baptisms and two weddings. The first wedding was for the young lady who sat next to me on the train. She married the man I mentioned who found a vein of silver and became a millionaire overnight. He donated a thousand dollars to the building. And the girl donated her gold. I often wonder if I shouldn't have been spending a little time looking for silver and gold! Ha! Although I feel I have already found my gold and silver. I found my fortune in that London rectory where I learned about God's purpose for me, a calling that will serve me well all the rest of my life.

The second wedding was Horace's. He married the girl who played the bird in the Bird Cage Theatre. There was some problem over the identification of the body that was found in the Cosmopolitan Hotel. It was charred to a crisp after the fire on May 26. Though the identity has never been fully determined, the people at Bless House swear it is Horace's first wife, who never returned to pick up her baby. The brothel is raising her child now, and it seems to have lifted their spirits. It is amazing what a little child can do for us all.

I am leaving just in time to miss an outbreak of measles. At first the doctors thought it was smallpox, but luckily it's not quite that bad. Also, the fires I told you about last time will not be a problem anymore. Just this week, the water company put in a fire plug and celebrated my departure with a spectacular living tower of water that shot several hundred feet into the air! Bless the living water! Right?

I love you, Frances! I hope you still have a corner of your heart left for me to occupy. If the train doesn't dally like a snail out of his shell, I will see you in a little over a week.

My fondest regards,
Cotter

About the Author

Marilyn McMeen Brown is fascinated with history. She believes in her "butterfly wing theory," that every human being who ever lived—no matter how seemingly insignificant—makes choices that impact our lives today. Storytelling is a way to give immediacy to those who have passed on. Their lives can inspire us to focus on our own critical choices.

Marilyn earned master's degrees from Brigham Young University and the University of Utah, and has garnered many local and state writing awards. She established the annual thousand-dollar Marilyn Brown Novel Award (UVU.edu/marilynbrown) for unpublished novels. She hopes to inspire others to write genuine stories honoring the actual figures who have influenced our lives.

For more information about Marilyn or her books, please visit www.marilynbrownauthor.com or contact her at marilynbrown@dishmail.net.

Praise for
The Rosefields of Zion

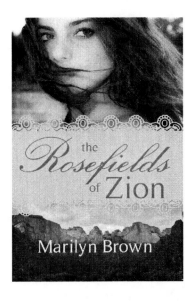

I was held in this book's spell from start to finish—transported to another time and place where author Marilyn Brown used just enough hope to tell a story of heartbreak, music, and heritage. There's a reason Brown is heralded as one of the great Mormon fiction writers of our time, and The Rosefields of Zion *proves her timeless ability to retain that title.* —Josi S. Kilpack, author of the Sadie Hoffmiller Culinary Mystery series

Fast-paced and well-written, The Rosefields of Zion *illuminates the Zion National Park area's legends and landscape at the same time it tells a page-turning story about a family in conflict with the U.S. government's urgent need to purchase their farm. A poignant fictional tribute to Southern Utah's breathtaking preserve.* —Veda Tebbs Hale, author of *Ragged Circle*, biographer of *Giant Joshua*'s Maurine Whipple

Marilyn Brown is one of the Church's literary treasures. The Rosefields of Zion *is a touching story of a young woman's struggle to find love and happiness in the face of overwhelming loss and crushing circumstances largely not of her own making. If only we could all demonstrate such patience in suffering!* —Elizabeth Bentley, Parables Publishing

Accomplished author Marilyn Brown . . . knows the formula for successful literature: a subtle plot with levels of meaning, an important site, and well-crafted sentences. Many legends of the park bring the locale to brilliant life. The writing is mature, crisp, and rich . . . a wonderful read! —Douglas D. Alder, president emeritus of Dixie State College, author of *Sons of Bear Lake*

The Rosefields of Zion *is a beautifully written story of a family and their fight against the federal government's creation of park lands in the early decades of the last century. Marissa, Michael, Carter, Morgan, Joey, their parents Ellen and Bradley, Blair Harper, Wade Keller, and all the other characters are totally believable and add an attractive dimension to this story that cannot fail to engross the reader. The plot moves convincingly to the story's rather sad but quite realistic ending.* The Rosefields of Zion *should be on reading lists everywhere.* —Alice D., reader, Readers' Favorite Book Reviews and Award Contest